REMEMBERING

A novel by

William R. W. English

For my parents, who lived through both World Wars, and raised three children during the Second World War.

Copyright William R. W. English 2020

Front cover drawing copyright: Sophie Claire Cooper 2020

Richard and Margaret Ward are caught up on opposite sides of the world, divided by a war that was none of their making. Richard is a P.O.W in Burma, while Margaret is prey not only to German bombing raids, rationing and snooping neighbours, but also the predatory attentions of her bank manager. While Richard is watching his comrades being executed one by one, Margaret is unaware that he has been attempting to send messages home to her; messages which have been intercepted. Can remembering the fun they used to have, help them keep their love for each other alive during all the hard-ships they endure?

PART ONE

Chapter One

1942

'Cigarettes,' Richard whispered to the face just visible in the bushes. 'Paper and another pencil. Dried meat. A needle and black thread - .'

'Whisky, sir?' The man might still have been serving him in the Mess.

Richard shook his head. What they called whisky was a dangerous and volatile juice which assaulted badly starved stomachs. He looked slowly round. Sudden movement was dangerous, betrayed you. No guards in sight. He still stood over his task, shovel in hand, endlessly preoccupied with eking out his sparse strength in a pretence of making a road. It was an effort to stand, let alone shake his head at the offer of whisky.

He had often tried to examine the surprising fact that the Burmese with his darkly serious face trusted him. Here was a man whose face did not betray a mind set on survival, a mind which, while it would keep a low profile, would at the same time always be open to deals and opportunities which brought forth profit. Thus, having to deal with the occupying Japanese did not preclude the odd deal with British prisoners; the two things were secure in separate compartments.

Richard also knew that Ashin respected the probability that the cheque which an English prisoner offered still represented the honesty and integrity of the British Empire: an empire on which the sun had not so much as set as suffered an eclipse. Eclipses do not last forever - the Japanese must eventually leave Burma, as had all invaders down the centuries. Which might leave the British still here, before they, too, went back to wherever they came from. Or the other way round. Either way, it was a good idea to continue to deal with both if at all possible. Be careful, cautious and wary: this was survival. If British P.O.Ws. could pay, Ashin would find a way of smuggling in those goods they wished to buy. The cheque would find its way home in a month or so; his account here in Malaya would be credited and all would be well.

The compartments into which Ashin had placed the British and Japanese were in their turn enclosed within a wider sphere outside which he preserved the life of himself, his family, and the wider kin of the extended village group. This was the extent of his interest in the prisoners. There was no sentimentality, no loyalty. Just the knowledge that the British were, from his experience of them before the war, oddly honest, particularly the officers, such as this one. Ashin's job in the Mess before the war started had not only paid well but had been paid each month, as regularly and reliably as the rise in glory of the hot sun each morning. Both events had filled him with a sense of wellbeing, moderated at times by surprise. Ashin, as his manner suggested, was a patient man, and knew that the cheque would take a long time to clear. But it would clear.

'Anything else, sir?'

Richard shook his head. Peripheral vision indicated movement somewhere down the road to his right, so he kept his head down and moved the shovel a little. The British P.O.Ws he was in charge of were strung out widely left and right.

'Right you are, sir. Jolly good.'

Ah, the accent and the phraseology learned in the Mess. With the shovel propped against his leg at an angle suggesting labour, Richard bent over the writing of the cheque using Ashin's pen which had to be shaken every few letters or numbers to encourage the ink to flush the nib. Richard had to control his irritation and write: one pound, three shillings and eight pence.

'As regards the goods, sir,' Ashin whispered, 'will supply without delay as you are good customer and cheque's clearance not doubted.'

The notion of a Cadbury's chocolate bar drifted into Richard's mind as he hid the cheque book in the pocket of his tattered shorts. But Ashin had gone, and the chirps, squawks and chattering of the jungle reasserted themselves as if nothing had happened.

'Mrs Ward?'

Why had the telegram boy held on to the envelope too long? Was it that he felt compelled to present the wide eyes of youth to the world; that he was not yet old enough to be sucked up into the military mincing machine of war? His head was slightly tilted back to free his mouth for speech: to talk, to chat into oblivion a few tedious moments of the morning, when all the rest was the lifeless slotting of envelopes into letter boxes. Or perhaps rendered bored, or worn down by the death and disappearance he peddled so many times up these Crescents, Meads, Closes, Avenues, Drives, and Walks, as if Street, Road and Lane were denied, prosaic, passé. But it made no difference: the declaration *missing* or *dead* was no respecter of the fancy nomenclature of all these new streets of new houses which collectively held fast the dreams and expectations of a vanished time of peace.

'Not so bad - the weather,' the telegram boy had even tried. And he'd offered the envelope in this reluctant way so that they both held onto it. Margaret began to pull. The boy's voice rose, 'For the time of year ..'

Margaret pulled harder, and the tension through the envelope made her words a rush: 'Makes everything grow so fast!' and gave a final tug.

Released, the telegraph boy touched his cap, and scuttled back down the garden path. Even residual guilt at not having eased the youth's need for communication delayed her ripping open the telegram's envelope. And then it was done –

Dear Mrs Ward, I regret to inform you that your husband, Captain Richard Ward, is missing - .'

She found that she had to take the telegram with her round the house, out into the back garden to see if the washing was dry, or down to the shops to buy small amounts of grocery. But the huge question remained: Richard missing? How could he possibly be missing? How could words hesitantly printed on a flimsy piece of paper, folded so neatly, dictate that a man so real, so full of life, be missing? And why had the telegram boy knocked instead of ringing the bell? Why had she delayed opening the front door while she twisted the flattened metallic hemisphere of the bell to check that the spring was fully wound? As if this was more important than a man, more urgent than knowing what a telegram might hide. Then she had to sign for the telegram, fumbled with the pencil, had almost forgotten who she was, had forgotten that you have to sign for the folded, enveloped words, while pretending that this is as ordinary as an exchange of money for a chocolate bar: a penny ha'penny and a thank you. Then the hurried, almost furtive ripping of paper to discover the taste of Richard missing. How could she believe this? Why did her mouth keep filling with saliva?

Home. Richard thought the word bulged with, was crammed with - what was a better word - redolent? Home was redolent with meaning; was a part of you like a tooth you habitually touched or tasted with your tongue. It was a place which was cool, where you did not itch all the time, where scabs which came from a single scratch didn't grow into buboes of pus which you had to squeeze out from under a hard scab; where you did not feel so weak all the time that you wanted to lie down and wait for the end. Home was a clean bath and a crisp ironed shirt, newly mown grass, and a pale blue sky with billowing clouds which might promise a brief refreshing shower, not days of drenching, angry monsoon. Home was where the sun was gentle, not a furnace under which you cringed, craving shade. Home was a place where deadly insects and reptiles did not lurk under every leaf, every crumbling piece of wood, every stone. Home was where you belonged, where you had your being among the familiar, where life was ordered, rational, comprehendible.

Home was Margaret. Of all these things, but most of all, home was Margaret.

He thought of her all the time. It was as if she was with him when with aching back, he bent to shovel the stones he had so painfully shattered and separated with a hammer. She was with him when he watched over another and another and another of his men fade into eternity, skeletal with starvation and disease, or the random brutality of the Japanese guards, or simply beaten by an existence that offered no news, no future and therefore no hope. But most of all Margaret was with him through the racket of the jungle night, and the clamouring of his mind for her. Perhaps, though, he spoke to her most when he was forced to stand all day in the sun, beaten hourly because of something one of his men had or had not done.

Margaret and home.

Her voice so much herself, indefinably familiar and dear; her eyes animated, lively, at one with her giggle which was life itself. Margaret. And her hands: so quick that she seemed to use only the tips of her fingers – tip-fingering through the sewing and knitting and mending. The way she could conjure out of the bits of left-over pastry a heart and arrow with M and R either side: magic and love in pastry on top of an apple pie! The way she lay in their bed relaxed and easy in a way his tense male body could never emulate. The way he would wait in the morning for her to surface from the calm, clear waters of sleep so that he could begin to rouse her into love.

Margaret and home. Home and Margaret.

Even so, his mind could still not encompass the enormity of separation, or the enormity of childlessness: no child - call-up - Singapore - exhausting marches - a botched battle - surrender. A complete history, unbound and squeezed into the few words which could articulate a volume.

Margaret missed the bus to the High Street because the siren had wailed its baleful rising and falling notes of death and destruction. Instead of
hurrying down the road to the bus stop, her scurrying feet took her reluctantly back to share the neighbour's Anderson shelter. Mrs Hipperson - Elsie, but Margaret had never been invited to use the name - and her younger daughter were already inside.

'Here she is!' Elsie was a woman who revelled in stating the obvious. If she encountered Margaret plodding back up the slope of Dicksons Rise with a basket full of shopping she'd tell her that she, Margaret, had been shopping. Margaret had long given up tidying her tiny front garden because of being told she'd done so; the implication being, About Time Too.

Elsie, in all her glory, was the eyes and ears of the Rise. Some hidden corner of her mind was likely to harbour the notion, 'Well, if I didn't, who else would keep an eye on the Rise?' A well- built woman who, despite rationing, had an enviable amount of weight spread over her body.

This time Margaret managed to avoid catching her head on the ribs of the galvanized steel roof of the bomb shelter. Even so, as she sat on the bench next to Elsie, her neighbour sighed and leant sideways to tweak the old carpet back into its proper place across the shelter's doorway. Margaret had long recognized Elsie as a woman whose sighs, sniffs and snuffles were another part of her way of managing everyday life, which together with the statements of the obvious constituted her approach to life. So far, in the few seconds of Margaret's time in the shelter Elsie had managed one of each: one comment and one sigh.

Even if it seemed quiet outside, this was not to pretend that nothing might happen up there in the aerial firestorm of ack-ack gunnery and the rival whistling of falling bombs, the earthquake crumps of obliteration below the delicate tracery of death as tiny machines wove heavenly skeins of white cloud into a delicate tracery of death. While below all this Elsie concentrated on keeping her family safe and warm, even rushing into the shelter with the hot water bottles kept ready, particularly for nights. 'Well, someone's got to keep the Home Fires Burning!' she'd repeat. All the while her daughter, Anne would be slumped on the bench with her eyes closed, bored and silenced by the weight of her mother's authority and enforced proximity.

'The jumper finished yet, is it?' Elsie wondered. Meaning, you've been knitting that for ages. By the light of a candle

Elsie would knit blanket squares from jumpers and scarves she'd unpicked, gleaned from neighbours and jumble sales Margaret had long known that Elsie had a range of knitting on the go both in the shelter and in the house. Further knitting was kept in her shopping bag so as not to waste time when queueing in the High Street for things which were rumoured to have just come in . Chatting was not included under the heading of wasting time, because she could chat, queue and knit at the same time. It was a performance which sometimes brought her muted acclaim in the shops as the shopkeepers carefully cut out the squares and oblongs from her ration book.

'Er, I've just sent off another batch of socks.' Margaret tried. But Elsie had some wool to be rolled up into balls. Trapped below ground like this had Margaret endure holding hanks of washed, unpicked wool for Elsie to wind into tidy balls before knitting them into socks for seamen, or pullovers for airmen. Margaret sometimes fell asleep trying to maintain the tension of the wool between her outstretched arms tight enough, and the ball Elsie was winding up would falter and become misshapen. At such moments Elsie's irritation with her could be worse than her irritation at the regular onslaughts of the Luftwaffe.

'Any damage last night?' This was in order to tell Margaret of the displaced tiles. 'Reg is going to struggle with ours at the weekend, with me holding the ladder!'

Margaret knew how her neighbour liked to impart information, particularly to strangers in queues; how she liked to present herself as a person who never wasted a moment of this God-given life because you never know what might be round the next corner. Corners were useful things to Elsie because they included the positive suggestion of turning them and all being well again. She enjoyed being cheerful about this, and regarded it as a further visible contribution to the war effort.

Twenty minutes, or even half an hour later the diminishing sounds of ack-ack, whistling bombs and thumping explosions was beginning to be obvious. But Mrs H. wasn't going to let go yet.

'And Jenny only just gone,' she added. But she never seemed particularly worried about her eldest daughter going up to London to work. Someone would let her into a shelter somewhere or she'd follow the crowd into the nearest Underground station.

Margaret had the impression that Mrs H worried even less about Reg, her husband, because he was in a reserved occupation with the Admiralty and could therefore not be killed by the Germans in some foreign field. The bombs they daily dropped on the docklands or factories now included the new suburbs, particularly from those Germans pilots dumping their bombs and fleeing home. She ignored exceptions to rules - the German hostile machine gunning of streets and random bombing of domestic housing. She liked to give thanks that her children were grown up because women pushing prams were particularly vulnerable to such attacks.

'I haven't looked at mine,' Margaret tried, but roof tiles had already been deleted from Elsie's agenda.

After a silence during which Margaret's mind had drifted back to the jumper she was knitting for Richard, and she said, 'Nearly.'

'Nearly what, dear?'

'The jumper.'

'What jumper?'

'The one I'm knitting.'

'Oh, that one, for Richard.'

Although Margaret had long since accepted the inconsequentiality of any attempt at conversation with Mrs H, she continually fell into the same trap. She noticed than Mr H had the same problem. Margaret glanced at the daughter: Anne had not said a word. When addressed by her parents she produced sparse, monotone sentences of essential words. Margaret could see the girl becoming so reserved that she was in danger of losing touch with life. The thought disturbed her, as if she had been describing herself.

"And all these Canadians coming over here," Mrs H. said, assuming that her visitor would be permanently tuned in to the continual broadcast of her mind, and would disapprove of such wild and unpredictable interlopers even if they were here to help us win the war.

Then all-clear proclaimed an end to potential or actual death and destruction in its rising note of triumph and optimism.

'Huh!' Mrs H. said, 'that didn't take long. Almost another false alarm.'

Margaret scuttled out of the Anderson shelter. Anxiety drove her to run to the bus stop - as if the Germans plotted to fool everyone as they left their shelters, and at any moment might rain bombs out of the sky.
She was still out of breath when she reached the bank. Moreover, her usual anxiety about repeat raids and finding the bank closed made her feel as if she had run the whole length of the High Street even though the bus had set her down a hundred yards away. Pushing open the heavy oak door was almost too much, and added to the sensation she always had of entering an indifferent, almost hostile and exclusive world where money was manipulated secretly and unseen, its only trace left as spidery black marks in journals and ledgers. She never understood the carefully hand-written statements describing her account. In her frugality she seemed to make no unreasonable demands on the money available and which continued to appear monthly as if Richard still ate his way through the daily shopping. So that now she had come to place the statements unread on the pile of such documents on the writing surface of the bureau, adding to the pile which Richard had started.

Although lit from above by bulbs below wide-brimmed green Perspex shades, the pecuniary oppression of the inside of the bank, reinforced by the heavy wooden counters and panelling, always overwhelmed her. From the moment she stepped inside the place she wanted to escape. As if to delay this, Mr Bailey, the old cashier, retained from his expected retirement because of war and the lack of manpower, was so slow counting out the money, and always double- checked: one green one pound note, and in case shop keepers didn't have sufficient change, four half crowns, one florin, one shilling, two sixpenny pieces, four thruppenny pieces and six one penny pieces. Occasionally, a newly minted coin was offered like a small, unexpected, glowing gift. At home she would buff up the warm copper of a new penny or the moon-glow of a half crown and leave them displayed like trophies on the kitchen table until reluctantly compelled to spend them.

In addition to being slowed by age, Mr Bailey seemed so overloaded with courtesy as to almost seize up and become incapable of functioning at all. Margaret recognised that this was his way of trying to express deep sympathy for his customer: a young woman whose husband was missing, possibly dead, in the Far East.

All through the transaction Margaret had to avoid looking at her watch. It was ingrained in her that every second in town was dangerous. The German bombers had once kept conveniently to a timetable, but the randomness of their raids now was more terrifying This had started months ago when she had been walking past the police station: the siren had punctured her wrapped thoughts with its lament of death: so low a sound, so elemental as to pierce her soul and add itself to her repertoire of nightmares - the wail of loss, the rising lament of destruction. Or in bed, bathed in sweat, she would lie awake for the rest of the night, forcing herself not to obey the siren's urgency and scuttle into Elsie's shelter. Instead, she would lie in bed not daring to call out Richard's name. And now, here in the bank, all she wanted to do while Mr Bailey's face concentrated on accuracy and sympathy was to run and get the week's shopping over with, frustrating queues, coupons and all, and back to the security of home and memory, even if this was in the security of the Hippersons' shelter.

Today, to make it worse, Mr Long, the manager, had appeared behind Mr Bailey to add a face of studied compassion to his cashier's genuine one. Then, without warning, Mr Long lifted the heavy counter flap to step out and down onto the herringbone floored territory of his customers. At first Margaret assumed that Mr Long's presence and actions had nothing to do with her, that there must be some other reason, some other customer which had made him emerge from the inner sanctum of the bank. Still pushing her purse securely into the bottom of her bag, even with her eyes downcast she knew that Mr Long had moved across the floor to the door. Perhaps to open it for her. But as she stepped slightly to one side to allow for the arc of the door as it opened, she became aware that he wasn't going to open it. His hand on the brass handle was slack, or slightly inclined towards the door so as to trap Margaret. She saw that he stared at her intently.

'Any news of Richard?' he said, trying to moderate his curiously high pitched, false customer voice, 'If you'll pardon my asking?'

'No.' The word slipped out, carried on a tone careering towards a squeak. But somehow this prodded Mr Long into pulling open the heavy door.

Freed, Margaret fell into her usual urgency: back to the house quickly, put the butter and cheese in the kitchen wall cool box with the bacon. Then the apples in the Claris Cliff bowl, one of a set which Richard's parents gave them for their wedding. Back into her cave, her hideout where she could think of Richard and what she'd tell him in her next letter.

These were herself squeezed into words. Outside these letters herself in words was the humdrum response to crisis: her reluctance to plunge beyond the voluntary work to help the war effort in the careful communal knit and pearl of blanket squares, then graduating to socks for seamen. She shunned the almost public making of cups of tea in the Methodist Hall to raise money for extra food and clothes for our boys fighting abroad; or donating comfort smiles and quiet words at the hospital for men torn by war; or checking on the old and mowing elderly lawns; above all, waiting and dreading being called-up for work in a factory or on a farm.

She was waiting for Richard.   The whole world must wait as well.
But the letters. It was as if she forgot each time she started to write and was not prepared: a floodgate of the mind would burst and the tumbling, flowing tide of words were free - but somehow stifled of passion, anger, frustration and love.

Down the high street were the usual queues but one longer than the rest - oranges this time. I got two and had half a day and the daffodils are growing when I went down with the peelings and the bombings are still coming, and I go into the shelter and hurrying down the shops and only to the ones where they'll got shelters I hope you are all right I am keeping myself well. Oh, and you know that little hop-up Dad gave me?

When the pressure ceased, when she got to the end of the page, or if she was interrupted by the air raid siren, the barrier snapped shut and herself became once more the words of the Margaret you might meet in the street and talk with of the weather, the war, the scarcity of this or that, apart from the rationing, and where she'd heard you could get a jar of Marmite, soap or baked beans because they had only just come in.

Chapter 2

1943

'My hat,' Mrs Long said to Dr Simpson, "is it necessary to remove it?"

'No, no, of course not.' A little abruptly. The good doctor was used to hats being worn during a medical examination, though as a young doctor it had amused him. Men always removed theirs.

In common with most doctors he liked least doing internal examinations of middle-aged women who were gracelessly descending into an older category. He preferred the hope in the eyes of young men, women and children, even in time of war; but, there again, he liked many of the elderly, particularly the ones who still referred to the saving grace of the doctor in heaven when earthly medicines and cures failed.

Mrs Long wanted to keep her hat on during the examination. To a certain extent her coiffure relied on the support of the hugging brown felt, and could be disrupted by the removing and replacing of the hat. What to do with the long and dangerous hat pin though? Pushing it back into the discarded hat always seemed to her something like an act of violence. She spent a lot of time arranging her folds and hanks of long greying hair with an assortment of grips, clips and clasps so that it was confined to the shape of her head and the approximation to the fashion of thirty years earlier when she was still young. This word had a particular meaning for her: it embodied all that she had been and could have been and might have been and had not been or become, even though she shied away from too close and destructive a definition of all the coulds and mights. It was enough that she retained a feeling that it could all have been so much better; and even, at times, that it would have been better if she had stayed young and full of an undefined kind of potential.

It was a time when she was perfect. Now the word made her sigh several times a day. Without willing or wishing it, or in any way making it happen thus, life became more difficult day by day, month on month, year on year: her parents, the neighbours, her husband, and now her body. The war she ignored. Even if Mr Long marched off awkwardly in his Home Guard's uniform, he still belonged to the bank and that was unlikely to change because of his age.

Dr Simpson cleared his throat to indicate that he was still in charge and was about to proceed with the next part of the appointment.
'Please place your lower clothes on the chair behind the screen and lie on the ..'

That smell of the aging female body, though worse in aging men, had already filled the consulting room. For professional reasons he would have called his wife to sit in, and to perhaps chat with Mrs Long while she dressed and he escaped. A certain weariness, or lethargy or the knowledge that he had known Mrs Long for years, that Mr Long was his bank manager, that the woman was unlikely to get hysterical about such an examination, prevented him from bothering.

But he again allowed himself the little diversion of wishing he was ten, fifteen years years younger and could be patching up soldiers somewhere far away - in North Africa, for instance, where Monty was driving the Italians and Germans back. On the other hand. he had stopped wishing that he was a few years older so that he could have done his bit stitching up soldiers in the Great War. The mud and gore of that conflict contained for him not an ounce of romance or glory; besides which he had lost an older brother and two uncles.

Mrs Long lay rigid in her pulled-up petticoat. Thinking ahead to this moment she'd omitted her corset which required considerable squirming and tugging to remove; not the sort of performance which could be done quickly while the doctor waited. In the event the examination which did not need to take much time: it was fairly straight forward. Dr Simpson tried to make a few comfortingly professional noises to reassure her that he was on the right track and that she could feel easy, or as easy as possible in the circumstances. She would need, as women of her age often did, a hysterectomy, but not yet. Aspirins would suffice.

For her part, Mrs Long, relegated for a few minutes to the passive role of a patient with a gynaecological problem and feeling completely in the professional power of Dr Simpson, considered it right and appropriate to drop her guard long enough, in case it should have some bearing on her condition, to confess, 'Er, Mr Long does not trouble me at all now, doctor.'

'Thank you,' Dr Simpson said, either to indicate that the examination was complete, or perhaps in acknowledgement of her confidence.

He stood and walked across the room to the sink where he could wash his hands with his back towards his patient to allow her to feel more confident about rising half naked from the couch and moving behind the screen to get fully dressed.

A little shocked at her own audacity, Mrs Long wondered, as she carefully pulled her dress over the hat and slip, if she would regret her admission. She wondered if this was something she should offer to God in church at the end of the service when you vie with your neighbours in other pews to see who would remain longest on their knees in Protestant prayer. But this was also tinged with a sense of relief. At a certain age she was sure men were expected, and indeed expected it of themselves, that the time had come to leave their wives alone.

When you were young it might be different, there were children to conceive, but after that - she shuddered. Thirty years ago, her mother had told her what a messy business it was, how it all ended in agony and blood, and men were like beasts really, and all that was the burden, the lot, of women.

At least she hadn't mentioned to Dr Simpson the separate bedrooms.

Why should she? She did all the things a good wife should do: cleaning, ironing, mending, cooking. Fortunately, the enforced intimacy of the bomb shelter was not a problem.

It was too damp and cold, and presumably anxiety would also have a deflationary effect on a man.

She took care dressing behind the lacquered Chinese screen as if to give Dr Simpson and the world in general not the slightest hint that she had minutes earlier been lying half naked being examined. She was also beginning to feel slightly self-congratulatory about being resolute enough to inform the doctor at the beginning of the appointment that she would keep her hat on.

When she emerged, Dr Simpson was at his desk scrawling words onto a piece of paper beside a manila folder. He looked up and said, 'Ah.'

Composed and confident, she sat opposite him for a more detailed diagnosis. A few minutes later she strode out of the consulting room in her thick dress of impenetrable brown and the matching hat with the one diagonal dark green feather which had survived the experience unscathed.

It was not that Mr Long had been a friend. Richard, as far as Margaret could remember, had got on well with him in a client relationship, and had once or twice played golf with him. To the anxiety of being caught away from home and Mrs Hipperson's air raid shelter was now added the anxiety of seeing Mr Long, in case he repeated his sympathy act.

Although she had not yet acknowledged a thought or feeling about it - there was something she didn't like or trust about the man. Yet at the same time she didn't have the energy to confront this impression. To do so would suggest, or stronger, require her to do something about it. Without stating so to herself, she tried varying the time of day but the manager's office was furnished with a glass door with MANAGER and SOUTHEASTERN BANK in gold lettering. These did not prevent him from closely surveying the work of his clerks and noting which clients had come in. All she could do as time went by was remind herself that there was something about the man she didn't like, something which made her feel uneasy. But it slowly became obvious that he now looked out for her as assiduously as he looked out for errors on the part of his clerks. Once, as she entered the bank, she heard a voice slightly raised from somewhere among the working desks behind the oak panel room divider which separated the clerks from the customers' counter.

'Mr Fielden,' the voice was saying, 'Entries must double. Which is why our esteemed system of accountancy is termed "double entry". There is no other way.'

'Yes, Mr Long,' another voice said, 'Sorry, sir.'

If she had thought quickly enough, she might have been able to pretend that she had forgotten something and crept out of the bank to return later. As it was, Mr Long had spotted her and made towards the door leading to the counter as if it had been his intention all the time. Before Mr Bailey could speak, Mr Long asked her if he could help. She felt forced to give him the cheque. Mr Bailey stood back watching helplessly, eyes downcast, as Mr Long counted out the money. Mr Bailey could have been her father, indeed his reaction to her was very similar.

Each week after this it appeared that Mr Long took it upon himself to give her the money, personally, and then to release himself from the confines of the counter and hold open the bank's heavy door for her. In addition to this as he passed her the cash, he had taken to holding on to it just long enough to extend contact, and risk the possibility of his fingers touching one of hers.

'Would it not be easier for you, my dear, with the bombing now so unpredictable,' he suggested quietly one day, trapping her in this new way he had perfected, 'if I dropped the money round to you of an evening?'

She would not speak to anyone for days if the air raids had not propelled her into contact with Elsie; or the compulsion and expectation on her to take her knitted socks for seamen and blanket squares for the Russians to the gushing and grateful W.I. women, who then pressed voluntary duties on her: teas, sandwiches, jumble, sorting and packing frayed, faded books, As it was, in the intervals between these events, days and memories merged, faded and lengthened.

Sometimes she forgot to get up in the morning because the house was so dark with the blackout curtains still drawn. Sometimes she forgot what day it was and couldn't ask anyone, and had to listen to the wireless to discover which of the identically dull days was Sunday, because that was the day she spent with her parents, a bus ride away at Stoneleigh. It became easier to leave the blackout drawn until Elsie's critical comments in the shelter forced her to conform to the convention that all curtains should be opened during the hours of daylight. At such times the morning sun could be painfully bright, the day would stay too bright, unless blessed rain dulled the rooms. As a counter to this constraint she stopped opening any windows as a good wife should do in order to get rid of germs and foul air. Elsie, however, apparently didn't notice this. In time of war small victories can mean a lot.

Richard's shirts needed regular ironing because creases have a life of their own, and his casual slacks and trousers needed maintaining. Every few months she thought about taking his suits to be dry-cleaned, but the longer she thought about this the spark of actual action dimmed. Were clothes still dry-cleaned in wartime? She knew she could have put moth balls in the pockets or on the floor below the hanging turn ups, but she hated their peppermint smell of absence, exile, death.

Everything she did in the house reflected the presence of Richard: not a chair or cushion could be changed round or altered, a picture rail painted, a wallpaper they chose could not be changed either. When she sat at the same place at the kitchen table, the times she remembered to eat, it was opposite the place where Richard should be sitting; where they could gaze fully at each other. She only went into the dining room to clean it: on her knees with dustpan and brush to sweep the plum hued, patterned carpet with the stiff hand brush, collecting mysterious fallen dust particles in the tin pan. Then to feather dust the delicate walnut cupboard which contained, like holy chalices and wafers, their wedding gifts of the Japanese porcelain tea set, the Worcester dinner service, the silver cutlery set, and silver napkin rings, two of which had been engraved with their names; the set of six looking to a future in which more of them would be named and used by a large and noisy family. Dust inexplicably settled inside this cabinet as well as outside and forced the occasional evacuation of all their precious contents for a spring clean, irrespective of the season; when, or rather if, she had the energy and inclination.

Or she would find herself wandering in the back garden, shrinking from involvement with the front garden borders where Elsie could see her and later, in the shelter, inform her what she had been doing : 'Tidied up the front bed nicely, didn't you? Or tried to!'

In the relative safety of the back garden she tugged at weeds and left a desolation of dying roots to join rusty leaves on the slimy concrete path, on the lawn woven with couch grass and punctuated with dandelions, and on the slightly disturbed raised weed patches which had once been flower beds. It was enough to push the mower, suppressing the pungency of memory in the new cut grass. To heave the box onto Richard's heap was to trample too much onto the shape of something he had left, even though it would rot down in a way that memory might not. So, dispensing with the box, she left the cuttings to brown the lawn, and in colder, damper weather succumb to slime. Gradually, and unnoticed by her, Richard's vegetable plot became part of the lawn, stretching a green square into a rectangle.

But ever-present memory could stop her hurrying feet in the street, or with a plate held half washed up over the sink. She could walk the entire length of the High Street wrapped in the thumb-sucking comfort of memory, and find herself unable to remember the shop she sought: was it Willis's for the bacon or Poulton's gaudy stall for potatoes? At such blessed times even Elsie's probing statements disguised as inconsequential comments, even the threat of bombs, could not deflect the warm consolation of memory: like the time they hiked to Brighton.

Arm in arm, hand in hand, with their new haversacks they had strode out past the half-built or nearly finished Crescents, Meads and Walks sold to gleeful people who thought they'd be living in the country which was in the process of being destroyed all round them. The hard lines and texture of new brickwork prepared for the thousands waiting in London for their share of country air and the freedom of space and light were left behind on the Downs as the gentle hills of chalk stretched out before them.

Because hiking was the new thing to do. The novel feeling of being up-to-date lent a spring to their step: among the first liberated young people to stride across the soft curves of hills and the pastel shaded meadows of Surrey and Sussex. First to reach the light and soft green of the beach woods of the North Downs, below which lay the thick wooded Weald and the far-off glimpse of their eventual goal, the South Downs which concealed the ultimate aim of the adventure: the blue and beckoning pearl-shot English Channel.

It was not that they didn't notice the drawn faces of the farmers' wives in the flint cottages, or the crumbling wattle and daub farmhouses. It was not that they didn't consider the pittance payment for bed and breakfast: one and six a night seemed to be acceptable. Sometimes the sum humbly requested, sometimes the sum gratefully received on a grimy outstretched palm. What was it? Margaret wondered endlessly now that she had time to remember. Some isolation, some insulation engendered by the wealth of the new ring of building round London?

It was so easy to put this rural poverty aside or pretend it wasn't there: they were newly-wed, newly joined, newly together having fun. The bacon and egg with sausages and onions flowing from the large breakfast server, crackled blue willow-patterned, brought through from the hot kitchen gave a misleading impression of plenty.

Near the end of the hike they had to crawl the last yards up Chanctonbury Ring to collapse in the shade of the beach trees covering the ancient hill-fort. Below them the world was spread out: The Channel in the near distance dazzling with promise, the fields and woods of Sussex so lush and green behind them. It was a defining moment for her, a recollected picture as surely and securely delineated into memory as an oil painting hanging on a wall. Oh, Richard. And how, stifling giggles, they had muffled their voices and bodies in the dowdy farmhouse bedrooms: the lumpy mattresses, the warped frames which crowded them into the middle of the bed, the random detonations of weary springs, or the groans and squeaks of floorboards which traced their progress across the room or down a dark corridor, to carefully carry a pot out to the privy in the garden. How, when bronzed and fit from the week-long hike they had laughed at home about it all and bathed together, shrieking over the slippery soap, and finally to bed naked - how modern, how daring! What fun.

You know that little hop-up which Dad gave me? Well, the light bulb in the kitchen flashed and went out. I fell off the step, but do not worry I caught hold of the kitchen table and was all right. Oh, and I mowed the lawn but miss all the vegetables you used to grow and I found that shirt you liked to wear in the summer the one with all the blue lines and It had a button missing. How did I not notice that before?

Or the time Leonard and Estelle picked them up, complete with gramophone and picnic hamper, and drove up onto the Downs. Richard got on well with his brother-in-law, and adulthood had successfully masked, if not banished, Leonard's old irritations and quarrels with his sister. Sitting in the dickie seat of Leonard's Austin Eight, Margaret and Richard joined in with 'Run, rabbit, run'. The four of them singing so loudly that passers-by had been stopped in their tracks. Leaning back in the dickie seat gave them the mistaken impression of privacy so that cuddling nearly became a public act of promiscuity which was able to confirm older passers-by in their opinion that the morals of the young were in sharp decline. One old man defiantly waved a walking stick.

Well on the other side from the Epsom Grandstand they fell out of the car and set up the gramophone and picnic. Each time memory supplied her with the clear blue sky of early summer, a day daubed with bright expectation in the wildflower meadows beyond the green sweep of the racecourse: a profusion, a drift, a gathering together of triumphant yellows, purples and blues - vetch, campion, buttercup, ladies fingers, bluebells, stitchwort. Richard wound up the gramophone, fitted the trumpet and put on a Charleston. The needle rose and fell with the gentle distortion of the cellulite which serenely created crackling jazz to fill the air round their gyrating, jerking, skipping bodies. When Leonard flicked the speed catch to SLOW the co-ordination of limbs became deliberate and difficult. But they laughed even more as the unwinding spring in the last moments of its coiled life ground to a growl, and the antics involved in keeping time had them collapse on the cool grass, aching with mirth. Aching.

Day and night, she ached for Richard. Day and night, she remembered the fun.

Richard had learned that to discover something in passing could threaten to be more shocking than the death of the man whose words you were sharing an hour before. Even though such a man might have told you of the girl at home, or his old dad deafened in the trenches the first time, or his mate Reg who'd been knocked over by a Japanese guard and never recovered.

'No, sir,' Ashin had whispered, 'there is no postal taken, sir. Some come in. To the commander only. He send some of his out. That is all.' While his voice was controlled, his dark face was sweating, drops coalescing at the tiny junctions of creases. He glanced left and right.

Movement somewhere down the road had him slowly withdraw, subtly blending like a jungle animal into the deeper gloom.

Richard knew Ashin would not go. Would wait for more business. But could not know how Richard shook with the pain of yet another door closed to him. He, they, many of his fellow prisoners scratched at torn bits of paper with the stubs of pencils. But even stubs measure time and indicate a future containing no further words. Their few frugal sentences they wrapped in approximations of envelopes: greasy paper, ragged remains of newspapers each with too great an expense of pencil lead further depleted by an address which had to be painfully thickened to make any impact at all.

His letters to Margaret. All those letters to Margaret.

Written as if they were public statements, 'We're bearing up, and kept very busy all day. Could all do with a good bath though. I'm getting quite good at mending my clothes, and have even become a dab hand at darning socks. Of course, we don't wear them much here, the heat is considerable, day and night ..'

From time to time when he'd written to Margaret it was as if a little light had shone dimly somewhere in his head to remind him that this was not enough. But this light would not suffer the transformation into words, so that while it shone and tried to tell him, his hand continued to write on the surface of the paper as if determined to exclude anything between the lines, let alone anything to shred the heart of both the writer and the remembered reader.

All those letters to Margaret; all his men's to their wives and sweethearts. How could he tell them, how could he kick away these men's last props? He felt spasms in his throat as if silenced words were fighting for freedom. He knew he'd have to tell them; he knew he couldn't. Slowly, it sank in, possessed him. It was as if in propping up these cripples' crutches that his own would stand firm.

From the jungle shade, Ashin's quiet and reasonable voice resumed the commercial transaction. 'And, as previously transacted, sir, your usual consignment of cigarettes?'

'Yes.'

'As regards other items, sir?'

Richard tried to bring Ashin back into focus. In those moments he'd sought, as happened more and more often now, the sanctuary, the ease of mental escape, a random flick through his life at Home, his life with Margaret. This time he was standing in front of Leonard's Austin Eight when it decided not to start. He rehearsed the ritual of easing up and releasing the catches, then lifting the whole side of the engine cover so that its hinges on the other side would open in reverse to the ones at the top on your side, the two parts co-ordinated to reveal the glory of the silent engine. You touch leads and pipes, press, push and pull. You return to the starting handle. It is as if the motor needs those few minutes of devotion or affirmation because it now springs into life. But this was only a temporary reprieve.

Back to business, he, Richard, had the goods; to be hidden, but too soon consumed. Some given to men whose days faded before their eyes; some to men beaten to a pulp; some food left over to preserve himself.
'Thank you. That will be all, for the time being.'

Ashin's silent nod, only just visible, indicated that another cheque would be required; that there was no time for further orders, that time was dangerous. Richard had already counted: he had seven left. Somehow seven cheques had to be stretched into an unknown future of unknown duration. Like the stubs of pencils, the experiments with wooden nibs and charcoal ink, the cutting up of old tyres into the shape a man's foot, and the preservation of a thrown away piece of cloth for some imagined use in the next minute, hour or day. Your whole being sunk into the invention of survival. Or the creation of a future where none existed.

But a question drawn itself up in his mind, 'Look here Ashin, if a cheque can get through, why can't you take letters?'

Ashin's silence became active. His face, thrust forward, shook. Richard saw the lateral movement of a forefinger drawn left to right across a dark throat. The finger joined its fellows to reach out as a hand for the cheque. Time for the secret and planned experiment was running out. Quickly Richard wrote the amount he owed on the cheque. His mind spun with words: words that smelled of flesh, of hair, of his hands touching hers before sliding down to her waist, her eyes closed, and then her gasp. That blessed moment. Now, endlessly his mind had to erase from memory, oh God, a hundred letters written and unwritten, thousands of stilted words signifying little or nothing, but everything to him.

Sweat dripped off his face; a drop fell onto the cheque, grotesquely magnifying part of the tiny word, South-eastern, before beginning to dissolve the three letters. Automatically, the little finger of his left hand swept across the threatened cheque, delicately removing the drip, obliterating it with an opposing thumb; a drip of time forgotten in his urgency to tear the cheque from its stub and turn it over. Words rang in his mind, clamouring for precedence, racing to be first.

Bracing the back of the cheque on top of its inert successors he wrote, 'Please tell Margaret that I am well.

Tell her I think of her all the time.' The very cement of his being, where he drew himself for a blissful moment away from this hell and placed himself beside her, say, in their garden, a walk on the Downs, in quiet contentment on the settee listening to a Home Service concert, Holtz, Elgar, or Vaughan Williams. The quiet remembered contentment. The fun.

Chapter 3

1943

It might be that the sound of attack, assault, or death can be immediate: the tumbling of a heavy weight onto the stomach, the fear, the flight. Or it might take in a slow drip of time to become a volcano of terror flowing red hot through the whole body. In this way the air raid siren would hurl Margaret from the oblivion of sweeping, dusting, cleaning, or staring at the wall. Or as now, in the middle of the night. It was a physical rising within her of the force of fear which coursed through her body. Its rising and strengthening note of warning could reach her throat before she knew what it was. Yet familiarity was no comfort.

The creaks and groans of the house at night had frightened her after Richard had gone - the airing cupboard in the bathroom, the chest-of-drawers and cupboard in the bedroom had all ticked, moaned and groaned their particular litanies of separation. And the very stairs themselves whispered of an intruder creeping up to attack her. Over time she had isolated each, one by one, so that the knowledge of which was which could no longer wrack her body in beats of hot panic. She tried to cling onto this small triumph. But each time the air raid siren jolted her out of sleep it was because it was too elemental, too much like her heart crying. It threw her out of sleep, or out of any sunken state in the house or the garden, or walking down to the shops. It propelled her feet too often to the earth of Elsie's shelter.

Elsie consciously managed shelter time. Each time it seemed as if a different tack was to be introduced, some agenda of her own mind's making, a reflection of her inner monologue, her war tinted preoccupations. For Margaret, entering the shelter now resembled being late for a meeting: the apologies for absence had probably already been covered, and perhaps by now Matters Arising were being attacked, following the minutes of the last meeting during a particularly nasty bit of bombing.

That night the meeting had been convened at quarter past two.

Margaret stumbled in, barely guided by the failing battery of Richard's bicycle lamp.

'There you are, at last,' Elsie announced as she shuffled along the bench to give Margaret room. 'Budge up,' she told Anne, 'in case your dad gets back early.' Air Raid Wardens sometimes didn't. She looked Margaret up and down to fully register the two coats, Richard's oversized socks and the exhausted bedroom slippers. Her face winced with the effort of not saying anything about the slippers and the muddy garden path down to the shelter.

Outside, beyond the hanging carpet door and the rigid curve of the galvanized steel roof, the real world rumbled and thumped, but did not yet approach to blast them into eternity.

This evening's agenda included neighbours in general. War had not diminished Elsie's sense of rumour: the Smiths a few doors away: Mr had lost his job, probably through incompetence or idleness and a son, William, had been taken into the Navy. Elsie's opinion about that: 'You'd be safer in the Army'. The Smith's daughter looked as if she might be getting married, Hitler permitting, to a man who had been courting her, but whose work was top secret. That this was conjecture did not matter; conjecture was close enough to fact to satisfy Elsie.

Further down the Close the husband and father, Mr Lethwade, at number ten, had simply disappeared. Working hypothesis: probably secret work, involving parachuting into enemy territory. Mrs Bythe, widowed some time in the 1920s, was going to resign from the W.I. , and that lady at the bottom of the street, something like Mrs Derbyshire, with all those children, most of whom would soon be reaching serving-in-the-forces age, had a man, not Mr D, seen to be entering and leaving the house at odd times of the day and night. And her great with child, one after the other. Across the road, the Fullers, she'd seen cracks of light on at least two occasions. On one of those occasions it seemed to go on and off like a signal. What was more, there was an air raid a few minutes later. If it happened again, she was going to report it to the Air Raid Warden, and if he didn't do anything about it, she'd go to the Police.

No one stirred, reacted or tried to think of better things which could be offered up in an air raid shelter. But suddenly the carpet door was thrust aside and Reg pushed his way in. He crammed in between his wife and daughter and stared blankly at the curve of the corrugated steel roof, while, slouched in blankets, they faked sleep to dissociate themselves from war, from the proximity of parents, a neighbour and the conjecture-filled air of the shelter.

'Thank the Lord for small mercies,' Elsie muttered. But Margaret had closed her eyes, the better to listen to the strengthening of the explosions which seemed to be wandering nearer like a summer storm. She'd brought nothing to knit.

With the unpredictability of the duration of this air raid, Mrs H. didn't to get to A.O.B., or even the date of the next meeting because Matters Arising covered all other preoccupations, even if they were clothed in the hand-me-downs of others. This was also because she had been nursing an all-embracing and final give away: those new people, the whatdoyoucallthems, the Northies and the Bowes:

'They're the sort who don't do anything for the war effort - youngish and fit, and who should be reported as well.'

But at the same time Elsie often sought to demonstrate how her humanity lingered close to the surface of everyday life in time of war.

'And you, dear,' she added quietly, in a post-AGM fashion when tea would be taken, together with the cupcakes of further local scandal. 'And you, dear,' she repeated, 'heard anything yet?' Margaret shook her head. What more could anyone say of a man missing on the other side of the world? To her the absence of further telegrams meant that he was still missing, so why did everyone ask? Was it something like that man, a dentist, who'd been found dead on the heath? He'd been missing for months, nearly a whole year, why did everyone keep asking about him?

'Oh, dear,' Elsie said, 'with you fit and able, and with them desperate to fill all these jobs for the war effort. Haven't they written to you yet?'

Even Elsie could not know that the letter asking Margaret to report to the employment office in the town centre was still lying on the sideboard in the kitchen. For days it had lurked there like a threat: You've got to do this, the authority says so, within the next few days.

Mrs Ward, 28 Dicksons Rise. Dear Madam   Yours faithfully, squiggle.

Last night in Mrs H's shelter I finished your jumper. The Sherwood green one. Mrs H lost some tiles but that could have been the wind she says. I bought a few apples and nearly made an apple pie ...

In keeping with his status as branch manager, Mr Long knew that he had total control of the post. However, in a wave of enlightenment, partly induced by wartime initiatives towards achieving greater efficiency, he'd delegated initial sorting to Sheila because she'd worked hard for the bank but had no hope of rising further than a junior clerk. She would never, in other words, get to serve customers behind the counter, like Mr Bailey. His was a position of great responsibility. Despite changing times brought on by the second war, Mr Long still felt that it was not right for a woman to be exposed to the danger of such responsibility: a situation where she might come into contact with male customers.

A few years ago, Mr Long had hovered round Sheila like a moth, finding the light she emanated attractive. She had entered and occupied a place in his fantasies. But he couldn't think exactly why it was, because in the fantasy Sheila never got into bed with him. When the war came, she somehow began to fade, lose shape, her hair greying overnight, her clothes tired. Her body, despite wartime rationing was, in his opinion, no longer comely; her place in his fantasies taken by Mrs Ward - so sad, so tragic, so much in need of help.

Mr Long was probably a bit early this morning. Eager to open his post and begin the comfortable routine of the day, he stood over Sheila as she finished sorting it: letters marked CONFIDENTIAL and addressed to the manager on her left, cheques, credit notes, invoices to the right, and head office directives and government bumph to the front because they'd be perused by Mr Long first and then delegated as appropriate. So, this particular morning, her boss hovered, shifting a little impatiently from one leg to the other, anticipating the pleasure of sitting in his office, immune to the world, slitting open each CONFIDENTIAL letter with a satisfying, rasping whisper of his silver letter knife styled, because of the dictates of fashion in his youth, like a diminutive Japanese samurai sword.

During the day Mr Long would often handle this knife. He liked to contemplate its difference, its overt if discrete sense of the exotic.

Clients and customers, he thought, might even be a little impressed. At the very least, it gave him a slight, but noticeable, frisson of power and potency, together with a hint of the forbidden - his country being at war with the Japanese. At heavy times of the day with his room darkened with duty, he fingered the silky sheen of the blade and stared at the handle's complicated pattern: the eternally intertwined line going everywhere and nowhere, the letter perhaps signifying some deep and barely comprehendible eastern concept of eternity. Sometimes he pictured himself swinging a full-sized sword of this shape and design, carving the air with flashes of steel.

His secret.

The envelope franked in India which Sheila had just picked up was grubby, faded and tired. Still leaning impatiently over Sheila, Mr Long felt an immediate sense of danger, a tiny but significant leap of the heart, before reaching out for the envelope. In that time Sheila had it open, and a cheque had dodged her quick fingers to float down onto the polished oak table. Unlike toast, it landed the right way up and both pairs of bankers' eyes immediately registered the worn paper, the faded date, some months earlier, and the signature of Richard Ward. One pound, three shillings and seven pence. Sheila gasped and the muted activity over busy ledgers and journals around her ceased. But Mr Long had pounced, in seconds had read the sixteen words on the back, and in a flurry of further seconds had realised all possible implications, and had snatched up the envelope.

'Please come with me, Miss Hurst.'

Mr Long closed his door and sat at his desk. Sheila stood before him, not invited to sit on one of the two seats usually reserved for clients. She noticed, but he hadn't yet, that he'd picked up his letter knife as if the envelope he clasped had not been slit.

'Miss Hurst, you are to mention this to no one. No one, do you understand?' His voice was quiet, reasonable, measured, even though he didn't notice that the knife swung left and right, imperceptibly conducting his words.

'Apart from the fact that this could be a forgery, there is no evidence that Captain Ward is still alive. This could come as a great shock to his wife, and she needs protection from any such thing. This matter is highly confidential and, I don't need to emphasize, delicate. It requires careful handling, and I may need to consult the authorities. I repeat, you are to mention this to no one!'

Sheila nodded. 'Yes, Mr Long.'

She even had time to reflect that secrets are rather nice. She'd have a secret which she could use to bestow upon herself a certain superiority and excitement otherwise totally denied her. The spinster. The way men looked at her, in some cases politely trying to conceal their pity, in other cases the opposite: a woman who'd be so grateful that she'd do anything for you.

'Yes, Mr Long,' she repeated. And while she was there with him and no one else could hear, added, 'Excuse me for asking, sir, but when you've finished with the envelope, would it be possible for me to have the stamp - ?'

Mr Long had forgotten that Sheila was a keen philatelist. His blank look was enough to tell Sheila that the request was so impossible as to require no answer. She turned and reached for the door handle.

Although sufficient time had not yet passed for Mr Long's daily foray into the territory of his juniors, he followed Sheila out to collect the rest of his post, and to linger on the floor long enough to ensure that the financial day had begun as it should continue - heads down, entries being assiduously recorded, accounting checks and balances meshing harmoniously and, above all, that the only audible expression of words was strictly limited to banking, in consistent with the high levels of efficiency and professionalism of the South Eastern Bank.

Margaret had not yet pulled across and fastened the blackout across each window; not yet shrouded the house in gloom so that indoor lights could be safely switched on and off. This was the in-between period, a premature twilight, where it was still light enough outside, but indoor tones and hues were fast dwindling into sombre colourlessness, and domestic clutter began to blur formlessly. As time went by, she found this transitional time, stretched in summer, brutally brief in winter, almost comforting, secure in the knowledge that, with the lights off, she could see out, knowing that no one could see in. If she could only clothe her life in such protection, she would be cocooned, safe, and wait. Wait. Waiting.

Day and night this transitional life strained at her consciousness, trying to force an entry, but barred because to face it in the sunlight of clarity would be too much. It was a time of wandering secretly through caves of her own making, which became a time of phantom echoes: 'Mummy, where's Daddy? Mummy, when's Daddy coming home?' For these were echoes which should have had real instigators, children running up and down the stairs, demonstrating that bed was the last thing on their minds. Then their laughter at being chased and hunted down behind a door, the teddy bear like a detective puppet finding the child, the child unable to resist it. The fun she could have had. The bits of Richard which could have been left behind.

Then the unanswered words she wrote to him.

Mrs H says we're keeping the home fires burning but I have not had a letter from you. She says send them to Singapore but the post office says no, to the Ministry. It is difficult to get any coal. And Mummy and Daddy send their regards and there was a bit of damage in town.

The scraps of paper left in the dining room, one after the other, lifeless in the bureau.

It was unusual to have this subterranean time interrupted, unless by the siren. Unusual to have the twilight was rudely destroyed when her feet fled, though increasingly reluctantly, to the shelter. Once, she'd just laid down on their bed, fully clothed, waiting for the end. Not making any kind of promise, not saying if I'm here in the bright morning I'll do so and so and change and never again live like such and such, when Elsie, clutching an armful of blankets because of the unseasonably cold weather, had banged on her door. Then used the bell to reinforce her pressure. Thump, bang, crash, and ring with the urgency of imminent death, long before it was actually raining down from on high.

So that when the bell rang, she was gripped with a panic which left her breathless. Even though Elsie might be the only one in the street who'd ever do this, the repeated agendas of frequent bombing had rendered casual contact redundant, saving it for chance encounters up and down the street or during expeditions to the shops.

Within moments Margaret had recovered sufficiently to think, to remind herself that she could see out, and no one could see in unless they peered closely, their faces shielded with two hands, their breath swallowed to prevent the glass fugging up. A thing that Elsie probably wouldn't do in case she was spotted by an alert neighbour and thus lose out in the battle for control of all local rumours.

The bell rang and rang. Metallic trilling clamorous, urgent, invasive, so much closer than the siren. Margaret ran into the kitchen. Even with the door shut the noise was still distressing. She thought of hiding in the spare bedroom upstairs at the back of the house. But this meant running the gauntlet of the front door - running past the bell itself. She knew she could not bear this. The kitchen was the only refuge.

It seemed like a long time, but was probably only a few swollen seconds when the tone of the bell began to flatten and fall, soon to begin to lose strength, dwindling, dying. Even this death was not enough to dispel its soul which still rang in Margaret's ears with all the terror, shame and insistence of its live self. It still filled the house as she opened the kitchen door and crept down the corridor, flitted up the stairs and threw herself into the main bedroom, stumbling against the chair in front of the mirror where these days she sat and looked at herself, discreet make-up forgotten and wondered who she was and what she should do. But she was not going to be reprieved so easily; a hard rapping took over from the death of the bell: a ratatat hammering of the door knocker. A hollow, dismal knell more terrible than the trilling of the bell. She felt the house shake; she felt her heart thump faster and faster as if the evil beat were climbing the stairs one by one to get her.

This was when she couldn't understand why she was lying on the floor. Silence exaggerated the colliding cartilage of her finger joints as she pressed herself upwards. This sound was submerged under the stretching of her suspenders and the crackling of her starched blouse as she unwound herself.

From the dimness of the bedroom window she watched Mr Long walk slowly and awkwardly backwards up the garden path, his eyes fixed intently on the house. He stopped and turned at the gate to open it. With a last look at the house, staring blindly at where Margaret stood, he turned and walked away with clipped, practiced steps. Even though she and the house still rang with the terror, the shame and the insistence of the demanding doorbell, she forced herself to go downstairs again. When she reached the front door, she stretched out her hand towards its gleaming bell. But no, she wouldn't rewind it: the bell had unwound to Mr Long's urgency, and she would leave it unwound, its springs uncoiled, its impotence paradoxically protecting her. Later, under the protection of complete darkness she opened the front door, stepped outside and wrestled with the door knocker, twisting and wrenching, until it came off with such a scream of outraged screws and wood that she thought Mrs H would surely have heard.

The padre had died. His face had become pallid with the sickness for which there was no doctor to define, fictionalize, or treat. The eyes always followed this lead, paling into insignificance before giving up. Richard could see it coming because this was what happened to them; one by one they weakened. Gave up, were the words used at first, as if in resisting a sick man could deflect or at best postpone death. Slowly, under the weight of approaching morbidity, their words were crushed out of existence. The eyes of dead men were irresistible; stared as if seeing but not understanding, and had to be gently closed. Yet, before this point of no return, Richard saw lost souls in living eyes all round him. To him it seemed as if souls wanted to vacate the shell long before death, or liberate themselves at a time of their own choosing.

With each death Richard was reminded of their emaciation as a mirror image of his own. They'd need a supply of fat cheque books to keep them alive. He had only a few cheques left, and resisted the temptation to count them because this would have seemed like pacing his own end: his life stretching the length of two, three, four cheques. But even this ignored the random nature of the sickness which took you: skeletal men might clatter on in life day by day, month by month. The strongly built, on the other hand, could be quickly stripped of flesh and felled.

The Padre's book was thrust into his hand in a gesture impossible to refuse; so that Richard now read the prayers over the emaciated young bodies. The Book of Common Prayer, proclaimed in copperplate writing that it had first belonged to William Stackwood in 1897. Then the names of the Stackwoods who'd used it since, Walter, Stanley, and finally Peter who could no longer use it. He'd had to cajole, persuade and bribe with pieces of chocolate the men he ordered to dig shallow graves.

Man that is born of a woman hath but a short time to live, and is full of misery. He cometh up, and is cut down, like a flower; he fleeth as it were a shadow, and never continueth in one stay.

Each time the words which Richard read rang in his ears as if someone else were reading them. They would continue to swirl in his mind while he pretended to hack and dig, carry and dump. The road they were building had no end; even its beginning had been forgotten. Increasingly he felt the presence of Margaret behind him as he bent to work. Just that. He'd be with her somewhere unidentifiable and he was supposed to be filled with ..... what? Then, if he tried hard, he could speak to her; but this would often get confused with the conversations he initiated with God. In any case, the words of the burial service would inevitably reassert themselves. He knew them by heart, as if that forlorn organ was the only place where they'd stick.

thou makest his beauty to consume away, like as it were a moth fretting a garment: every man therefore is but vanity.

Chapter 4.

1943

Margaret had made a decision. It had come to her in the fretful watches of the night when she'd again wakened from a dream she couldn't recall. Or perhaps that was the point: it was a dream made waking flesh, cleanly incised onto a more illogical and arbitrary world. What happened was that she felt empowered to pursue the first sentence of a story into a complete narrative in which she was to be the main character, the protagonist. She would visit the bank as usual, as if Mr Long had not exhausted her front door bell; as if he'd not battered the front door with the knocker she'd later wrenched off and which lay just to the left of the door handle on the tiny table with the long legs where in other houses a telephone might have been placed, instead of hung from the wall next to the door.

She would impose her own order on the situation. She saw herself walk in, not creep in, holding herself more erect than usual, wearing her best brown coat, the long one, with the brown hat that went with it. The hat with the matching brown band and the two discreet but significant green feathers, to be worn at an almost jaunty angle, pulled down to the right. She would go straight up to Mr Bailey and will him to serve her as he usually did. She would make herself ask him in sentences larded with, 'If you could be so kind, Mr Bailey. Yes, the weather seems to be improving'. She would force herself not to catch Mr Long's eye if he lurked among his clerks. Mr Bailey would serve her in his usual sympathetic way, and the story would end when she swept out of the bank, into the sanctuary of the high street.

Even so, she quickly recognized stage-fright in the emerging tightness of her stomach - an emotion either new to herself or not experienced for longer than she could remember, even though she had had time to mentally rehearse the act several times during the walk down the slope of Dicksons Rise, through the park and along the High Street, not taking the bus as she usually did. Could actresses, she wondered, clothed in the security of carriage and composure, wearing the right disguise, confident of a trained and well-modulated voice, still feel like this?

The 'Good morning, Mr Bailey, I hope you are well. The weather shows signs of improvement, does it not?' went well. Mr Bailey smiled, looking at her fractionally longer, as if at a new Mrs Ward, and replied that he was well and hoped the weather would maintain its improvement throughout Sunday, when he'd have a particularly large amount of gardening to do, it being the time of year. He carefully counted and smoothed out the pound note, and checked the half crowns, and small change, sorting them into a pattern on the gleaming wood surface the easier to check twice that the amount was correct.

It was going so well that Margaret dared to raise her eyes to meet the gaze of any of the clerks moving hither and thither behind the partition. She smiled a mask at Sheila, and at another, a short middle-aged man, neat in starched collar and dark grey suit. Mr Long was nowhere to be seen.

'Thank you, Mrs Ward,' Mr Bailey said. His smile was not such a mask as hers, perhaps because not so over-rehearsed. He did, though, seem to have something else on his mind like some unfinished business. This went as far as a gentle, forced cough, with one hand in front on his mouth as if to protect Margaret from some indiscretion. 'Your husband,' he whispered, 'any news, if I might enquire?'

Even though this was an unscripted addition, Margaret coped, readying herself to depart with dignity, stage right. But Mr Bailey's question almost threw her. All she could do was shake her head, because peripheral vision showed her that all was not well, that the rehearsed action of sweeping out might have been subverted by these mere seconds of valuable time wasted. She was right because as she turned, she saw that Mr Long had somehow appeared behind her. This eventuality had not been rehearsed, but was a subplot which should have been, and this angered her. The possibility of a conspiracy between Mr Bailey and Mr Long rose before her like an unbelievable flame she would have to douse. Even so, she surprised herself. She saw that Mr Long had taken a deep breath to speak to her, but she spoke first. He may even have spoken as she began, but his words were lost on her in her heightened state of emotion.

'Thank you, Mr Long. I am in a hurry, if you don't mind.'

Margaret extended her right hand toward the large polished brass handle of the door. Stunned at being brushed aside, Mr Long reacted like a servant caught neglecting his duty. He sprang past Margaret to open the door. She swept out, and ran the length of the High Street, her bag so tightly clutched to her side that her running motion was distorted, her legs felt as if they were carrying her in an awkward way which must have been evident to every passer-by.

By the time she arrived home, flustered, bothered and too hot, something else had happened. At the back of her mind it was connected with Elsie, though this was obscure. It was also connected with her every departure and arrival to and from home: that Elsie would be watching. If not watching, she'd usually know, because even if an air raid didn't offer a day or night time meeting in the shelter, Elsie would catch Margaret in the street and inform her that she, Margaret, had just been shopping, had been gardening or going into town because of the latest rumours of the unexpected availability of marmalade or even more oddly, cheese off-ration. What happened on the surface was that Margaret, as if impelled by the energy generated by her defeat of Mr Long felt she must go straight to the letter still lingering on the lounge mantlepiece next to the telegram about Richard missing. She'd report to the war effort place the next morning, or the one after.

I am managing quite all right with the rations and Daddy is growing spinach. Mrs H has got vegetables all round and over the air raid shelter and I am still helping with socks and blanket squares and I wish I could hear how you are .....

Two days later Elsie hammered on the door. Even though the siren was wailing, Margaret took some time to check that it was not Mr Long before opening the door. Elsie was terse, tense, 'Are you deaf?' and scuttled quickly away. With the door open the siren sounded as if it were braying in the next street, or at the bottom of the slope of the Rise.

In the shelter Elsie's agendum was to remain silent to show Margaret that she disapproved of something, or of many things. Although Margaret knew it would all eventually come out, she hoped it wouldn't.

She knew how Elsie would knowingly trample over anything she wished concerning Margaret, and that she would want to know why.

'Are you going to have it mended?'

Should Margaret be defensive by asking her what? But she feared the answer was likely to be sarcastic, you should know. Don't need me to - .' Was it the knocker or it was the bell?

She capitulated and said, 'Yes.'

'Who's going to do it?'

'I expect I'll find someone.'

Elsie's replying sniff clearly indicated that something far more definite needed to be declared.

'Father,' Margaret lied, 'I'll ask my father to come and repair them.'

To ask when her father was actually likely to present himself with tools was a mark which Elsie could not overstep in the presence of her husband and daughter. She changed the subject.

'Heard any more about War Work, then, dear?'

Margaret, bowed over her knitting so that her eyes were not visible in the wavering candle light, shook her head, 'Not yet.' It was an act of defiance she rather liked; to knowingly conceal something from Elsie was to keep part of herself intact, out of the way, completely her own. She'd tell in her own time. If anything came of it; that way she'd not have to admit to failure and endure Elise's probing backed up by compulsory advice.

In fact, she had heard, though in person. She made a decision, somewhat in the spirit of the one she'd made before going to the bank: she'd see what would happen, and she'd keep this to herself. The day before she had gone to the War Effort Exchange - a small hall attached to the Methodist Church; a place which, despite a couple of unhappy light bulbs, effectively expressed the gloom of the winter's day, if not a dusty smell of abandonment.

In the middle of this hall, below the stage, stood a single trestle table covered in small piles of paper. At it sat an older man, say Dr Simpson's age. Because he sat at a table where information was displayed whose particulars had to be summoned up and reasonably proposed, the man had an air of responsible preoccupation, as if the whole war effort rested heavily on his shoulders.

Half a dozen wooden chairs had been placed along one wall at a right angle to the table. The age darkened floorboards of the place cried out for occupation, for a Bring and Buy, for a meeting about a church fête in six months' time and a toddlers' session where exhausted mothers could commiserate with each other over a cup of tea. At the back of her mind was mention of the hops held here - the depleted local dance band with their quicksteps, waltzes and foxtrots to alleviate the waiting, watching and worry of wartime.

A woman of Elsie's age sat apologetically on the second chair: the first chair could reasonably be defined as being the one nearest to the table. Whether or not out of a sense of modesty, or because someone else had previously occupied the chair which unquestionably proclaimed them as first in the queue, Margaret could not tell. She carefully selected the fourth chair, because that left a polite gap between her and the woman. As Margaret discretely sat, the woman turned and smiled at her. Words such as hello or good morning were obviously out of the question in so serious place as this . Smiling back, Margaret recognized her as Mrs Fuller about whom Elsie had said certain things, but she had forgotten what. Was it a vanished husband? Or some man seen in and out of her house, or merely the one who'd lost her ration book?
Rising to his feet, the War Effort man spoke a little above a whisper, 'Madam, if you would care to -'

As Mrs Fuller stood, Margaret noticed the smaller chair opposite the clerk's table.

In the hollow hall words would have to be exchanged in the form of writing if there they were not to be broadcast for all to hear. And so, it was that Mrs Fuller's name, address on her identity card were publicly confirmed.

'Thank you, Mrs Fuller,' the man said, 'Would you please be so kind as to indicate such skills and experience as you may have acquired.

This should allow me to match you with such work as may be appropriate.'

Margaret sat in a state she knew as jitters: she'd be asked the same question. Her answer would sound as void and unhelpful as Mrs Fuller who spoke of mending, housework and washing. Because her mind stormed with what to say and her legs began to insist that she flee, she missed what the man suggested Mrs Fuller might do for the War Effort. She was aware, after an indeterminate amount of time, that Mrs Fuller was making small crackling noises with a piece of paper she was pushing into her bag.

The man looked across at Margaret. 'Madam, if you could be so kind,' he said, indicating the small chair.

Between bouts of fever, Richard wondered if his illness was getting worse. Were the attacks becoming longer, and the relatively well time in between becoming shorter? He found it almost impossible to quantify time of any sort within a day or night, let alone in terms of days, months, or years. The worst thing was having to work when the fever chose to reassert itself: to wield a pick, push a shovel, sort stones. At such times he crammed his mind with Margaret, their house, their garden. Particularly the garden where it was always Spring. He'd look from the dining room French windows or the kitchen window over the washing-up towards the bottom of the garden. Here the Bramley serenely waited, biding its time, while the Victoria stood braced for blossom burst. The daffodils below were triumphantly first, just beginning their gentle nod towards the long spears of their leaves. Among them, the bluebells he'd planted had pushed up gentler blades, more vividly green, their flowers not yet ready to dance on slender stalks. If he stepped outside through the French windows, the sun from the east, might feel just that welcome bit warm on his face. This whole thing was an image he thrust at his mind, a rigidly compulsive picture he had to gaze at as long as he had the strength to retain it.

But, of course, Margaret was there beside him now in the garden. They weren't doing anything in the garden, just being. Being together. If he allowed it to distress him, he knew he would be lost - because he couldn't fully see her while he was looking directly at the flowers and she stood at his side. He knew how he wanted her to appear: a gentle presence, say, in that new floral dress. But she wouldn't fully materialize. He had to force himself to be content that she was there. Sometimes, though, when he tried to invoke the sound of her voice, not even real words, this wouldn't come either. Instead, their place was now filled by a kind of babble which could have been almost any woman.

If the bouts of sickness and fever closed the gap completely who would read the holy words over his own grave? Would anyone even think of placing a wooden cross in the earth above him? Also, he'd looked, he'd counted: he had one more cheque left. She must know. She must.

The laundry was on the edge of the Heath. The garden-girded ranks of new housing facing the heath were held back by the retaining belt of Ashtead Road. Not so the laundry; how the laundry came to be built where it stood in solitary glory on the other side of the road on the otherwise inviolable heath no one knew or cared about in time of war. It cleaned mountains of clothes for the town and now for the newly arrived Canadians, and it employed people who, instead of having to risk the journey up to London, had only to walk or cycle to work. There it steamed, incongruous and utilitarian, in whitewashed concrete block walls and corrugated iron roofs, washing and cleaning for all it was worth; a steamer moored among a wreck of tired grass, and islands of spindly hawthorn and delicately stunted silver birch.

Two years ago, the Battle of Britain had droned and whined above the Heath, the sky laced with white exhaust, punctured by the black smoke of stricken aircraft, and graced by the occasional lucky white flower of a parachute. Once an airman had pushed open the front door as Margaret did that first morning, he asking for a telephone, she for a Mr Barnes.

Mr Barnes, she understood, ran the place which meant that he didn't have to get soap suds on his hands.

She found that she was standing in what looked like an office which had a desk each end submerged under bits of paper with random vertical spikes where more paper was skewered. At each desk sat a man in a brown suit. Both had worn, brown trilby hats on their heads. Set into the long wall opposite a partitioned office was a large walk-in cupboard. Next to this a large notice-board intruded, crowded with yellowing sheets of paper whose curled up corners had become a faded imitation of embryonic dried flowers. Margaret waited, thinking that one of the working men might acknowledge her existence. After a few moments one of them stood and, without a word, with scarcely a glance at her, walked slowly across to the partitioned office. He knocked moderately on the glass door of the partition through which Margaret could just make out the darker shape of a man rising.

The boss, Mr Barnes, as his name might imply, was a large man who had to fold himself to accommodate life: getting his head safely through his office doorway then avoiding the threatening steel beams in the office as he walked across to Margaret. To Margaret he was like a leaning giant who, instead of peering at you down a long nose, bent down, staring querulously over the top of his glasses.

'Who are you?' he asked.

Margaret tried to explain about being sent here, and how she'd had a puncture.

Mr Barnes sighed, and persisted, 'But who are you?'

She told him her name and about the man in the Methodist Hall. 'And he sent you?'

Margaret repeated her bit about the War Work Office at the Methodist Hall, omitting this second or third time the subplot of the bicycle which she'd have to push home.

'Do they have a telephone?'

She searched her memory for a trace of dumpy black Perspex on the desk, or the hazard of a flex snaking across the floor. On the other hand, of course, had there been a wall mounted set?

'I'm not sure, I - .'

The man who'd not summoned the boss now stood and handed Mr Barnes a slip of paper. 'Ah, yes, of course,' the boss said, putting it in his jacket pocket.
That settled, Mr Barnes looked round the office. 'Now,' he said, 'didn't we used to have a table, the folding one - ?'

This was the moment that one of the clerks, Margaret was later to know as Garner began a loud clattering of his calculating machine, whirring the handle viciously, crashing the carriage forward and back with the tens and hundreds lever as if the shredding of numbers was part of the war effort. It startled Margaret, adding to her unease, her desire to escape. But, as if under this noise screen, the other man, she'd later know as Savory, rose from his desk, strolled across to the cupboard, opened it and pulled out a collapsible picnic table together with its accompanying folding chair. Carrying these into the centre of the office, he paused and looked round. Margaret could see that he was engaged in a troublesome and possibly vexing inner debate. His face was closed up so as to avoid consulting anyone else; he was going to place the table in such a position as would not inconvenience himself at all. His decision made; he laid the table collapsed on the floor in the alcove made by the part of the office not included in Mr Barnes' partition; likewise, the folded chair. At the same time the detonations of the calculator seemed to rise to a climax before an abrupt stop as if it had completed its destruction of all known numbers. Mr Barnes turned and walked back to his office, Mr Savory to his desk. In their impenetrable trilbies both Mr Garner and Mr Savory resumed their work. Over to you, their silence and preoccupation with invoices and payments proclaimed; you mind your business, we'll minds ours.

As Margaret stood by the collapsed table and chair a memory in which Richard had put up a table and chair like this fell into her mind. Was it Richmond Park, by the river? Rich-ard, Rich-mond. She hid inside this memory while she bent over and fiddled with the catch to lock the legs of the table in their supportive position; then, after a couple of bungled attempts, the chair also conceded an affirmatory click . Careful not to scrape the chair legs on the floor, she sat in her coat and hat and waited, bathed in the comfort of a reborn memory, until they told her about the work she'd do here at the Laundry. Before the picnic Richard had rowed them in a hired boat along the Thames. Although rocking the boat was still largely a male preserve, she'd dared to do so and Richard had laughed when one of the oars he was pulling snatched at air, nearly unbalancing him. She could even recount this as Richard landing legs up in the bottom of the boat. Thereafter memory would probably concur. People walking the tow path had laughed, but the last thing Margaret would do was play to the gallery. Richard delayed her stint at rowing until they turned about at Isleworth Ferry and had the tide with them. This was when he remembered the Brownie Junior and took a photo of her. She reciprocated, unexpectedly a little unbalanced and took the slanted snap of him. Smiles and laughter back on the towpath, even over the primus which was reluctant to settle to a blue flame and boil the water for the eventual resuscitating cup of tea which would accompany the egg sandwiches. In these moments of detachment while she waited to find out what they wanted her to do she wondered if she'd have the courage to go to the drawer in the living room press and look out those photos, rediscover them. Or would they pull out with them too many other memories from the bundles in which they were stored? Bundles tied up with red tape, abandoned among empty albums awaiting the regeneration of a procession of happy moments in the lives they depicted, as if such a cavalcade was the whole of those lives. Somehow, she'd always assumed that photographs willingly conspire in this deception, subtly distorting memory, reluctant to let the fun fade out of those days.

'Well, as it happens,' a powerful voice made her start.

'Sorry,' she said, as if she should have known that Mr Barnes was going to speak to her at any moment.

'As it happens, Mrs Ward, there is something you could do for us. Fiddling job which drives me - .'

Margaret couldn't think what, but rose from the collapsible chair partly out of worry for its reliability and partly so that she might better understand what Mr Barnes was trying to say.

'It's a checking and cross-reference job,' he said. 'Come tomorrow at about noon and I'll have had time to get the stuff together by then.

After that each day would suffice, would do nicely. Unless, of course, unexpected contingencies intervene.'

Mr Barnes clumped back into his office only just remembering in time to duck below the lintel. Margaret, standing, worked out that she didn't need to sit down again, picked up her bag, looked at Garner and Savory who refused to acknowledge her existence or her impending departure, and crept out of the hut.
Somewhere in the middle of the prison compound a Japanese guard stood looking up at Richard. Richard waited, eyes down because he knew they didn't like full eye contact, particularly when they were much shorter. The guard spoke in that urgent way that their language seemed to demand. Or it might have been some military habit which Richard interpreted as such. But there

seemed to be some indication in the man's urgency that Richard should follow.

The gap between Richard and the soldier kept widening and the man was growing impatient with having to wait for Richard to catch up. Half way across the compound it became clear to Richard that he was being escorted to the Commander's house. He searched in his mind why this might be; but found a mind which could not speculate, could not imagine anything worse than everyday common brutality, sickness and death. And he couldn't walk any faster than the speed of a crawl on hands and knees; couldn't do anything to assuage the guard's guttural irritation.

The Commandant's accommodation was removed from the huts of the soldiers, and even further from the hovels of the prisoners. Richard assumed it had once been the home of a rubber planter and the Colonial style was evident from its regular windows and neat, sharply angled, wood tiled roof.

A shove with the soldier's rifle pushed Richard up the steps to the veranda stretching the length of the front of the building. The front door was open, as it usually was, and Richard was prodded towards it. As he was about to enter the soldier barked more barbed words and pushed past him. Waiting, he heard from inside the room the staccato voice of the soldier and a quieter, briefer one from the Commander inside. The soldier reappeared and, grasping the remains of Richard's sleeve pushed him through the doorway.

The bus was either late or cancelled. Margaret wished she could have saved time by walking into the centre of town where she could get the bus which went directly to Stoneleigh.

As she walked up the Sunday afternoon street of nearly identical bungalows, Margaret, pretending not to, tried to avoid catching the eyes of the Lord's Day gardeners she might have known when she lived there as a child. Most looked up from a preoccupation with couch grass and ground elder, but only a few went as far as a smile from a crouched or doubled up position. She found that a slight wave sufficed. One bungalow was a levelled heap of rubble. The bungalows either side apparently unscathed, their neat gardens ignorant of war, or at least of the odd stray bomb.

Walking down her parents' short drive she glanced left and right: yes, paint was difficult to obtain, or had got too expensive. Or in her parents' case, just maintained a flaking pace with time. Rose, her mother, opened the door, as she usually did, this time launching into an expression of worry because Margaret was late. Margaret hadn't the energy to explain: everything and everyone was delayed these days, never turned up, or had died.

'Well, you've arrived, that's the main thing, love.' Mouthing tea, she ushered her daughter into the living room where Margaret's father was slumped asleep in his easy chair, yesterday's Morning Post collapsed into a ruined pyramid on the carpet beside him.

Waiting for the offering of tea and not wishing to wake her father, Margaret sat and got out her knitting: Richard's jumper. Moments later the dissonant clacking of the needles dredged her father out of his doze. Sighing, Frank pulled himself together, his eyes finding his daughter.

Assembled, he said, 'Ah, there you are.' Picking up and reordering his paper, he resumed reading, as if the presence of his daughter required some space, some garnering of daughterly topics before conversation could begin. 'Ah,' he eventually announced, as if of a conversation interrupted and folding the paper in half, 'At last they're being rolled back,' Margaret paused from her knitting, found her tape measure and checked a measurement. But her silence had him add, 'The Japs.' From the kitchen came the muffled sound of the kettle whistling with that rising note which no one had noticed was so like a minuscule version of the dread sound of a siren.

'Ah.' Margaret's father offered as a counter to the silence between them. 'What has it been doing out there?'

'Trying to rain. But the sun came out for a few minutes. Around lunch time. I think.'

Frank, grunted. Whether about the weather, or not knowing what to say, Margaret couldn't tell. But, as usual, coming to the rescue, Rose bustled into the living room, 'Just a cuppa, love, to get you in through the door. Proper tea later.' She breathed heavily, automatically demonstrating the exhausting feat of having to speak, carry and organise on a small side table the entire contents of a tea tray.

With the unnecessary aid of a red handkerchief, Margaret's father began clearing his throat in preparation for both speaking and drinking tea.

Later, during proper tea of sandwiches and cup-cakes in the dining room overlooking the back garden, the sun burst forth, converting the lawn into a vivid green, inviting square. Margaret's mother was thrilled, 'We can leave the washing up and all sit outside in the afternoon sun for the first time this Spring!' Her face glowed with the righteousness of her daring suggestion. She must have thought that Frank looked doubtful and added, 'But, dear, the deck chairs won't take a moment!'

But this took more than a moment because the third one was found to have dangerously worn canvas. It was a crisis: three people, only two deck-chairs. Various suggestions were made about possible chairs that could be brought out: a kitchen chair, or the one in the bathroom upstairs might survive the assault of garden dirt, but certainly not the posh dining room ones. Margaret knew well the signs of impending argument between her parents and that the only way of diffusing this emergency was by taking matters in hand herself.

'The rug,' she said, walking rapidly back into the bungalow before counter alternatives were offered. Margaret found the travelling rug in the bottom drawer of the press in the dining room where it had lived for the whole of her parents' marriage. It had been taken out only a few times in her lifetime, but its presence in this drawer had, however, remained an immutable truth: it was kept here and not with other blankets in the spare room chest because its use in the garden or in a car separated it irrevocably from its bedroom kin.

As Margaret placed the blanket carefully on the grass so as to make a triangle with the deck-chairs her parents would occupy, her mother was seized with sudden inspiration to scuttle indoors and find her camera. 'Well, love, we've still got several snaps left on that roll! And goodness knows when we'll be able to find another one.'

Frank, standing awkwardly muttered, 'There's no shortage that I've heard of. It's just the new colour film which you can't get, which in any case, is far too expensive.'

Margaret silenced a sigh of relief: at least her presence had so stimulated her mother that she desisted from offering up for general debate the availability or otherwise of camera film before receiving or being denied permission to take a snap. It was not that she couldn't decide things, it was just that it was so much nicer if everyone else thought it was a good idea as well. This, Margaret knew of old, merely legitimised things, and that made everyone feel better. She said, 'The roses. In front of the roses. There are a few early ones out.' Margaret's mother heaved herself up, groaning, but seemed happy to comply. They took up a position together near a side panel fence with the roses either side of them where Frank had daringly extended the gardener's compulsion to think in terms of squares and said, 'That would be nice, before we settle down.'

First Margaret and her father were snapped smiling in the deck chairs, then Margaret and her mother. Finally, Margaret persuaded her parents to have a snap together. As these her parents composed themselves for the photograph, Margaret didn't know whether to laugh or cry. Her father stood like a child unaware that he'd present himself better if he pulled his stomach in; her mother got into a dither about her hair, pushing and pulling, smoothing and patting. Suddenly noticing that she still wore her pinny, announced coyly, 'Frank, you could have told me!'

Margaret bent her knees the better to snap her parents straight on. She found it difficult to see through the view finder, not because it gave her the usual shrunken image of wherever you pointed the camera, in this case at two awkward figures, but because it was the tears and not the laughter which had apparently won: these her parents who had hoarded their rations to give her a good tea, the highlight of their week. Her father exhausted from fire-wardens' nightly watch; her mother exhausted with worry about her daughter, the new V2's and the relentless years of war.

Yet here they were, her parents, Frank and Rose, nearly Ruby Wedding, forty years, as they'd sometimes admit over a cup of tea, while world-wide people were being blown up and gunned down. And here were her parents shyly smiling at the camera with their hands seeking each other's, to touch for the split second of the snap before pretending that they hadn't. In these few seconds, although the sun seemed to shine briefly in her mind, Margaret knew that the roses would not have their potential stunning colour recorded, neither would the sky be blue. 'Colour snaps,' as her father had said, 'are too expensive.'

When Margaret was finally seated on the rug and her parents in the deck-chairs, her mother said, 'You're looking pale, dear. Your father and I were wondering if it would help if you moved back with us. You know, dear, until the end of the - . or until Richard, er - comes - .'

Standing in front of the Commander, Richard's back began to ache even more than usual. The Commander he saw had the chairs and table of the former owner pushed to one side. In their place stood a low table with several cushions serving as seats round it. A large piece of white paper hung from the wall behind the minimal table. This was decorated with five huge Japanese characters.

Richard tried to take in the rest of the room, but the backache was becoming unbearable. He found it impossible to work out if this was part of the illness, whatever it was, that was making him feel weak all the time; or the malnutrition. Standing on the road he was supposed to be making, he was usually able to shift position: lean on his shovel, move it from near his foot to a few feet away, simulating what he hoped would look like work from the short distance to where the Japanese guards stood grunting at each other.

From time to time, out of boredom, a soldier would wander up the road to inspect Richard's work, and on the way push, slap or shout at a prisoner strung out along the road. When this happened and the guard drew near, Richard would carry out a planned series of movements which he hoped would not leave him light headed from the heat and sweated loss of liquid.

Richard knew that the backache was rapidly becoming unbearable. He also knew that, whoever you were, when you stood in front of the Commander you had to wait for instructions, implied or direct. But another notion crept into his mind: was this the final test? If he failed this one would he be merely the next man to be beheaded?

The moment came when his legs, or his whole body itself intervened to decide his fate. With this came light headedness, and a complete surrender to whatever was about to happen. He sank to the floor, where his mind wandered about in some shifting corridor of darkness.

Margaret knew she was getting careless. She had begun to ignore the battering of her front door by Elsie, from the bedroom window a ghostly figure shrouded in a light dressing gown, to a background of the siren wailing the destruction of the world. At the end of the working day she would creep back from the laundry, round to the side door which let in to the kitchen, rather than to the front door where the act of unlocking the door was dangerous and exposed her for the few seconds Elsie needed to pounce from the jungle of her preoccupations in controlling the top of the close. The

V2s you heard, the ones that missed you, were getting closer, day and night. But at twenty-seven, or was it twenty-eight, she felt that the colour of her life had become grey. Indeed, a random grey strand would confront her in the morning mirror. At first, she thought it a trick of the light or some aspect of shade against a bright summer morning. She learned how to isolate a single strand of grey between thumb and forefinger, wrap it round her finger, yank it out and hold it up for the verdict of the real light of day. Not so much grey as white.

Slowly Margaret recognised what had probably become obvious to outsiders: that she was diminished. The sleepless nights in the shelter had taken their toll, even though she had now stopped fleeing bombs, and there were signs that Elsie was giving up summoning her to the shelter. It was the tension of every living moment, of not knowing, that had wearied her to the bone. Returning home from the laundry at the end of each afternoon she took to her bed, curled up and waited. In waking moments when the summer evenings had darkened, she rose, found bread and spread it with the jam her mother had bestowed upon her. It was odd how sometimes delicate spots of blue were revealed, hidden inside a loaf, or to have pocked-marked an abandoned slice of bread. The near turquoise spots and smears closely matched the Chinese colour of the breakfast crockery.

Then there was this other thing: she fought to remember something missing, something to do with Richard. Not the endless yearning for him, that undiminished part of her, but something else. It was a long time before it came to her, unbidden in the marches of the night, merely popped into her head as if it had been there all the time and had merely bidden its time: letters to Richard. How could she have forgotten to write them? How could she? It felt like a betrayal, a deliberately evil act which tugged at her body like a pain almost manifest. In the morning she would write. And when it came to morning and she found a pencil and a piece of paper torn from a notebook the words would not come, would not write themselves, would not reveal themselves in scratches of meaning on the paper.

Chapter 5.

1944

When you work, as Margaret discovered, homecoming if you allow it, can acquire a small element of pleasurable anticipation: often late now, the postman might have been. Her mother wrote two-page letters each week. Although only one or two short bus rides away, Margaret knew without reading between the lines that these letters were really making the point that in these dangerous times they lived too far apart. The dangers and privations of war had distanced mother and daughter; that before the war, the words between the lines reminded her, they used to meet in Kingston or Croydon, she elevated to the status of a married woman, and spend the day window shopping, chatting all the while about the new fashions, which might have been resurrecting pleats and a slimmer profile, or back to good, honest flares, or hats almost brimless. Or they'd go up to London to window shop in Oxford Street and then down Regent Street. Despite all this, Margaret did look forward to the letters, to become absorbed in her mother's world - what she'd queued for, how she'd heard where wool she wanted was unexpectedly recently stocked, and where bananas had somehow got through the U-boat infested ocean.

Pictures of her mother smiling in those pre-war days were so easy to summon: they had walked past, and sometimes round shops as if they were on holiday, testing the balance of crockery, stroking clothes, sliding a hand over the dark blue or medium brown enamel of a new kettle.

That was it, remembering the companionship of being an adult daughter with her mother. It was like remembering a time of extended holiday where the sun shone and there was little to worry about. At times this could come close to the cloying embrace of remembering the fun with Richard. But the crash of the letter box startled her. The postman. Or post boy.

Automatically switching off the kitchen light against Elsie she left the kitchen. In the gloom of the hall she found a letter. It was a little darker in tone than the white envelopes her mother used. Back in the kitchen, with the door to the hall closed so that the light could be switched on her heart leapt: it was buff and shouted OHMS in big letters. Underneath this printed proclamation the words *Mrs M. Ward, 29 Dickens Close* were smaller, uneven, as if typed by a hesitant, war-weary machine.

She stared at the envelope, holding it with both hands in case there was something fugitive about such a communication from on high, even if something damaging. They could play with her life if they wanted to, they could make mistakes and not care. They could send her the wrong information; they could lie. They could torture her mind.

The OHMS telegram which had preceded this envelope by nearly three years remained as evidence on the mantel-piece of how she felt. The telegram was propped up next to the wood framed clock which Richard used to wind up every four days; and which had long ago stopped because he couldn't any longer wind it up with the wide-winged brass key which lay willing and ready on the mantlepiece in front of the clock. If she passed the mantelpiece too fast, say, when in the morning she remembered to draw back the blackout, the telegram would waver and fall off onto the green tiles of the fireplace hearth, or capture the dying disturbance of her passing by achieving a little soar before landing soundlessly on the carpet.

Later, if she'd missed this involuntary flight and found the letter disturbing the tightly organised carpet pattern, the sight of it fallen became an omen which could distress her for the rest of the day. Paradoxically, she could not hide the letter in the bureau or in some forgettable drawer somewhere. This would be like trying to forget Richard.

Standing, as if before an altar, she looked at the telegram and experimented with how she'd feel if she put the envelope over it, superseding it, or next to it for support or comparison. This became too complicated in a mind too anxious to be able to think straight and which now veered obliquely into other labyrinthine passages: if she had not opened the telegram those few long years ago she would not have known that Richard was missing; she might even have retained the bright colours of hope all this time. Instead, she could only summon up the word, grey, the ashen hues of hopelessness and helplessness. And what could come after this - only leaden, murky, dingy, defeated black? Or some kind of death? If she opened the letter would that mean that she'd killed Richard, would that mean that he'd disappeared from her mind and therefore her life for ever?

Time that had stood still somehow passed as she stood in front of the clock that no longer measured it. After a blank of indeterminate length, Margaret was left with one notion which cleared itself into a thought, a decision: she would not open the letter, she would not risk feeling worse about herself, and even bleaker about being informed of Richard's death. Thinking this felt so like an admission of finality that she couldn't stop tears springing from her eyes, coursing down her cheeks. As one thought pulls down another you didn't know was tied to it, so her tears wrenched sobs from her throat, her stomach and then the whole of her body.

The sound *thunk* was sometimes hard, sometimes soft according to the force and skill of the Japanese swordsman. Richard would watch the stance of the executioner; the sword lifted a couple of feet from the bared neck, then lowered with great care, to delicately and gently stop within an inch of the flesh. The sword would rest there for long seconds, memorising the exact place where it would descend for a second time with such speed that in falling it would vanish, born again the other side of the severed neck. With his engineer's mind automatically matching force with distance travelled, he knew he could do this; he knew he'd have the might: even if it used up his last, final strength. It was merely another mystery, but one which he didn't or couldn't question. It was just that he could feel his hands gripping the leather of the handle, raising the sword high, feel his arms swinging the weapon downwards, flexing his wrists to wring out of the downward flight of the sword that extra force and finesse.

Should a second cut be necessary, the space between the two would sometimes be filled with a falsetto scream, cleanly cut by the coup de grace. Richard knew that the commander became irritated in such circumstances. The man would growl a length of crushed vowels and consonants which sounded no more like words than the grumble of a tiger. Outward emotion, particularly when you were being executed was a thing he abhorred. In his own mind Richard agreed.

As the senior officer, or rather the only one surviving, he had to take a list of remaining prisoners each week to the commander. He didn't question why. He would knock and wait for the commander's aide to admit him. Sometimes this happened immediately, sometimes he knew he'd have an indeterminate wait, slumped in the shade of the veranda and carefully placing as much of his mind as he could somewhere else, that somewhere else which was Margaret. The being of her. Her presence, though growing weak, was still there, was still indisputably her, but rendered almost transparent, remote, as if he could reach to touch her but find that his hand would slip through her body. Or he'd be merely in the English summer landscape where they'd been - perhaps Dorset in a painfully intimate corner of a meadow of delicate wild flowers, green grass and protective trees, the air full of scent and bird song, a cloth laid out for a picnic - ; or a village of thatched houses sufficiently relaxed to avoid straight lines and horizontals, with flowers in profusion all round them, climbing clumps of soft pink roses in cosy humps over the wattle and daub. And somewhere, just out of sight, Margaret sat and waited while he opened the hamper to reveal the ham sandwiches, the freshly cooked currant buns, the thermos of hot tea.

Summoned by a military word barked in his ear, Richard would rise and salute in case that was required and walk in through the door, hand over the list with a second salute, turn back with the practiced British Army parade step, lightly stamping the left foot back to make a pair with the right foot and attempt, if the energy was there, to march out. This procedure could take up and dissipate his meagre bank of strength and he'd have lean heavily on the rail leading down the steps from the veranda.

However, the last couple of times an alteration to this ritual had arisen. He found himself saluting the commander's back. Instead of at his desk, the commander was now seated cross legged on the floor with his back to Richard. Richard had to salute the back and wait with the list. The commander meanwhile, head slightly bowed, appeared to be in communion with a Buddha a foot or two from him on a low table against the wall. The first time the commander slowly raised one hand, fingers open for the list; the second time he'd remained in contemplation, or prayer with the statue, leaving Richard to revive the static dream of Margaret summoned outside on the veranda. In this state he stood waiting for the commander to raise one hand. But standing still made his back ache. Eventually he had to sink to the floor. He thought he did this soundlessly, but the commander's hand had immediately risen in an arc, fingers spread. After the third or fourth time of presenting the list, Richard noticed the great sword. It rested on the low table in front of the Buddha, supported along its length by a piece of polished wood cut so as to hold the weapon horizontally with the sharp edge downward, hidden. It interested him the first time he saw that the commander kept the execution sword here with him behind the statue but sharing its altar. After that it was just another detail which could be cancelled from his mind.

Thunk!

The blood shot crimson in one burst as the headless body toppled where it had crouched, the head tumbling forward down the execution slope. Since he read the words of the internments, Richard was also expected to retrieve the several head and reunite it with its body. As he carried each head back up the slope half articulated words rang into his mind: *Me next, me next, or when I'm the last, when I'm the last, with no one to pick up - .* It no longer surprised him how heavy a head was; how the hair, or the scalp on the bald ones, was wringing wet. The sweat of death. The sudden eruption of death-sweat before the quiet breath of the falling blade.

Up at the laundry Betty was a breath of fresh air. Even more, the only air ever to penetrate the office. She had to come in with forms for Garner and Savory and to talk to Mr Barnes about orders, customers and problems with the machinery. She entered as if it were her god-given right as a woman to invade what had long been a male preserve, fought for over the decades since Mrs Pankhurst. Despite the relatively recent appearance of Margaret, she made it clear by the way she spoke, the way she thrust her energetic bosom into the office that she was entering male territory, propelled, empowered and validated by the force of the female ones in the steaming rooms behind her. She once told Margaret, 'If I did the dance of the seven veils, love, those two dried up old sods wouldn't notice'. This with a female audience in the drying room, demonstrating everything she said, with her overwhelming bosom taking up the rhythm, swaying in sympathy. Rewarded with shrieks, she was encouraged to remove her overall and allow it to float down to the floor in a sensuous parody of the first of the seven veils to be removed.

It was only Betty's unpredictable appearances which made the days bearable for Margaret. Mr Garner and Mr Savory, Margaret soon learned, enthroned in trilby-ed stiffness sifting through papers supplied them by Mr Barnes, hated each other. Entries were made in journals and ledgers, bills for services rendered were prepared, contracts were tendered and serviced, for instance for the Canadian camp nearby.

Papers whose duties had been completed and whose services were no longer required were put to death on one of several spikes both men had ranged before them. After a period of public humiliation, the entire contents of a spike would be lifted off and buried in one of many box file coffins stored for all time deep in the vault of the communal cupboard.

During the life of this entire process not a word passed between Garner and Savory. They knocked off for morning tea and read the papers; they knocked off for their lunch break, ate their sandwiches and read the papers. And they finished off the papers with their afternoon tea break. Their knocking off time was at half past five in the afternoon. To the second they would break the silence with a sound mid-way between a sigh and a groan, put on their gabardine macs, pick up their newspapers, gas masks, lunch boxes and leave. Apart from frequent trips to the toilet in a shed outside, they saw out their days silently chained to their work stations, quietly consumed with dislike for each other.

Margaret too sat in a silence only relieved by the forced entry of Betty who dispatched secret looks of female support and sympathy. Such papers as needed to be given to Betty, Mr Barnes began to delegate to Margaret, or queries about some problems with standards of washing were taken by Margaret deep into the women's territory in the womb of the laundry where they could be sorted out, where she would be given a cup of tea, where Betty held court among the red faced laundry girls with their bloated hands and swollen fingers.

'Well, gal, don't let the long wet weekend look get you!'

Up at the laundry Betty had no volume control. She was a walking megaphone, exuding a passionate energy, suggesting that life had to be attacked head on all the time. Her communications with a single person were for one and all.

'Those miserable buggers,' she'd tell Margaret, 'if you could get them these days, I'd put firecrackers up their arses. An' you, gal, comin' to the hop? Before they all get sent to France. Good. That'll make all of us, then.'

And swept off on urgent business elsewhere before Margaret could come up with a panic-driven excuse. At home extreme anxiety gripped her, transmuted quickly into terror. She had an interrupted night where she thought she'd not slept at all. In the morning, she decided, she'd tell Betty, she'd just say, 'No, I can't come.'

'You all right?' Mr Barnes noticed. But that was as far as he'd go, knowing as he did about women's monthly problems; knowing as he did that you should never mention it. Margaret spent most of the afternoon in a seething, anguished stew of her own making before Mr Barnes came out with a list of things for her to check with Betty.

But Betty was ready for all eventualities, 'Come on, gal, you need to get out.'

Margaret hadn't said anything, was about to utter prepared, forced words when Betty grabbed the list. 'Anything I can't find, I'll whizz back to you with. Righty- o?' Then she was off, compulsively bearing all before her. Margaret knew her only recourse was to hide. It had worked before. It would work again.

Knocking on Margaret's door again was a risky business, despite the long gabardine mac and the long-brimmed hat pulled firmly down.

Neighbours might accept one visit. But twice was practically lots of times, three would be all the time. If he tried to question the wisdom of these two visits, his mind refused to become engaged. If he said to himself, the best way is to look out for her in the bank and invite her into the office, his legs still impelled him to walk across the town and up the cul-de-sac where Margaret lived. Alone and in the privacy of her house; away from the formal atmosphere of the bank with its prying eyes all intimately known to him, all watching the boss, the manager observing and noting every breath and every step he takes.

But Margaret, convinced it was Elsie, didn't risk looking and therefore courting the added danger of being seen. She found herself in the dining room but couldn't think why. The lid of the desk was open so this might have been some clue as to what she had intended to do. Her hands found papers - her handwriting, but to whom? But there was no urgency, no pressing need to look, no compulsion to write anything to anyone. Instead, she turned, walked across the dining room where she very carefully, soundlessly, drew the deep blue long double curtains across the French windows overlooking the back garden, in case Elsie or anyone else should come round the back looking in to catch her. In the double gloom that drawn curtains gave the room she lay down on the carpet, drew her knees up to her breasts and held them there, folded and secure, to await the cessation of the knocking and the departure, for the time being, of Elsie, or even of Mr Long.

Aircraft, little more than low black shapes, hurtled through the air. They left in their wake like a disturbed flock of birds, a flapping cloud of what could soon be seen to be leaflets. These missed the camp, fluttering and blowing listlessly onto scrubby ground leading to the sombre jungle. Prisoners, trudging back from work on the road, were seen picking up the sheets, peering at them, until grunts from the prison escorts made them drop the paper. Other aircraft, much higher up, droned faintly overhead, trailing wispy exhaust. What could have been distant thumps of artillery would occasionally be heard. Restless gusts of wind were a reminder of the expected monsoon. It felt as if the growing heaviness of the air could be grasped, collected and rolled into a tense ball.

Richard knew that God sometimes spoke unbidden: like whispering air that filled the space round him with uncertainty. His uncertainty, not God's. An angry uncertainty sometimes, but at other times just there with no particular colour, weight or meaning. They could be words that sometimes conjured up Margaret, but more often were a jumble from the prayer book.

Even the list of prisoners was becoming too heavy, as if the dwindling number of names had taken on a greater weight than before. Sometimes he crawled into the commander's room, at others he could support part of his weight on a balustrade, wall or door. The commander still contemplated his Buddha as if he did nothing else outside the formality of attending in full dress uniform the dwindling number of executions. But the Buddha had moved. It was now elevated to the long, low table on which the great sword stood. Being bulkier the Buddha stood to the back, and the sword lay immediately in front, its role as if now protective.

How Betty managed to unearth Margaret is difficult to say. Perhaps it was her voice, magnified down the hall to the kitchen, when she bellowed through the letter box. That this had not been preceded by the terrifying impact of knocking was what may have thrown Margaret.

'It's me, Betty! Are you there, love? It's Betty! Halloo, oo-ee, hello dear!'

Perhaps her words drew Margaret, hypnotically, irresistibly, down the hall. With a foot expertly inserted Betty quickly enlarged the tentative gap which Margaret allowed when opening the door. Betty was immediately inside, overflowing with herself, filling the hall with smiles and relentless cheerfulness. Margaret didn't know what to say, what excuses to lamely present.

Whatever she'd said, Betty's reaction would have been the same.

'What, no glad rags, dear? Come on, let's see what you've got!'

She was up the stairs as if she came round every day and helped herself. Her instinct was true: the front room would be the master bedroom; in here would be the walnut or mahogany wardrobe, and inside that would be all the dresses that a woman possessed. Underneath these, all the shoes, and in the chest of drawers next to the cupboard there might even be a more serviceable and presentable pair of stockings than the thick work ones that Margaret usually wore. This was when there came the sound of a car's horn from the street. 'Quick,' Betty urged, 'into this.' She held up a floral dress of free-flowing green leaves and flowers. 'And these will go with it.' Dark green lace ups with a bit of a heel.

A few moments later Betty had Margaret by the hand, firmly leading her down the front garden path to the sit-up-and-beg Ford Eight waiting with its impatient engine fut-futting a low layer of pale exhaust drifting towards Elsie's house. As they drove away, Margaret glanced left. Elsie's front door was partly open and a figure, no doubt Elsie's, stood obscured in the evening gloom of her hall. Margaret felt as if she'd made some kind of escape, ridiculous as it might seem. She couldn't remember why Betty had done this to her; at the same time, she felt helpless to resist. Betty's ability to carry all before her now included her, Margaret.

Inside the car were two girls from the laundry, their hair piled up, home-made perfume wafting like brash drizzle cloud round their heads. Margaret tried but failed to match them with two girls in protective scarves and overalls at the laundry.

One was driving. Betty said in a loud voice, 'Driving for some la-di-da orficer, she was, before the laundry. Got him into trouble, I bet. But her dad runs the garridge.' The girls in the front giggled. And Betty laughed for the joy of going out with the girls to a hop, and for the gift of habitual effervescence with which she always clothed herself.

The Camp's hall on the Heath was like a large hut where you'd expect to see a crowd of boy scouts busy with knots, the flapping flags of semaphore and the checking out of their store of bivouacs and tent pegs before the summer hols camp. It stood to one side to proclaim its difference from the smaller wooden huts where the Canadians bedded down. Between the two was a desert of a tarmacadamed parade ground where a dozen jeeps were very precisely lined up.

Even before the engine was put out of its agony, Margaret could hear the thump of caged, enclosed music. Indeed, even the handrail by the wooden steps leading up to the door trembled with the rhythm and power of the music. The noise when Betty thrust open the door was like an unexpected hot gust of loud wind. 'Hey, girls, how are ya,' one of two Canadians just inside said Both smoking like chimneys, eyeing up the converging talent. The two laundry girls giggled; Margaret, trailing behind, tried to look as if she wasn't there. But Betty still had her by the hand. Inside the hall, the assault of cigarette fug and the new, amplified electronic music which she'd never before heard was overpowering, oppressive to Margaret but clearly liberating to Betty, the girls from the laundry and the men and women inside: a close-knit pack revolving cheek to cheek, couples shoulder to revolving shoulder with other couples. There was a makeshift bar on a table one side, the absence of chairs ensuring that no one sat out this one chance the soldiers had to dance. The huge loudspeaker stood next to the gramophone on a small table in one corner. A soldier stood by this, sifting through and peering at the titles of cellulite records stacked dangerously near one edge.

The time between the impact of arrival and what happened later was almost completely erased from Margaret's mind. She knew she'd been crushed in the melee of quicksteps, foxtrots and waltzes; she knew she'd been clasped by a succession of Canadian soldiers in their abrasive uniforms; she knew she'd had enough at one point, but not when this was, and had pushed herself out of the arms of a soldier and out of the crush near the door. She'd descended the steps into the remnants of twilight, aware of figures against the wall outside. She'd intended to maintain the momentum of her flight but was stopped in her tracks by the sight of Betty with her back to the wall and a soldier pushing against her. Then she saw Betty's legs revealed by her raised frock and the rhythmical movement of the soldier penetrating her. At the same time Betty turned and smirked, Betty for once silent, Betty for once doing the bidding of another.

In the second or two it took Margaret to understand this the door opened behind her and the soldier she'd been dancing with grabbed her arm. 'Fresh air,' he muttered, stepping down level with her and guiding her away from the steps. Margaret might have assumed she was free, but she wasn't. The soldier led her by the wrist, as if in the dance, the length of the hall and round the corner to where the light of residual sunset did not reach. The force with which he pushed her against the wall caused her head to crash against the wood so that the pain deflected her from what he was doing to her dress and knickers. Suddenly limp, tears wetting her face, she was too weak to resist, only just aware enough to know what was happening; only just aware that another soldier was pressed against her and then another, until a voice somewhere near her ear said, 'OK, girl, you rest up here a moment.

We'll get you a drink.' The muscles of her upper thigh felt wrenched, torn, her back strained, the back of her head pulsing with pain, her shocked breathing like the rasps of pneumonia.

Margaret tried to walk but fell onto the ragged grass, instinctively falling into a foetal position of ultimate defence. In doing so she felt the rucked-up dress, the ripped knickers hanging on to one knee, the shredded stockings round her ankles. She found swelling on her face, bruising on her arms, and a deep sense of tearing pain in her lower abdomen. At first, she crawled into the darkness across damp grass, anything to distance herself from the hall. A few moments later she found that she could stand, then painfully stagger. The north west sky still glowed weakly, laying cloying, colourless light onto the Heath. Beyond the aches and pains, she'd identified, and which wrenched at her body, Margaret couldn't feel anything, as if the world had become a place robbed of mental sensation, but filled with pain. She ordered each foot to follow the other, and this seemed to work. When the heavy bulk of the laundry appeared, it seemed put there by right, or for some purpose.

There may have been a day and then a night. Margaret slept, waking in the night to notions, ideas, sensations of Richard's presence; only to find that she'd been wrong. When daylight appeared for the second time and she consciously shifted, stretched in the bed, the impact, the full force of her torn groin made her cry out. She reached out to feel her face, her head, her arms, her legs, checking all parts of her body. She ached all over but in one specific place was it worse than anywhere else, a kind of grinding pain in her vagina. What surprised her was that her mind now seemed to have more life than her body; that it was detached, viewing her as if from above or to one side, that it had become, well, was cunning the word? That it was not going to say, this is the end: Richard gone, and now this. That she could hide things in her head in the same way that she had been hiding herself in the house. The two were the same, inseparable; the only way she could survive, the only way she could preserve something, whatever that was. An animal survival, clinging, dangling over the edge by its claws. Understanding might be beyond her, but this new sensation was there and couldn't be questioned or doubted.

Another night and another morning. Knocking on the door. A car revving away. Footsteps up and down the road outside. She ignored them all, and allowed herself to drift in and out of sleep, aware that these noises were of the working day. She limped to the toilet from time to time with her eyes closed, so that she could sleep again. She took water from the bathroom tap, and once with deliberately half open eyes felt her way slowly downstairs to the kitchen and ate all in one go next week's cheese ration from the cool box in the wall to the left of the back door.

Come another bright early summer's day, Margaret found her eyes open as if by their own volition, not hers. She closed them, but they sprang open again.

Creeping cautiously downstairs to look at the clock in the living room, she'd forgotten that it had stopped so long ago. She remembered her own wrist watch, but that was upstairs and she needed tea and bread before she could think of the stairs again. Vaguely she wondered what day it was, but this didn't seem to matter much. Later, she couldn't find the watch, and fell back to looking for time in the shortening or lengthening shadows of the back garden.

Chapter 6.

March 1945

Hunger wrenched Richard from the inside. The last cheque had been torn from its stub, had vanished into a long, dark cave from which no echo bounced back, whispering, I have arrived, I have reached Margaret.
Ashin brought the food, such as it was after these long spaces called years. He, too, was thinner, and new lines were pulling more strongly at his face: pushing and pulling, tucking and folding his outward character into a more unpredictable guise. At times he looked like the old man he might become in time of peace many years hence.

'Regret to inform you, sir,' he'd said, 'is not much food. I continue to pursue my enquiries, but unfortunately supplies limited.'

Doubtless there had been parallel problems in the mess those centuries ago, problems only revealed to the commanding officer, and which top brass military influence might have alleviated.

Prisoners develop their own strategies for keeping hunger at bay: particular ways of lying down, of resting so that the stomach feels disengaged from the business of living, isolated and left to cope on its own. Despite this, Richard's mind would lose its grip on his body and he'd move a cramped leg, say, or try to ease his back into a more comfortable position but the stomach would reassert itself and attack. He dreaded these attacks as much for the pain and because they cut off his mind's drift into escape, destroyed those long reveries of home, of Margaret, and which used to hustle time by in enormous chunks.

Increasingly, time would become void and empty and its cavern could only be filled by words which he knew were from God: sometimes punishing words, sometimes words saying this is what is and shall be and has been, but sometimes words of milk and honey which he could no longer understand. If, in the void, he could have thought of it, he would have beseeched the return of Margaret, because she was his core of self and memory. A core like a solid column inside him which was now so weakened that it folded to his fatigue, tucked and puckered to his habitual weariness and refused to appear when bidden.

In addition, the unpredictability of hunger pains seemed to conspire with the violence of the guards. Not all, but some, in these last days. Richard found that he had to squeeze this unpredictability into an alias predictability, so that when a guard began beating a prisoner at random it was not random, but expected. A man might not move to the left or right quickly enough. Or he might just look for a moment more a victim than others at that particular time; or might not be working on the road hard enough, or had collapsed. Richard knew that you had to lie on the ground and await the abatement of the attack. It could be of little consolation that each time might be the last time you'd be beaten: that you'd sink into endless slumber in a shallow grave, which other weak and weary prisoners would have to dig. Gradually, the sweltering shacks up Pall Mall, Regent Street, and Piccadilly lost their names as surely as did Hampton Court, Buckingham Palace and The Ritz, as they emptied one by one and had no tongue to name them, no mind to contain them.

The Commander still required his weekly list: if he'd been capable of thinking of it, Richard might have speculated about his figures being cross-checked. His honesty was not sustained by any moral sense - it was merely that his mind had not suggested an alternative, in the same way, for a long time, a map-less escape had never been thought off as an option. One thing he hadn't failed to notice: the commander seemed to be keeping him waiting for longer until he took up the list and slowly counted to check Richard's presented total. In this way Richard was allowed to slump on the floor against the wall behind the commander, instead of dragging body and soul out into the jungle to hack and hew, to sweat and ache, to watch the guards and wait for those blessed moments of inattention which would allow him and the other men a few moments respite.

As the days flicked past he began to see it almost as a kind of relief - in here, in the presence of a man contemplating a Buddha, Richard would also no longer be trying to tend sick men, listening to their last words which would be about the girl, the family, the home, or what they had once wanted to do out there in the adulthood of their lives.

He began to look forward to what must have become several hours, if not a whole morning or afternoon of escape in this way. There was another change too, as if akin to an evolution of something in the commander's mind: the Buddha was now alone again, but still elevated on the low table in front of the man. The great sword on its holder, however, had migrated to one side, further down the wall against which Richard leaned. It now stood in solitary confinement on another low table. If Richard had the notion of reaching to his right, he could now touch this table, and even feel the blade of the sword it bore.

Come Saturday mornings and filled with that sense of escape from work when she had dragged herself to the bank, Margaret was served, as usual, by Mr Bailey. As the war limped by the old cashier looked increasingly tired, as if his attentive sympathy had run out of energy, had been dulled by the grime and erosion of endless global conflict.

Margaret might have long accepted that sympathy wears thin, spread as it was over the three years of Richard's disappearance; but to the cashier this change felt more like a failure He was not to know that no one now, not even her parents, mentioned Richard any more for fear of upsetting her. It was like a death without a burial might be; the departed vanished, fallen into a past which would not be recalled; words stifled. Had she still endured bomb-storms in the shelter she might have preserved something of the past. As it was, she no longer had a half-knitted pullover to demonstrate to Elsie that she still had faith, still believed. Where the knitting had gone, she had no idea. It had merely disappeared along with memory of where she might have left it. In her inner core Richard lived on pale, drab and grey like a fading photograph, incapable any more of bursting into the colours of intimate dream and vivid memory. To friends and relatives who had moved on, Richard was almost an impediment.

While Mr Bailey laboured long over the checking and counting of Margaret's pound, shillings and pence, breaking them down into the habitual change required by his customer, Margaret noticed movement behind the low partition behind the cashier. Alert and apprehensive, she had to glance. Mr Long had appeared, moving across her vision, and now leant over the work of an unseen clerk. He appeared to show no interest in anything beyond whatever preoccupation he had at this moment. Margaret tried to quieten her mind, willing Mr Bailey to hurry himself. She still wanted to leave quickly, even if Mr Long had not invaded her peripheral vision. 'Thank you,' she said, with relief as she quickly arranged the notes and change into her purse, then struggled with the heavy oak door and escaped. 'You are very welcome, Mrs Ward.' Mr Bailey had laboured over the words as if this would redeem him from failing to recognise Richard's possible continued existence. But this gesture fell flat because Margaret was already out of the bank.

Escape is relative to distance achieved or shape shifted.

'Mrs Ward. I say, Mrs Ward!' Mr Long had followed her out. He touched her arm.

Margaret felt her whole being flinch inside her. This propelled her left arm upwards, shaking off the hand. She had to fight panic, possibly even fainting, because of this so public a manifestation of Mr Long's urgency.

It took the breath out of her; she was not prepared, had not rehearsed and could therefore not confront him as before.

'I must speak with you, Mrs Ward! I have something to tell you, and show you!'

Margaret heard the words, but not the meaning. Her breath during her time in the bank had returned. She ran. A procession of startled white faces flicked past. She bumped into one. Then Mr Long's sweating face unexpectedly bobbed up to one side of her, moving forward to cut off her flight. She side-stepped the threatened collision and scurried on, this time more strongly. The high street shops ended, and with it the succession of staring faces. Panting, she weakened to a slow shuffle but Mr Long was evidently no longer in pursuit. Even so, she dared not look back as if so doing would conjure him from the very dust of her fear. But her heavy breathing became sobs, and the ache in her stomach began to demand more attention than getting away from Mr Long.

Margaret struggled with the rest of Saturday and the whole of Sunday with the wrenching pain in her stomach. At times as she rested on her bed the pain would subside into manageable discomfort, only to unexpectedly reassert itself. She spent the weekend in bed, nursing her pain, nursing herself as best she could, unable to think through how she could live with what had happened to her, unable to confront it.

Food was forgotten, as was the blackout. But even the Germans wouldn't have known that: she hadn't once switched on a light.

Catching the bus to her parents' house was not something Margaret had thought through. It was Monday when she should have been up at the laundry. But it was a day when she felt so sick, so weak that she wanted to give in, return to the earth of home, of childhood, and lie down in a warm bed while someone else fussed and fed her. Anything to avoid Mr Barnes' cheerful assumption of her fitness or the vicious silence of Garner and Savory. Above all she wanted to create a distance from Betty as if that would lessen the trauma she'd suffered. Even though nothing had been said about the hop, even though Betty was still compulsively herself, Margaret felt dirty, filthy, tainted, as if what happened to her had been her fault. Within days of the hop, the Canadians had all gone, now fully trained to take on the Germans in the Allies' sweep into Germany. So there was no more mention of dances, as if they were something from the past, gone and done with, like the rockets and doodlebugs which had shot and lumbered overhead for years, and which now left the sky in piece, to give way to the endless squadrons of allied bombers heading eastward.

Having reached her parents' house, Margaret felt a little better for this achievement of a sort. As expected, and hoped for, her mother fussed and her father stood at a little distance, trying to understand. Perhaps it was because of her bearing, her demeanour, or her more-than-usual paleness that Margaret was put to bed, shivering, with two hot water bottles. At supper time she was given soup, her mother bringing through a chair to watch Margaret sip, while her father stood in the doorway. 'Frank,' he was told, 'do stop hovering. Do something useful. Margaret will need another blanket for the night.'

In the morning Margaret was sick, retching into the bathroom sink, her mother's hand warm on her shoulder. She couldn't eat any breakfast. There was a hurried, whispered conference between her parents in the hallway outside. Then her father came back into the kitchen with a set mouth. 'I'm calling the doctor, my gal.' Behind Frank, Rose's face was stitched with worry in a way that looked even more permanent than her husband's.

To Frank and Rose, Dr Simpson had always seemed a large man, physically, if not by reputation. While they were tending to shrink into the expected shape of old age, the doctor's frame seemed to have bulked up. Even his slight but developing stoop did not counteract this. He still filled a doorway, and the room he stepped through to never seemed sufficient to accommodate his outsize frame. Margaret was reminded of his heavy features, the dark eyes, the thick hair greying reluctantly, with streaks of white, harbingers of the advance of old age. She remembered her childhood fear: this large man, so serious in his homburg, whose face when it came close in examination was furnished with a moustache which looked as brittle and spiky as a hedgehog. And with all this came a frugal manner which could so easily be interpreted as irritation. There was a procession of illnesses which you had to have as a child: flu, chicken pox, measles and whooping cough.

Each one signalled the inevitability of another home visit, a brief examination, the close-up heavy breathing, the stethoscope cold on your chest.

Then the audible but enigmatic sigh as Dr Simpson completed the examination, offering no obvious feedback but culminating with the too quiet consultation with her mother on the landing outside her bedroom, behind her closed door. It was bad enough feeling the regressive pull of childhood at home; seeing Dr Simpson after so long a gap was like being seen anew as a child. The years between seemed to have vanished in an accepted and scarcely noticed state of reasonably good health. The fear might have gone, only to be thus revived.

Dr Simpson sat heavily on a chair next to Margaret's childhood bed.

Rose was outside again on the landing.

'Sickness,' Dr Simpson repeated, 'sometimes in the morning, but at any time day or night?' Margaret nodded. 'And feeling weak and listless.' This was for the third time of asking. There was no mention of Richard.

As close to him as this, Margaret tried to recall the heavy, almost laboured breathing, but couldn't. The doctor listened intently to his stethoscope. He looked into her throat, ears, took her hands in both his and, turning them gently over, carefully examining their palms and backs. Then he asked her to pull up her blouse and push down her skirt a little. He pressed one and sometimes two fingers into her abdomen to the accompaniment of further work with the roaming stethoscope.

Margaret had closed her eyes, opening them only when Dr Simpson spoke. She allowed herself to fall into that half-remembered reverie, a suspended state where she blissfully felt she had no control, no ownership, no responsibility for her body, or herself. Even though this was something which could only ever last a few minutes, it was like a briefly snatched moment of total relief.

Suddenly Dr Simpson's breathing changed. There was an intake of breath somewhere along the line of a sigh. Margaret opened her eyes.

'One of my first born,' he murmured. The hint of a smile slightly disturbed the powerful moustache. Behind him Rose sighed from the landing.

Dr Simpson summoned up a tactful cough. An explanation was perhaps called for. He said, 'At the beginning of my practice, what, nearly thirty years ago?'

If there was any significance in this careful and controlled dropping of his guard, Margaret didn't then notice it. Rose dared to add, 'A difficult birth.'

It might have appeared to Rose that the doctor ignored this, but Margaret caught a momentary flick of his eyes away from her. That was all. Walking across the room, he cleared his throat in a more decisive manner: 'I have something for this,' he said. Margaret couldn't turn her head round sufficiently to see what the Doctor was

doing - the medical clicks and clinks gave her no clue. Then he was back, and she saw that he held a syringe. 'This will be uncomfortable at first,' he said.
She felt herself tense even further, even though this was countered by a vague determination not to let Doctor Simpson down. 'I'm sorry, Mrs Miller, but I'll have to ask you to close the door a moment.'

The pain, when it came, was too much and she couldn't stifle her cry. First her legs and then her abdomen were filled with agony - it was like spilled boiling water, or being crushed by a heavy weight, or being ripped into by some terrible monster of childhood nightmares. Dr Simpson withdrew the syringe, pressed her abdomen for a few moments, grunted and stood, taking care to conceal the size of the instrument as he took it away across the room. He quickly left the room to reassure Rose who sat on a chair on the landing with her head in her hands and shook with weeping. Touching her shoulder, he muttered, 'It's finished.' He held out a small packet of pills. 'To be taken once in the morning and once at night. And, er, I'd like to see her in a week's time at my surgery.'

In the silence which followed, Margaret further adjusted her skirt and blouse, hauled herself up from her prone position on the bed, and Rose moved quickly across the room to assist her, the rigid set of her face clearly indicating that she should be told what the problem was. But it was clear that there was also to be no whispered parent/doctor consultation outside this time. This was now and Margaret was an adult. Dr Simpson was never a person his patients dared to question: what is the real matter with me doctor?

Shaman-like he worked his magic, and this was amply proven by the prescription of a pill (once/twice daily) or a bottle of medicine possessing an even more magical quality (one/two teaspoonfuls a day after a meal). The little box of pills or the bottle of medicine remained for the duration of its doses on the patient's kitchen table, prominent and important.

Unforgettable.

After three- or four-days Margaret had insisted on going home. This precipitated a crisis: she was not well enough to go on her own.

Margaret said she'd be all right on the bus. The three of them maintained these opposing positions all day. Night being a skilful aid to arbitration, a compromised was reached over breakfast whereby Frank and Rose would see Margaret onto the bus. This happened. Publicly, mother and daughter briefly embraced, and Frank leant awkwardly towards his daughter, missing her cheek completely.

Twenty minutes later, as Margaret stepped off the bus in the High Street, she felt a surge of tears suddenly overwhelm her. Weeping and walking was a public display she would have avoided at all costs. But she was incapable of suppressing one and the other was a dire necessity. Had Elsie appeared she would have walked through her to turn the key in her lock, slam the door and collapse onto the carpet of the hall floor. However, there was no visible Elsie, and no other neighbours loitering among the flower beds of their front gardens.

But a notion had seized her as if borne out of her distress: the letter. She had to know, she had to have it straight - was it Richard's obituary, the final confirmation she had fought so hard and for so long to deflect, that in ignoring it, it might have gone away? To have fought this long, these weeks and months, was to have kept Richard alive in a way that would not otherwise have been possible. This notion was hovering there just in front of her like a barrier she had to break through as she reached for the sealed envelope next to the dead clock on the mantelpiece. She could have found it with her eyes closed. She could have ripped it open with her eyes closed. Even so she almost surprised herself at her sudden calmness as she read it.

There was no steam wafting out of the laundry.

At first Margaret didn't notice because she was bent over the painful task of walking, not trusting her balance on the bike. Her mind told her that she shouldn't have set out for work, that this was folly, a stupid thing to do. The laundry would not collapse without her. She had no idea of the time because the lounge clock was still not wound up and she'd lost her wrist watch. No strengthening sun, or parting clouds were there to give hints about the time. But her feet led her. As she approached the office door, she noticed that there were no bikes in leaning familiarity against each other in the bicycle shed; nor was Mr Barnes's Austin abandoned round the side. Lowering herself carefully to sit on the doorstep, she knew she should think carefully about what day it was.

Vague memories of the passing of nights and days while she lay in bed sick at her parent's bungalow could not possibly have added up to a week. Or it could have. But time could not be compressed like this; a week was a long time. It hung heavy and weighed you down, filling you with obligations, routines, tedium. Or it could flash by in wilful deceit. She stood and walked round the side of the office to peer through a window. Despite the dust and mirk of the glass she could make out no one at Garner or Savory's desks. Peering over at her own, she tried to remember being there - when? As she walked slowly home, she became more and more convinced that she'd been at work the day before. More than that, she had a notion that yesterday was Monday.

It was as if Elsie was waiting in triumph for her at the top of the Close. But it wasn't the only thing. The first thing that Margaret saw was fluttering bits of colour against a grey sky - what was it - bunting? Some fete here? She couldn't conceive, think, guess what, why men up ladders were tying strings of bunting to the lamp posts, why women were hurrying hither and thither with trays to trestle tables set out on the turning circle outside her house. Children, ordered to take this and that: plates, knives and forks, glass beakers, jugs, and plates of sandwiches, chattered and laughed 'There you are, here she is!' Elsie was a woman who'd won, and was going to demonstrate this to the whole road, 'You're just in time!' she yelled, grasping Margaret's arm. Margaret caught a wince of pain just in time, surprised at her quick reaction when all she wanted to do was crawl into the cave of her home and lie down. Protecting herself against Elsie was so strong, so established inside her, so hard a kernel. So feral. Elsie, on the other hand, now felt she had the authority to push and pull Margaret towards a folding wooden seat at a table, even if she could no longer aspire to the permanent total control of her neighbour that she had long sought.

Overhead, the launching of the bunting into the air was soon completed: the lamp posts and telegraph poles were at last united to flaunt the gaudy face of the tarnished world of war. The children were pacified and confined at the tables, wide eyed with puzzlement and suspicion. Neighbours found themselves in random proximity and sudden celebration together, where before they had huddled in the separate fear of their garden shelters, or had only breached barriers with next door both ways. Littering the tables were cakes made with carrot and parsnip, icing with flour and saccharine and re-used tea-leaves in pots and chicory in the coffee: the whole street, under Elsie's direction, had pooled the ersatz, the make-believe, the imitation to satisfy palates long since dulled, stomachs simplified beyond the richness of the Canadian chocolate which lay in solid, grossly oversized cut cubes - such a gift from a compassionate and caring colony which had also willingly and unstintingly thrown its sons into the murderous fray.

Elsie's moment of consummate victory and achievement came as everyone sat and tucked in. She alone stood and surveyed her domain. Raising her glass of ginger beer, her voice boomed out over the street, the empty houses and the fluttering bunting, 'To the end of the war!

Three cheers for Churchill and the end of the war!' The three cheers hurt like nails being driven into Margaret's head. As the blows reverberated, she knew she had nothing to offer, nothing to add to the celebration. After she'd eaten some of the chocolate, ignorant of its provenance, crouching so as to be nearly invisible behind the row of sitting neighbours, she fled the grey skies of threatened rain, to fall through her door and retch in private.

Outside on the street, it sounded as if the whole world was singing God Save our Gracious King, not just once, but as a filler between repeated Rule Britannias and half remembered renditions of I vow to thee my country.

Inside her cocoon Margaret sat on her chair in the kitchen, unable to galvanise wit and energy into assembling water and kettle, teapot, a cup, saucer and spoon, plus the strainer, and the special brass caddy spoon: one for me and one for the pot. With the kitchen curtains still drawn she sat in the impoverished light trying to summon Richard. Not just Richard himself, detached, inactive, but Richard doing something; no, them, the two of them, doing something, being somewhere, enjoying themselves. It was like a person being asked not to produce one word but a whole sentence. In such a circumstance a mind full of potential sentences of endless variety cannot conjure up a single one. The same was true of Margaret's memories. She had finally to admit this to herself: for some time now, she had not had a single all-consuming specific memory of Richard. She couldn't make them go for a walk on a beautiful spring day, or picnic, or go up to London to see the Lord Mayor's show, or hike along the cliffs of the Seven Sisters in Sussex, or daringly hold hands in the picture house. Moving pictures of the mind were no longer projected because the lamp had failed. She felt crushed, belittled, bereft, bereaved.

Despite the cloudy, cool weather, the V.E. Day party continued noisily into the afternoon. Rule Britannia welled up again and again, as if war had forbidden it, as if it were now finally unfettered. Until she fled home, Margaret had sat among these her neighbours unable to party, unable to engender joy, unable to celebrate. Above all, unable to share her secrets, the deep shadows of her life.

One secret forbidden; two others not believed.

Chapter 7.

May 1945

The occasions when Richard was required to present himself to the commander might have appeared to come round with increasing frequency. But this was not so. Time can warp, twist and above all appear in retrospect to have contracted. In his mind Richard might have thought that he had spent whole chunks of time, whole mornings or afternoons, even whole days, slumped on the floor behind the commander. He could see past the man to where the Buddha was the centre of contemplation, and he too let his gaze rest on the serene features of the statue about whom he knew next to nothing.

He assumed the Buddha was a god whose face possessed a full mouth which ever so slightly hinted at a smile, like the Mona Lisa he'd only ever seen as a small print. The eyes, too, intimated the same smile, either immediately before or just after a greeting, or a welcome. This was reinforced by the relaxed posture of the body which the commander mirrored so carefully, with his feet pulled up and over the opposing knees in a way that seemed impossible and uncomfortable, yet suggested a commitment to sitting like this for a long time.

This god, Richard made himself think, did not hang upon a cross, had not died in agony, but sat at ease over this land, inviting the onlooker to share with him whatever it was that he wished to impart, or wished you to think in some eternal firmament around and above him.

If he'd felt better, if he had the energy that would allow him to sit upright in contemplation, he might have developed thoughts about the Buddha. As it was he had to concentrate all his remaining strength on two things: the first was squatting approximately behind the commander, albeit slumped; the second was ignoring the table which was now pushed so closed to the position he was expected to occupy that he could now reach across the dangerous space of a few inches not only to touch the table but the sword as well.

Mr Long slept fitfully. The town clock chimed a background to his sexual fantasies, rising in number to midnight, reduced to single figures in the latter part of the night. Such rising and falling fantasies did not include Mrs Long who slept in the second bedroom, the one at the back, with the door locked from the inside just in case. Although relieved of the *forced sessions*, she knew that men are prey to the sudden change or eruptions of what, tendencies? They had to be rationed or, in her case, completely denied such awful bodily functions. She was reminded of her mother, of how she didn't ever want to be like her: a machine which cow-like produced a child a year, punctuated by miscarriages; a woman existing in a state of total exhaustion, that pale face with thinning hair in a pudding basin haircut. Above all, that sack of a body, so lumpish that it forced an excess of bulk to slip down her legs, swelling her ankles and feet so that she limped and could only ever wear bedroom slippers. A permanent fag jaundiced her fingers, but was her only comfort, her only excuse to claw back a few brief moments and sit in a chair, staring at the wall.

In a desperate attempt in the watches of the night to lock onto a satisfying fantasy, Mr Long would return to Margaret. But she was no longer as pressing and convincing as she had been. She was no longer sufficient. The cheques and his desires had somehow become fatally entwined, mixed up, messed up, out of control. He was afraid, but wouldn't admit it, that she'd seen through him. He knew, but wouldn't admit it, that he should have told her about the cheques; should have shown her the messages which would have given hope to her wan and defeated face. Now it was too late: if he showed her one, she'd wonder if there were others; she'd asked each time she came to the bank if another had been received. The clerks would get to know this. Sheila would wonder why, she'd ask questions.

Sometimes he'd wake from dreams of running, of escape, but never of the women he'd summoned in a waking state and whom he was about to or had actually taken to bed. Waking dreams inhabited a different land, could not travel into sleeping dreams to give him some kind of short-lived peace and excitement. Even though it was against so much that he believed in, against so much of how he knew a man in his position, a bank manager, should act, behave, he could see no way out.

Besides which there was that last time he'd walked furtively up Dickens Close. Why had he worn that old trench coat? And the cap you see in photos of some distant shoot in the country. And who was that woman with the large florid face? Can't a person knock on a door and be left to his own business? It wasn't that she herself was large, it was her presence. Overpowering might be the word if you were forced to think of one.

'She's not there!' the woman said, or rather shouted for the whole Close to hear. One of those people who come right up to you, who come so close that you have to take a step backwards. Then, 'Who are you?' To be asked that of a total stranger in the street like that. His mind brought him straight back to the security of the bank - an almost hallowed space which customers entered at their peril. In fact, how much nicer it would be without them at all. Days passed in perfect peace in his manager's lair, while the bank itself managed the invisible flow of finance. At such times when an underling would knock, they would creep in when allowed, and speak in whispers. And now this harridan who shouted, 'Anyhow, she's not there!'

A few days ago, he'd been asked to visit head office in the City for a meeting of branch managers. The brief of the conference was to lift the curtain of peace time banking and peer into the bright new future which thus beckoned. This steering committee was to meet once a month. Feeling boosted, or rather privileged to have been chosen, it became the one bright day in an otherwise featureless procession of grey days in a bank manager's life. It also renewed his interest in London which, battered and wretched, was still the place of interest and pleasure which it had been before the war in his young days, his heyday as a junior clerk on the first rungs of the banking ladder. He allowed himself the self-indulgence of a few stations down the Central Line to wander on foot through the West End, Soho, and across St James Park. It was a revelation coming, if he'd thought of it in these terms, just at the right time to fuel his secret inner life.

At first Mr Long found the prostitutes in Soho intimidating. There was a totally different atmosphere in the place which didn't seem to chime with his impressions from before the war. The place seemed seedier, more run-down, coarse and raunchy. The women were perhaps more assertive, more aggressive. They stood in doorways and called out to each other in forceful sisterhood. As he passed, he caught whiffs of their body odour and what might pass for some kind of perfume. Their lips were ghastly gashes, their fingernails blood red. Strutting up and down, when not flaunting themselves in doorways, they dominated the back streets and, unlike ordinary women, looked men full in the eye, challenging, calculating. Mr Long was at once thrilled and appalled. At night he thought through scenarios where he took advantage of their services: the brief discussion of the price, the following of the woman up the stairs (usually), the tawdry room, the (probably) unmade bed - notions of a succession of clients. Then the actual act where the pleasure, fulfilment and release should occur.

Again and again both thrilling and repellent urges surged through him, sometimes in equal measure, but increasingly ending up in revulsion. This deeply disappointed him. He felt he was failing as a man; that he should be man enough, as were the men he saw peeling off from a purposeful walk with companion men: not a word exchanged, not even a gesture - one would approach the soliciting woman, exchange a few quiet words, follow her inside immediately, leaving the friend or friends to walk on, possibly to look for one they fancied, perhaps, who knows?

However, for a couple of months Mr Long persisted, drawn and repelled by equal and sometimes unequal measure. He was, however, beginning to consider that he would have to give up, somehow cancel this particular fantasy, find others, feel but never utter that he should rely on self-gratification as the only release. But then it happened that in Greek Street, he was approached by a diminutive, almost timid woman, much more modestly dressed, little make up, and more his own age. When she stopped in front of him, barring his way on the pavement, his first thought was that she was going to ask him directions to some street or establishment he might know. But her voice, quiet and almost a whine, appeared to be offering something, her face shaping a grimace masquerading as a smile. Aware that the woman was starting to repeat herself, he gradually began to make sense of what she was offering. At the same time, he found himself instantly, remarkably quickly in fact, compromising his fantasies, daytime perhaps lending a little realism or objectivity, downgrading them to something approaching this possibility. At the same time he found that he needed space to think this through, to run this new story through his mind, to attempt to assess whether or not he was going to be able to carry it through, whether or not it was going to satisfy him, whether or not this was what in the cold light of day he was looking for.

The woman watched Mr Long hesitate, attempting to come to a decision. He saw her eyes flicker, about to look past him for other opportunities. Something cut through each and every consideration his banker's mind was bringing to bear on the dilemma: the secret of jumping off a cliff is not to think much about it. Above all not to think about what follows the leap. He glanced left and right: people busy with the world walked briskly past, indifferent to a pin-striped, bowler hatted man trying to decide whether or not to go with an older prostitute. Mr Long nodded. The woman turned and he followed.

'   *to the uncertainty and confusion inherent in such a difficult situation, information is patchy or non-existent.*'

Margaret read and reread the parts of the letter which revealed the essence, the gist of the message. She didn't trust words to be fixed and straight-forward in their meaning. Words were too much like people who shifted shape, became someone you thought they weren't, or pretended to be ordinary and normal so as to deceive you.

'*Captain Ward was held as a prisoner of war of the Japanese Government until his release by British Colonial Forces in July 1945. All prisoners of war will be repatriated as soon as possible.*'

Margaret spilled more tears onto the letter. Where one fell onto the black typewritten words it grossly magnified a letter, or a couple of letters. Wiping away the blur from her eyes, only lasted moments before the next tear assembled itself and fell. She knew the words by heart but would still not trust them. They could change with her moods, or from strongly charged emotion like now, just back from the doctor for that scheduled follow-up appointment, which could alter the whole meaning. She had to check, she had to read again and then reread in case they told a different story from the one she'd told Dr Simpson.

'As normal communications are re-established, so will former P.O.W.'s be repatriated, Captain Ward among them.'

Was this the same? Could she dare to trust the letter? Repatriated meant home. Here. Home.

'Further information will be sent to you in due ..'

But her tears had magnified random letters out of all recognition among the lame words that followed. Without thinking, she brushed the liquid from the page with one hand. The typewritten words remained fast and would not be dismissed, even if the signature was smudged out of all recognition.

'And Richard?' Dr Simpson had pulled up a chair opposite the one reserved for the anxious mother, friend or adult child of the patient he was to examine on the couch. He was aware of his large presence. It had served him well in the First World War. But it was something that he lived with and therefore tended to take for granted and forget. This morning, however, he was reminded of his bulk, his possibly forbidding expression, only an hour after peering into the shaving mirror. Margaret looked terrified; she wrung her hands, she held her head low so that she had to force herself to glance up at him. He wondered why her mother was not with her.

Dr Simpson coughed politely, discretely and repeated more quietly, 'And Richard?' Margaret still needed time to answer. No one asked this difficult question now. It seemed as if words of reply would not grow and assemble coherently in her mind, let alone travel the vast distance to her tongue. One of her hands detached itself from the other and searched in the sleeve of her jumper, found a handkerchief and brought it carefully up to her eyes, then down to her nose. She made herself breathe evenly, willed her heart to slow.
Closing her eyes, she let flood back memories of her childhood, and the time when she'd become a woman outside when the child inside was still trying to catch up: how Dr Simpson could make everything all right. How when her mother, twice, was so ill that she'd caught her father weeping in the kitchen. How difficult it always was to make that decision - phone Dr Simpson. The last thing, the final admission that your own common sense, your own lotions and potions, the wisdom which your mother had passed on to you, had all failed.

The expense, always the expense. The juggling of money and health. The looming, potential disaster of a run of bad health, the inexorable decline more steeply tilted towards death.

'It's all right,' Dr Simpson murmured, 'in your own time.'

Margaret found herself nodding as the words finally came, floating on an audible breath, prompted, but not forced. Somehow, she understood that she could tell this man, her doctor, who'd brought her safely into this world; one of his first born.

'He's coming back.'

'I'm so glad.'

Dr Simpson caught himself staring at her downcast face, her hands clasping and writhing, the ankles crossed and drawn back defensively under the chair. He thought he'd count up to something like twenty, wait, and hope that this would make it easier for her. He knew how to let silence possess the consulting room; he knew when the weight of it could be lifted. 'And when will this be, my dear?'

After another long pause, during which he noticed Margaret's elbows twitch at her waist, he watched her shake her head. Silly of him, he thought, the war with Japan not yet over, how would anyone know?

'They didn't say.'

'Ah, fingers crossed, it'll be soon.'

He saw how she didn't agree or disagree with this wan piece of hope. But professional matters winged their way back and he murmured, 'As soon as you're ready,

Mrs Ward.' The examination was much the same as the previous week with the exception that Rose was not an anxious, almost ominous presence behind him threatening intervention at any moment.

'And your last periodic pain?'

Margaret had already worked this out for herself, not for more than a month, six weeks, seven or eight weeks. The almost forgotten relief of a flood of blood.

Dr Simpson was not aware of his sigh, but Margaret was. She felt it more as a judgement than a sentence. She felt it as something that would never go away, like war, disease, hunger.

The good doctor was not a man to consciously conjure metaphor. But images did often present themselves to him, unbidden. The ones which now insisted on an airing were in terms of skating on thin ice, of a balancing act on a high wire, of driving his Alvis too fast along the still novel Ewerton bypass, of unintentionally betraying a patient's secrets.

All men are sinners, he may have thought, and I am no better than any man. But behind these, entwined, enmeshed, was the huge difficulty of taking this consultation further, risking entering the realms of ethics, morals, right and wrong. Looking back to his young days as he often did, it all seemed in retrospect almost easy and straightforward in the trenches: you might possibly save this one who was unconscious, but not that one who was conscious and convinced that you could save him. Or with dwindling resources, choices about who could be given life and who couldn't because it would take up all the medication and blood that would save a dozen others. You played God and no one questioned this elevated role, this status.

Not for the first time in this new war had he been forced to acknowledge that some choices now were even more difficult - and these were civilians. But he knew that he must hold on, must not lose his ability to decide; at the same time, he had to know, because this could be the deciding factor. He sighed again.

'If you feel able, my dear, please tell me what happened.'

He heard Margaret catch her breath; saw her flinch, knew that he was cutting her to the bone, but could see no other way. He watched her face mirror her internal battle; he knew that no one else knew what she might or might not tell him. So, it was a relief to him when Margaret began to cry. She rolled over, away from him on the couch, brought her knees up to her stomach and, rocking slightly, quietly wept into her handkerchief. He knew that it was now only a matter of time. That it might, in the end, help her, despite what he had to do.

It was another day like the procession of so many others that it was indistinguishable in its own right. A slight difference could perhaps be discerned in Richard personally in that he didn't just feel well, but a little less unwell. He'd got used to these false dawns. They signified little and his life would dwindle as the sun reached its height and the heat and humidity bore down on him as he lay in his hut. They now no longer forced him to limp along the road to the end where it was still under construction. In fact, they'd gone quiet, as someone put it, and this was suspected of being more worrying than being beaten to continue working. Richard had still to take the list to the Commander, that was all. A grubby piece of paper, on this occasion torn from a book lying unclaimed in a corner. The name inside it, in fading pencil, was John Hutchinson, who had been a few months earlier on the list which Richard took to the commander.

The ritual was identical to others which merged with the forgotten, faded days: Richard sat and waited. The commander faced his Buddha; two men from opposite sides of the globe looking at a brass statue. Unblinking, the Buddha contemplated the two men. There was one difference: the sword had been turned round so that its handle now lay further from the commander's right hand and nearer Richard. The sword which had beheaded the now absent John Hutchinson.

Other differences became slowly apparent: the commander had removed his khaki shirt. He seldom wore his uniform hat inside, but tied round his head, just below his forehead hair line, was a red and white cotton cloth. Richard stared at the perfect skin of the Commander's back: not a blotch, blemish, wart or wen; olive smooth and hairless, clothing his torso in perfect harmony with his flesh.

As usual, Richard settled in for the duration of however long the commander wished them to both commune together before lifting his hand for the list. Richard remained on the floor, crossed legged, letting his upper body lean forward to find its position of approximate equilibrium where the strength needed to maintain this sitting position was minimised. Then, as usual, he let his mind go, he let whatever wished to fill it seep in; anything as long as it wasn't something distressing that clung to him, using up strength to dispel it.

If Margaret appeared by chance, she was now wraithlike, couldn't show him her face properly, couldn't speak, wasn't doing anything that he remembered they did together, or that she did round the house. It might be comfort enough, but was not fulfilling; its repetition had dulled its impact, and it had been left to fade away in its own time.

Other notions which wafted in were green fields so comfortingly hedged as to be divided safely and manageably, every now and then interrupted by a hummock hill crowned by a beech copse. Or the golden straw stacked after harvest, before being built into haystacks, those houses of straw quickly assembled onto a golden landscape.

This was all; it didn't mean much, because he couldn't walk across these fields, couldn't bring a particular one on a particular occasion into his mind, couldn't put Margaret in it and see her clearly. Above all, he couldn't hear her voice.

The sudden appearance of an alien sound can be disruptive and disturbing. What began as a low drone, as removed and remote as before, became more powerful and purposeful. Suddenly it was a roar, directly overhead. A snarl which like a wild animal begins and ends abruptly, but is then gone.

Richard felt his body react as if the sound had shoved him off balance. Automatically, he countered this and looked at the commander, but the commander had either not heard or intended not to take any notice. Immediately after this, there was a single shot, near enough to be inside or only just outside the camp.

Soon other shots rang out, shockingly near, jarring the air, shattering the turgid quiet. The commander shifted slightly but didn't change position. Richard's mind ran ahead to make sense of these new sounds, trying to put himself into a picture where his own safety was paramount.

More shots thudded in his ears. Men's voices, raised above shouting, screamed; boots thumped somewhere near. Richard, in uncertain panic, struggled to his feet, fully expecting the commander to have already done the same thing, his forehead fiercely furrowed, to stride out of the hut issuing staccato, faultless orders in that strong voice of his. But the man remained squatting with his upturned feet knotted in that odd way. But now, instead of quiet contemplation,

Richard could hear the Commander making a low, repetitive ululation, words as if they were on a revolving loop, or the needle on the celluloid leaping back each revolution, flicking back onto the previous groove in an endless repeated cycle. What was more and which startled Richard was that the commander remained in front of his Buddha with his head bowed: the exact attitude he had required of so many prisoners immediately before being beheaded. More shots rang out, now sounding as if they were from all sides of the camp; more screaming, more shouting. And still the commander did not move. Sitting where he was, Richard had only to lean a little to one side to reach the handle of the great sword.

Whether the voice was from the outside commotion, or the turmoil in his own mind, Richard never knew. But the voice inside him was strong and insistent, as if he read out aloud from the Holy Book:

'I will smite the sea peoples of the plain, for in the eyes of the Lord they are sick and worship false idols –'

He looked past the commander at the Buddha. The eyes, half closed as always, were gazing at him in an accepting but quietly confident way. They were telling him that whatever he decided to do was in accord with the spirit of the place, and his own soul. He reached for the great sword.

She didn't get the bus home, but walked to the High Street and out her side of the town, a woman for whom shops did not exist, a woman whose belly ached: 'This will hurt a little,' Dr Simpson had said.

Afterwards he'd urged, 'Contact me when the pain begins, tonight or tomorrow, and I'll come immediately.' He had looked into her face, so removed, so distracted and repeated the sentence until she'd nodded. 'The time, night or day, is of no importance. I'll come.'

Margaret walked. She wanted to get home without having to ask for, pay for, comment on the weather, or react in any way with anyone else. There seemed no other way of removing herself from contact with others even if she'd do anything for a chair or, better still, a bed to collapse on.

Two days followed in which Margaret fought to remember how you live: how you have to rise in the morning and organise soap, a flannel and towel, bring up the kettle and pour hot water into the bathroom hand basin. How you have then to make choices of what to wear, bearing in mind what mood you're in, what the weather's doing, where you are going or who might be expected to visit. How you have to organise a plate and cutlery at its simplest, or lard a frying pan and watch a slice bacon sizzle and an egg fry. How a house needs sweeping, dusting and cleaning.

Oh, and how there is an accumulation of clothes in the clothes basket which need to be washed, rinsed, painfully put through the mangle and hung out to dry in the garden, or on the drying-rack hauled down from the kitchen ceiling in winter. How there are the shops to visit, and, mindful of the constraints of the ration book, foodstuff to be bought and carried home - a whole life which she knew she couldn't perform because she was so assailed by an immense weight of pain and anxiety. A pang so great that fighting to contain it was life enough. She had no energy for anything else.

As she lay in bed for most of the days and all of the nights, the only defence she could muster failed lamentably: she could not bring back the vivid colour and life of sustaining memory. She could not put herself with Richard somewhere, like Alfreston in Sussex on the beautiful village green, or up on the South Downs where you could see the shimmer of the blue sea. But nothing would flow from this, no warmth, no consolation, no memory of what he said or did. The scene of his proposal to her in the garden of Hampton Court would seem like an inanimate, colourless picture, lacking movement, scent, atmosphere, warmth. A cold black and white film you paid to watch. It had become nothing, and was like the destruction of her final defence. She lay and waited for what she knew would inevitably be pain; a pain that would be totally new and terrifying.

A soldier in faded khaki with a wide brimmed hat pinned up on one side called down the steps to another about a stiff and a gallon of blood.

'Good move that, cobber,' he said to Richard.

The second soldier in faded khaki who stood below the veranda steps seemed to be complimenting Richard as if approving an accurate throw of a dart, or a nice stroke with the bat. Richard stood two steps above him outside the commander's room trying to understand, trying to remember the significance of the wide brimmed uniform hat with one side pinned up.

'OK, mite,' the soldier continued, 'gi's the gin. Fill me in.' Richard stood at attention, gazing over and past the man.

'Later,' the soldier muttered to the one who'd spoken first, 'zombie.' Then to Richard, 'Like a cuppa and a snort, mite?'

Movement across the compound caught Richard's eye. A ragbag of tattered figures, little more than skeletons - sharp elbows, swollen knees, large eyes staring out of shrunken features - seemed to have gathered in the middle of the parade ground. One might be wearing a tattered pair of shorts, another only filthy underpants, a third in a vest and something strung round his groin; a few had a shredded piece of cloth somehow attached to the tops of their heads; only a man here and there wore anything resembling a pair of boots, a few others had sandals of cobbled bits of rubber tyre; a puny bunch awaiting orders. The soldier looking up at Richard asked, 'So where are all the others then, mite?'

The smell of the room and the woman's body through an imperfect veil of cheap scent forced Mr Long to supercharge a particular subplot in a particularly obscure and little visited invention: the one where he was seducing a nun who was in full kit, where each garment he removed had innumerable buttons which were quite difficult to undo. The stir of excitement was in the undoing of the buttons which, in resisting, heightened deferred gratification.

The room itself was surprisingly ordinary, and could easily have been a bed-sit or a room in a small hotel in a depressed seaside town in Kent or Norfolk. The carpet was so dark as to obscure any pattern it might have been supposed to possess. The wallpaper a rather formal pin stripe in a colour difficult to identify; the double bed was probably turn of the century with a scroll moulded bed board stubbornly curvaceous, framing an offering of arranged leaves. A small, dark oak Victorian tallboy, two almost rural wooden chairs and the usual, faded Victorian prints of clean nineteenth century country children playing with puppies and spinning tops, watched over by a venerable old codger in buttoned- up britches. Mr Long had only been offered a narrow range of services - from a grope (2/6), through a bringing it off (10/ -), to the whole way (£3).

While she took off her dress and unfastened her stockings, he took out his wallet, found the three-pound notes and placed them on the tallboy to one side of the bed. Then with his back to the woman for decency's sake he began to remove his own clothes, placing them neatly on the chair nearest to him: the black shoes under it, before hanging the dependable black jacket on the back of the chair, and carefully folding the reassuring pin striped trousers onto the seat, followed by his black socks, grey suspenders with the dog-tooth pattern, and pallid, lifeless pants. Finally, he reached both sides of his waist to hoist up his thin vest.

'Keep your vest on, if you please, dearie.'

Mr Long was a surprised because this requirement didn't feature in any of his imaginings. When he turned back towards her, she was in the bed with the sheet and blankets pulled up to her waist. She was still wearing her petticoat; under that he could make out the ghostly form the contours of the stays and bones which shaped her brassiere.

'Gentlemen,' the woman said, glancing pointedly at the tallboy, 'usually imburse following services rendered. But don't worry, dearie, nice of you.'

As he approached the bed he found himself looking more closely at her face, grey in the subdued light, the lines etched on her forehead and how the crow's feet stamped round her eyes were unfairly exaggerated; how her cheeks had already begun their slow journey downwards to touch the base of her old age. Nevertheless, he was gratified to see that it was a face etched, he thought, with a history of passion and sensuousness, particularly her lips; this excited him into beginning to make plans in the way that a banker is long accustomed. Good accounts merit regular perusal and frequent checking.

'I see, love,' she said afterwards, 'so you'll be coming up once a month. Regular.' She laughed. Not the cackle Mr Long might have expected, but a pretty ordinary, everyday one, even if stretched a bit to make a joke.

As he replaced and adjusted his clothing, Mr Long refused to contemplate the possibility of the laugh reinforcing an intended pun. He'd accomplished the act, and that was all that mattered. A new account had been opened, to be serviced once a month. At a cost of three pounds sterling.

'Oh,' and what's your name, love?'

'Long,' he said, holding the door open, but avoiding looking at her.

Margaret could tell Dr Simpson about pain, but not about the phone cut off. It might have been a strategy to avoid further complications, if so, it was incomprehensible to her. The pain did not start on the first night, but the second. It was so bad, so debilitating that she thought she'd never make it to Elsie's. The only thing the agony did for her was that it prevented her from constructing any strategy for procrastination. It came with a bang three days after she had seen Dr Simpson and she had to react instantly. It was something she knew she had to do, the first and only thing to stand out sufficiently significantly from a deep well of apprehension and foreboding.

When Elsie opened the door, Margaret was clutching the knocker. The motion and inward swing of the door made her hands slip so that she fell into Elsie's hall, breaking her fall on hands and knees. Nevertheless, this was sufficient to satisfy Elsie's hunger for drama to fuel her thirst for the acquisition of juicy news. Here was something to get her teeth into, grist for her mill.

'Oh, dear,' was sufficient. Elsie immediately grasped Margaret under the arms to prevent her from falling sideways and ending up flat on the floor. Taking Margaret's weight, she made soothing words, 'It's all right now, dear, we'll just get you in here.' Her daughter had come out from the kitchen. 'The lounge door,' Elsie commanded, lifting and pulling Margaret in, over the maroon pattern to lower her onto the settee. Here she fussed with cushions, lifted Margaret's legs, felt her forehead, and wondered where she'd put the thermometer and the Epsom salts. Her daughter hovered until told to put the kettle on.

Margaret lay on the settee, groaning, her hands clutching at her abdomen. Elsie saw all this and pondered upon it. She was sure a secret was not so much in the making, but had been created and was in the process of being revealed. At the same time, she was determined to keep this to herself until such time as it would be useful, or had acquired a certain incremental value. She left the room in silent search of the travelling-rug they kept in the hall cupboard for unforeseen circumstances. This she placed carefully over Margaret so that when Anne came in reluctantly asking if she should make the tea, she was not able to see what Margaret was doing under the blanket.

'Do you feel well enough for a cuppa?' Elsie was dying to get Margaret to react, if not speak, so that she could get more of an idea what was the matter. She knew the doctor should be called, but needed to buy just a little time, not much, for herself alone.

Margaret shook her head. 'Dr Simpson,' she whispered, 'Dr Simpson. Please, quickly.'

Elsie was disappointed, secretly blamed but then excused herself. She wanted to be the one to make that decision. She wanted to be the one to advise, persuade and finally and resolutely not be put off from calling the doctor, 'For your own good,' were the words she wanted to use, 'it's always best to get these things checked.'

Dr Simpson's car could be heard on the gravel of the front drive.

'That was quick,' Elsie commented. She wanted to add, 'Almost as if he were waiting for the call,' but checked herself. Opinions could be used as facts. Facts and rumours of facts were her currency, but she had to be sure that they were finely-minted before storage and eventual use.

Elsie reached the door before the doctor could reach the door-bell or the modest brass horse-head knocker. The prying ears of neighbours might thus be excluded. 'Come in,' she whispered, both from a surfeit of respect for the doctor and a desire to be seen to be showing grave concern for his patient. 'This way, please.'

Once in the lounge Dr Simpson's every move seemed to be to suggest that there was no need for panic, or even mild concern. With an eye on Margaret, who gazed up at him from the settee, he prepared himself slowly. First of all, he took off his homburg and placed it carefully on the chair which Elsie had placed near Margaret's head. He followed this with his black overcoat, folding it and making sure it was placed carefully over the back of the chair. Then he lifted his bulging brown leather bag and placed in on the seat of the chair in front of his hat, and opened it ready for business. 'Could I possibly trouble you for a chair, please, Mrs Hipperson?'

Elsie bustled out with studied, short steps. She liked her image of herself as a helpful busy, co-operative woman.

Dr Simpson leant over Margaret and took her hand to feel her pulse. He whispered about pain. Margaret nodded. Elsie returned with a spare chair and sat on it at what she considered to be a respectable distance away from doctor and patient.

The doctor cleared his throat. 'Ah, I do apologise, I meant for me.'

Elsie stood, confused.

'Thank you so much,' Dr Simpson murmured, reaching for the chair and lifting it to where he could sit and examine Margaret. There was a pause while he reached into his bag and lifted out his stethoscope. Glancing round at Elsie who stood behind him, he said, 'If you don't mind, Mrs Hipperson - .' His back demonstrated to her that there was no possibility of this request being ignored or disputed.

With Elsie gone and the door closed, Dr Simpson listened to Margaret in the stethoscope, and felt her abdomen. 'How long,' he asked, 'since the pain started?' Margaret had to think hard over and through the pain. She didn't want to have to work out or calculate anything. How long is pain? How do you measure it? Pain is just pain. She struggled in terms of morning or afternoon. How long are they singly or together? She guessed, whispering, in case Elsie could hear through the wall, 'Three or four hours.'

Dr Simpson paused and thought a moment. "What we'll do is get you over to the surgery.' He made it sound like a pleasant stroll but added, 'Do you think you'll be all right in the car?'

Margaret nodded. The pain had withdrawn a little, biding its time.

As Dr Simpson and Elsie helped Margaret out into the car, the doctor took the opportunity to speak to Elsie in quiet, confidential tones, implying that she was party to private matters that it would, in all likelihood, be unnecessary to mention to others. He spoke in terms of the probability of hospital and a suspected acute appendicitis with complications. He watched the face he spoke to so confidentially lap up his words like a contented, even if slightly wary cat; a feline expression which told him that this condition could last for a lifetime.

PART TWO.

ARRIVAL

November 1945

Margaret felt sick most of the way in the train to Portsmouth to meet Richard. She shivered uncontrollably even when the incinerated dust of the sporadic heating system clogged her nose, brought persistent coughing to her throat, which in turn brought back painful stomach spasms. At night in bed every movement she made to turn on one side, the other side or return onto her back could precipitate an agony she had to work hard at controlling. The pain detected her slightest movement. It wouldn't retreat unless she lay stock still. At times it even seemed to know when she as much as thought about shifting position, and gathered itself together for an immediate strike. As each day progressed the aching muscles would relax a bit longer, so that she was given hope. But each night they bided their time, tightened their grip and have their revenge. Even so, they were still eager to remind her of their presence in the day, if she was careless enough to cough or try to lift something heavy like a plate, or a packet of flower. Careless meant not planning the operation of lifting so that the muscles and nerves were not in any way inconvenienced, were not asked to do something difficult or different. It was like living with a dangerous and cantankerous lunatic, who had been biding his time, who had occupied her hidden self all her life.

The railway carriage threw her from side to side, threatening pain unless she took charge and propped herself awkwardly in the corner by the window. Then the train would slow, or even stop at some remote station where one person might step hesitantly off, and two climb wearily on. At such times she would try to relax herself sufficiently to remember where she was going and why she was travelling through the black laced winter landscape. Richard, she must concentrate on Richard.

He kept slipping from her mind. Yet she'd spent a lot of time choosing what to wear: some kind of balance between the dowdy and the practical for a winter day near water. That meant the thick woolly stockings and the brogues, wearing which she could face puddles and mud. To go with these, it would have to be the tweed jacket and skirt which would complement more or less anything, enlivened perhaps with her dark red jumper. Finally, the best of two coats, the thicker winter one which went with her woollen hat which had once been fashionable. In these days of coupons no one would give you a second look anyhow.
The truth, she tried not admit, was she was dressing as if for someone she didn't know. But, nevertheless, she automatically clipped on the ear rings he'd bought her before they were married: small and gold, shaped like leaves.
Leaves long fallen.

The day before, as part of her preparations, she'd tried to cram Richard back into her mind by taking out all the photos and going through them, one by one, set by set: the wedding album where she thought she looked like a child in a party dress. In one photo where a gust of wind had caught it, the flare of white to one side made it look as if she'd just rushed back from a game, skipping or hiding somewhere.

That face: she stared at herself looking directly back at herself. What was she thinking? Feeling? Hoping? Wanting? She couldn't divine, or guess a thing; this is me, like so many others at the beginning of a journey which was called marriage, was all she could conclude. And once she found that an image of thousands of other women came to mind - staring, as she did, at their former selves and the wartime man who no longer existed standing at their side. Weeping should have made her feel better but it didn't. She was trying to get Richard back before tomorrow; she was trying to remember him, remember all the things they did in their life together, trying to remember the fun. But these things would not come: the joy she was sure she felt at their wedding: herself the centre of attention, the compliments, the admiring looks; herself triumphantly displayed to the known and the half known relatives; her mother so modestly deflecting compliments about the wedding dress she'd made and all the food she'd prepared; her father like a worried loose part who'd have to function in public as the father of the bride and say appropriate things with all eyes on him, all ears hanging on his every word. They'd be comparing this speech and occasion with other weddings attended; they'd be watchful for the lost word, the inappropriate comment, the exaggeration. Then the honeymoon in Scotland: the fathomless lochs, the brooding, clamorous mountains, the glory of roaring waterfalls - did she then ever consider the future, the possible future? Did she ever bother to cast a thought to what might or might not happen after this? In the end, all she could do was weep that she knew nothing; weep that life was trying to claw back something for her and she didn't know what; above all, weep that a notion was hovering there, just beyond her reach: that the end of an ordeal is almost more terrible than continuing to endure it.

Once, waking in the carriage and not knowing that she was even capable of sleeping in such circumstances, she found the carriage full of sailors, all staring silently at her, all smoking.

She felt like a trapped animal in a primitive smoke-filled cave. Her throat suddenly collapsed and she bent over wracked with spasms of coughing. At this moment the brakes of the train began to grind an approach to a destination. She had to concentrate on keeping secure in her seat, not only because of the cough but because the deceleration combined with lurching and crashing as the train ponderously clanked across points, all conspired together to wrack her with pain.

Then sudden movement all round startled her: the sailors were on their feet as the train nosed into a station. They swung canvas bags down from the luggage racks, muttering about the weight of their sodding packs. 'Ta, ta, darlin',' one of them said. But Margaret was oblivious, still engaged in a titanic battle to stop coughing, to prevent the wrenching, twisting and torturing of her guts. She nearly missed noticing that above the hurrying platform the word 'Portsmouth' was writ large.

Margaret stood on the platform wondering which way to go. So did a platform full of others, like her facing the next hurdle: women with children, women with older people, or older people on their own. A quiet crowd, subdued with separation, standing on alien ground.

She still felt bad about her parents. The least they could do, their faces told her, was come with you to meet Richard. You need support, dear, after these awful war years. We'll come and help you. And Richard, of course. After all, you've not been yourself this last year or so. At one point, in desperation, Frank said, 'I'll talk to Tom. I know he's got a lot of petrol coupons saved, for a rainy day, he says. He could take us down, and then we could go straight there, instead of waiting for two trains, and then straight back. Less tiring for us all, particularly for you, my dear.'

Earlier from the kitchen, she heard her parents muttering to each other. They left doors open these days. Rose was saying, 'After all, Frank, it's her husband she's meeting. If that were you, I would want to go on my own.'

Then Frank countering about health and strength. When they came back into the living room with a tray of tea, she pretended to be asleep. The thought of having to get through the whole thing with parents and Tom in tow filled her with horror. She had to get this right; was the one thing she knew. If she had to go through tears, a scene of some sort, then she was determined to do this on her own in the anonymity conferred by strangers on an unknown quay side.

The word strangers had connotations she refused to contemplate. This was disloyalty almost writ large, how could she and Richard ever be strangers to each other?
With the tea cup in one hand and the other hand occupied with the saucer and balanced spoon, she felt sufficiently in charge of herself to be polite but firm: 'It's very good of you, but I'm going on my own.'

There remained another three hours before they'd see her to the bus. This eternity of time was spent carefully avoiding the subject; with Margaret consumed with guilt, Rose and Frank trying to be cheerful and solicitous to cover up their feelings of inadequacy and the huge vacuum they could not fill with well-intentioned help. They would have to wait, Margaret knew, until such time as she felt she could bring Richard to see them. She couldn't explain that she didn't really know who she was going to meet. Or, indeed, who this person was that Richard was going to find. Then there was also the unpredictable onslaught of pain to hide.

Slowly, as if some hidden internal communication existed, the crowd of travellers on the platform gathered themselves together for a move towards the exit where the ticket collectors waited to clip their tickets. Few would surrender their tickets, because most would be back for the return journey. Margaret was caught up in the middle of the thinning crowd as it stretched itself into an orderly queue. 'Through the main door,' she heard repeated by the uniformed men at the barrier, 'a bit of a walk, unless you get a twenty-two going the right way.' Once out of the station the walk was as slow as happens when there are more than one or two gathered together. Yet she was relieved by this: an amble, the last few minutes to think through what she'd say, how she'd face an unknown length of time stretched out from this confrontation with the rest of her life. The inevitable putting off of the agony of facing up to whatever it was that she'd have to cope with: some terrifying new knowledge, but the unknowability of it all.

Who knew which way to walk across the devastated town centre Margaret had no idea. Ahead of her people picked their way across broken streets lined with rubble. Here and there a wall stood and revealed, say, that a downstairs room had had pale green wallpaper as a background to a display of tiny buttercups, and upstairs a warm blue with discrete pale waves tumbling into the distance. In one ruined house an upstairs fireplace with no floor or other walls to warm remained dependably in place ready to be lit. In some rooms wallpaper revealed the rectilinear ghosts of pictures past. In the rubble that was the broken soul of each house black patches of charred wood remembered roof and floor trusses, furniture, lives. Less intimate were the piles of bricks and concrete which had further to spread, more space to fall onto: the flattened warehouses and stores. And, behind it all, the massive grey bulk of a troop carrier, strangely mobile among this static destruction, appeared to be edging towards somewhere that might be flat and rubble-free enough for a ship to moor. Tugs hooted, their self-important reminders immediately thrown back, echoed, from the Downs behind the city, followed by fainter after-echoes ricocheting off more distant hills, sounding like landlocked vessels all joining in for the hell of it.

Repeated by the insistent tugs, this became a huge orchestration, a fanfare of announcement making of the place an immense soundscape, a momentous arrival.

The welcome: a waiting crowd , stamping their feet, shivering. No band to greet and celebrate the returning heroes, no flags, no bunting. Dockers, smoking and leaning in attitudes of boredom, stood ready for the leading lines to be thrown, would have to stand in for indifferent dignitaries. The huge ship was so ponderous, so massive a grey steel bulk; an enormous whale at which three tugs heaved, adjusted, readjusted, persuaded drift or wallow this way and that. Time seemed irrelevant. Nearer and almost persuaded to do the exact bidding of the tugs, the ship began to list towards the dock, crowded with white faces, puny arms waving, feeble whistles, with here and there a small hand held union jack, a few attempts at a cheer. And still the ship had not reached home. It had to be just right, exactly right, as if there was no point in it all unless a perfect mooring could be achieved. After an age of ropes adjusted, secured, wound round pillars of iron, the ship's siren suddenly and totally unexpectedly blasted the silence of the waiting people. Its explosion smashed against the remaining dockland walls and the ever-ready Downs and was hurled back in a repeated impact onto the thin crowd below. It was like a slap. Here and there women wept, or steeled themselves to remain desperately as they were, unaffected by this assault, determined not to break down. Not yet. Unlike the tugs, the ship's herald of return seemed to have no end and continued to be hurled back cruelly from the surrounding hills: I have arrived, here I am, I exist. Somehow, the silence which eventually came, was more terrible than the clamour of creation and its rival echo because of the immanent impact of the coming together of those waiting and those arriving.

With tearful eyes Margaret searched each deck, each crowded port hole. All or any of the faces of the returning men could or could not have been Richard. Around her people were getting excited, 'There he is, that must be him!' and pointing. Soldiers waved, some called. She heard 'Pat!' several times, and 'Anne!' but not Margaret.

It is always a long time from the perceived docking of a ship and the lowering of the gangway until the actual disembarkation. That the one should logically quickly follow the other is thought to be the case, but those waiting always forget this. The delay, after the arrival, seems as long as the voyage itself. Then, as if to make the point that nothing can be hurried, a single uniformed man will pick his way cautiously down the gangway. He'll ignore the crowd and may walk with a degree of self- importance and certainty towards a building. Perhaps he's carrying a briefcase, or a small official leather case. He'll disappear into the building, never to be seen again. Next, a few men descend: sailors. Why, what are they going to do? Then there's another pause before a blur of khaki appears: men with roll bags uncertainly balanced on their shoulders, the supporting arm partially hiding their faces, the other hand steadying themselves on the gangway rope. The line of khaki becomes more concentrated. The watchers and waiters begin to calculate their chances of being the lucky ones, the ones whose wait will be the shortest. The line descends, and walks upon England's hard, grey concrete. Here and there arms are flung round the lucky ones, but it doesn't seem to happen much and the line of khaki clefts a lonely route through strangers. It dawns on the small waiting throng that there are going to be far more men than there are loved ones waiting for them; that some men still have multiple train journeys yet to endure.

All this is but a prelude: there's another delay. The massed waiting faces on the stacked tilting decks become more restrained. There's a small, subdued gasp from the quay side when the first stretcher appears, slowly and painfully edged down the gangway by orderlies.

The waiting relatives had not bargained for this. Like Margaret, they'd constructed and preserved pictures of a reunion with a walking son, husband or brother in possession of all four limbs, in reasonable enough health to re-join this depleted life, to forget, to put behind him whatever has happened, assured of a fresh start. The line of stretchers become endless, only interspersed by the halt and lame on crutches. Military ambulances and civilian coaches behind the waiting relatives have nosed quietly in: this isn't really happening, no need for anyone to be concerned or worried, everything is in hand.

Margaret reacts like other waiting loved ones: oh God, is this him, stretchered, or limping with a crutch? She's pushed against other anxious relatives to search each white, wasted face. She's eaten up with anxiety. At the same time there's an energy in her she's not noticed before, a determination: if one of these invalids is

Richard, no one's going to take him away, he's not going anywhere else, he's coming home. There's steel inside her she never knew she had; it's sharp enough to kill.

Richard waits on the top deck. He has stood on the faded boards for a few minutes each hour to see if the fog will allow him to see if *Home* exists. He wants to see England grow from a thin, dark horizontal line into something that is the living land he can recognise: Home. A few minutes is all he can stand; in both senses of the word - he's weak, he's cold, he's frightened that this land, his country, might not be the same, might not hold within it the same people. He's frightened that it might be illusory, that it might just fade away, disappear into nothing; that it's been so long coming it might not be real. But he knows that if he forces himself to watch it grow it'll remain there on the horizon and continue to exist. If he does this Margaret might even continue to exist. Whether or not she's the same person he has no idea because he inhabits a world where anything and everything can change shape, alter, not be what you first thought. Later, he thinks that in any case, she might not be among what must be a dark crowd of people waiting on the distant quayside.

Although he can't fully articulate it, he's frightened of confronting what he has yearned for and waited for these four long years. If he could quantify this huge length of time a ship takes to sail from Burma to India to the Suez Canal to Malta to Gibraltar to Portsmouth it might help. It might allow him to approach understanding. Days and weeks on this ship were little different from the years in the camp: they were merely days and weeks to be endured, like now in the crush of men on deck, or in the crowded cabin, or the overflowing mess, the porridge hard to keep down, or queuing for the toilet, queuing for an overcoat when they reached the Mediterranean, and always out there the endless and indifferent horizon.

Then the ship would reach somewhere. He was not interested in where because it's not *Home*. He stands looking down at people in small colourful boats laden with trinkets, calling 'Hey, soldier want a – ', who row round the ship and try to get on board. These men have the dark faces the returning soldiers are used to, but the energy they're not used to.

By Gibraltar Richard thinks that he's got the strength to disembark and have a look round. He follows other men up a narrow street that looks like Home and reaches a small square. Here he has to sit down because a dark sky has lowered itself close to his forehead, just above the eyes. He's aware that a voice is offering him tea or a drink, or Whisky, sir? but can't do anything about it because the darkness pressing on him is too powerful. All he's aware of later is leaning on the shoulders of a couple of soldiers, being coaxed back up the gangway.

He can't remember when it happened but later assumed it was after Gib. that he and all returning soldiers were told to gather in the mess hall at a time which was neither breakfast, lunch nor dinner. He was one of those who could walk and follow a line of men filing in slowly, silenced by the weight of the unexpected summons as much by crutches, sticks and endemic bewilderment. A sergeant points to a chair and he sits, even though he'd rather have stayed propped on a deck rail gazing at the horizon for hours as if to persuade it to offer a distant, grey glimpse of England.

Around Richard on unsteady wooden seats sit men of all ranks gleaned from the Far East. He knows battered souls when he sees them. The sergeant's face twitches and his left hand kneads his shoulder and head as if trying to make something of the damaged dough of his body and mind. Surveying this slow procession of broken men, an officer stands, waiting, behind a small desk on the raised part of the hall where the ship's officers sit for meals safely separated from the other ranks . The officer's desk is covered with the green felt which looks like an English lawn, on which rests the comfort of a glass of water.

The Major clears his throat and bends slightly to reach the glass of water in order to signal the start of the meeting. The men have filed and limped in quietly, muted by the change of their sea gazing, card playing routine. A minority mutters and mumbles.

The Major rises. 'Good morning!' The residual sound of men dries, dies a natural death. 'Gentlemen,' he says loudly, 'I'm sure you will all like to know that we are now less than four hours from Home, depending on the wind and weather. We are due to dock at Portsmouth at about twelve hundred and thirty hours.' He pauses, as if for himself as much as for the men to take in this news. His hands tremble a little and he reaches for the safety of the jug of water in order to top up his glass.

'But what I have to say to you this morning is of the greatest importance.' He pauses, as he practiced all those years ago in staff college. Then looks from left to right at the blur of faces peering up at him, and takes a deep breath.

'Gentlemen, you are the lucky ones.' He pauses to let this sink in. 'Many thousands of your comrades and friends are not. You are returning home, they are not. You will all have a picture in your minds of Home, England, and of your homes, your neighbourhoods, the shops, the public house round the corner where you used to meet up with your friends. But, most importantly, your nearest and dearest - your families. For many of you, thinking about these, the most important things in your lives has been the one thing which has kept you going, whether you were prisoners of war or on active duty fighting the Japs.'

The Major pauses, drinks from his glass, and finally wipes his ample moustache with a handkerchief. 'But I have two things that I want to put to you all before we dock. These are very important, and I hope will help during these first few days of your liberation from both the camps and the war itself.'

Richard was startled by a grunt, or snore from the man sitting next to him: a man with a drooping military moustache and completely bald head, slouched in a faded uniform of the Royal Signals. The man's eyes are closed, and the snort is an irregular snore. Glancing along the line of seated soldiers he sees that, here and there, some slumber, their heads nodding, their arms folded as if this would protect them from whatever bad news there might be. 'Gentlemen, you will be returning to an England greatly changed. While you, on the one hand have endured hardship with great fortitude, so have those left behind in England - they have had to endure relentless Nazi bombing throughout the War, they have had their food drastically rationed, they have had to rely on themselves without you all this time. Many have been bombed out of their own homes, many have lost sons, fathers, and husbands in the theatres of this terrible War. Because of these privations, gentlemen, you may find them changed, and this is something that you will have to come to terms with.'

He paused again, but this time looked at the men before him, as if so doing would somehow help his words resonate in the minds of these returning soldiers. He drew another large breath.

'Gentlemen, this is not all. I now return to you. You, too, have been through experiences you may never have expected to endure: imprisonment, starvation, illness, cruel treatment, battle. You, too, will have been changed by this. You, too, may seem like a different person to those closest to you, as well as your friends and neighbours.' Another pause.

'And here, gentlemen, I come to the point. Think about what I have said to you. Think about how you are going to fit back into the life you had before this enormous upheaval. Think about how you will fit in again, into life in peacetime as civilians. Remember that you and your families will have suffered this distressing separation in different ways, but now have the chance to come together again and build a life back together. Gentlemen, I'm sure that by being understanding you, too, will be understood. With all my heart I wish you good luck and prosperity in this new England, this post-war Home with your loved ones who are so looking forward to having you home at long last.'

Several hours later, despite Richard's fears, England begins to grow, to resolve itself into the sombre lines of distant buildings, one like a fortress, with the soft curves of remote hills behind. He hears this all round him being called, The Solent, and look ahead, there's Portsmouth! It's so cool that his teeth chatter, and he's shivering uncontrollably.

There's no one else back in the cabin. With relief he lies down on his bunk. Sometime later the ship sways enough to make him aware of a change. In addition, the ship's siren screams and is answered by its own feeble, distant others echoing from the reliable Downs behind Portsmouth. He drags himself off the bunk and because of the dangerous tilt of the companionways grasps rails to balance along lengths of steel walls, door handles, as he stumbles and sways to reach the deck.

Up here the slope of the deck is disturbing. Although he cannot reach the railings because of the press of men leaning over them, he doesn't want to confront a chasm leaning out into space, trying to propel him into the void. Here and there, between heads and shoulders, he can see a roof, a bit of wall, gaps where you'd expect a building, a crane or two above it all, and beyond them the dirty green of the chalk hills.

The sky of England is uniform grey, a weight of indifferent frigidity. Someone says, 'Time to get our kit, lads.' Richard follows them back into the straight corridors and the tiny cabins they've lived in for so many weeks that it seems like forever.

A tall, painfully thin man stands in front of Margaret. His lips, stretched to breaking point, are trying to smile. Somehow the man retains the ghost of Richard's features, an older impression of the man she's waited for all these years. He's staring at her as if she were someone else: say who you are, introduce me to this person. Above his eyes, above the unexpected lines of his forehead, she takes in the white hair. Pure white. There's a split second where she thinks this must be a hat he's wearing. But she watches how his hand passes up over his forehead, brushes over his head so that his hair is disturbed. And it really is white, a shock of white hair where it should have been light brown with here and there a hint of fair, which would lighten in the summer. She is instantly deflected from this: how can such thin wrists hold up his hands, make them work?

Richard can't hold the smile: it's a forgotten action which should have been rehearsed, as if someone had just asked him to vault a hurdle because he'd been good at it at school. This woman standing in front of him, among a few older ones, a woman whose face is an impression of Margaret, lined and somehow altered as if she'd sketched herself inadequately and hadn't bothered with the colour wash. He knows he must speak because she might go away and then he would never have known.
'Margaret.' This is neither statement nor question. She hears her name in a voice she struggles to remember, and is tired, like an echo of itself.

'Richard.' He hears his name spoken in a voice which is so thin, so simplified, that it could have reverted to childhood.

Margaret sees that he possesses only himself and a small khaki pack which has fallen off his shoulder and lies abandoned on the oily surface of the dock.
Richard sees a woman who is flabby and grey with the weight of waiting; a woman who must be Margaret, but a woman he can only stare at in an attempt to reassemble her features, the way she stands, the set of her shoulders the way she looks up at him.

'   ,' he tries.

'   ,' she tries.

Next to them a soldier and a woman clasp each other. Richard knows he should do the same. He raises both arms and leans towards her. Distantly, Margaret finds that her arms don't work, but feels both of his briefly touch her upper arms but fail to pull her by the shoulders towards him. They step apart like strangers and continued to look at each other. Without knowing why, but still with this new and strange sense of being empowered, Margaret leans awkwardly and picks up the khaki pack in such a way that the pain in her stomach will not know. She half turns and points to somewhere behind her, and they walk stiffly, slowly away from the ship and the few remaining quietly waiting people, to try and find the way back.

In the train Richard sits bolt upright, stiff and unmoving, intently watching the green fields and filigree winter woodland flow by in a pastoral procession of England. The smoke from the locomotive dips across the window from time to time, obscuring the sight of what he had for so long yearned, so that the landscape becomes every now and then a phantom of itself. As if she understands this hunger, Margaret lets him sit next to the window and settles herself against him, mirroring his sitting position, absorbed in his silence, her right arm linked with his left. To her he seems to neither react to nor ignore this contact. To him it is something he wants but cannot acknowledge or believe is actually happening.

Presently she allows the little finger of her left hand to cross over and find one of his. There's hardly any reaction from his finger, but she keeps hers there, from time to time giving his the smallest tug.
When the darkening suburbs of London take over from the dimming fields of twilight, she takes her arm from under his and reaches over to take both of his hands in hers, searching among memory for this touch. Richard's hands seem to retain their weight, but not their feeling. His fingers scarcely react. Richard, too, is fighting a way through the corridors of memory. These are so numerous for him to navigate a way through, paradoxically too clamorous and combative to allow any single one the strength to dominate. He knows he should say something, should comment on the voyage, the train, the empty stations where the train stopped, the landscape. Above all, he knows he should say, 'How are you?' Above all he knows he should try to smile; he should give her that. But even this will no more come than the conversational niceties that were for so long unexercised, and had died. Margaret watched Richard in

the bus from the station. He'd close his eyes, as if the darkness outside, inadequately lit by the still newly awakened street lights, was not worth looking at. To him this was simple exhaustion; to her it was perhaps an inability to engage. It was different when they alighted from the bus. As soon as they began walking up the slope to the top of Dickson's Close, Richard had to stop every few steps and shore himself up for a few moments on a garden fence, or against a lamp post, just to gain the strength needed for a few more steps. 'Not far now,' she said, knowing it was as much for herself as for him; she knew that it was simple exhaustion and she began to blame herself for adding to it.

Nearly at the top, in sight of the house, a figure approached them down the hill. It stopped in front of them. It began to speak loudly, insistently. Elsie wanted to justify herself, wanted to vindicate the fact that her business coming down the road like this on an early winter's evening was innocent and public spirited.

'It's Mrs Bolton at the bottom again,' as if they'd know about the other implied occasions, 'another turn with Arnold - .'

Elsie paused and drew herself heroically out of the Close and her own preoccupation with rumour and fabricated news, 'And Richard back,' she sang, 'Thank the Lord!' Then adding, 'Oh, yes, we've kept an eye on her all right, we have.' As if this was not enough, and to fill the dread silence which ensued, trilled, 'Oh, yes, we've looked after her for you!'

Richard had just had a rest, propped up against the telegraph pole three-quarters of the way up Dicksons Close, and didn't know who this woman was who seemed to want to prevent him from reaching home, lying down and allowing the balm of sleep to give him blessed relief from the trials and tribulations of travel. He pushed himself from the lamp post and wasn't going to stop. Elsie looked up at him as he was almost on top of her, exclaimed 'Oh!' and side stepped. It appeared to Margaret that Richard didn't so much as not look at Elsie, but had detached himself from her existence, would have not noticed that he'd walked through the woman. As it was, she was holding onto his arm with one hand, and carrying his pack in the other. Although her back was beginning to ache, she felt stronger than she could remember for a long time. In order to help Richard, she had to keep in step with him, and this meant leaving Elsie staring at them in the baleful light of the few street lamps which remained lit. All the same, Margaret was confused between a compulsion to apologise and a resolution that this was none of Elsie's business, and that she'd have to make her peace with her neighbour sometime soon because she'd taken a fierce and, to her, reasonable decision not to tell Elsie or anyone else in the Close that Richard was coming home.

It was a part of keeping a secret, a superstition that if you let one out the rest would all come tumbling out, one after the other, like a visceral rope of blood and bones. Not that this was going to help much: by the morning the whole Close would know that Richard was back. And now there was the front garden gate and the front door to negotiate, to persuade to open, despite their wartime neglect.

Somehow, she got him onto the kitchen chair where he used to sit, and told him about food. She'd got powdered egg, bread, the rest of the week's butter ration and some of her mother's jam. The frying pan was ready with two rashers of bacon, the water in the kettle, everything including the cutlery was already laid out. All she had to do was light the oven for warmth, stir the egg powder in the saucepan into a semblance of scrambled egg, fry the bacon and boil the water: the ghost of a wedding breakfast almost forgotten, the feast after the slaughter.

The sound of frying and boiling, together with the whisper of stirring and the growing aroma of bacon, filled the kitchen. Richard watched, his elbows on the table, his chin propped up on his hands, trying to think, trying to get all this into his mind: on the one hand nothing had changed, and these were the food and same utensils being operated by this woman who on the other hand was supposed to look like and be Margaret.

The powdered scrambled egg and the two rashers of bacon, together with two slices of fried bread Margaret placed on a warmed plate on the table to await distribution while she warmed the teapot, carefully measuring in three, instead of two, spoonsful of tea leaves followed by the boiling water and a good stir before finding the one thing she'd not thought of in advance: the tea cosy. When she turned back to the table, she found that Richard had eaten all the scrambled egg, bacon and both pieces of fried bread. As this sunk in, she saw that he was wiping his mouth with the back of his hand.

Slowly, to give her time, she placed the teapot on its stand on the table. Words, propelled by feelings, were just there on her tongue, but were killed by a huge surge of emotion which blinded her eyes with tears. If she'd let it, a second surge would have had her howl and her stomach swirl with pain. Instead, she reached for the bread - this might stretch to one more day; her next ration would be in least three days' time. Thinking, 'Oh, God, when would rationing stop?' she watched as he spread the rest of her ration of butter on the slice, she thought she had cut for herself. She cut a second one and spread her mother's jam on it. Richard looked at the sugar in the sugar bowl, lifted the curved sugar spoon and gazed at it, turning it over as if it were a new thing he was wondering whether or not to buy. 'Part of one of our wedding presents,' she whispered.

They ate in a silence so huge as to drive all words from their heads. At least eating uses up time. It's either a lubricator of communication or an excuse not to. Chewing can fill the head, crammed as it was in Richard and Margaret's minds against the enormity of four years of separation. Robbed of this time, robbed of the time to generate the talking, the sharing of lives in which it was necessary to negotiate each day, week, month, year in a companionable and loving way, all that is left is silence.

Less than an hour later this silent, rigid man lay with her in their bed. He smelled of rough, unwashed things, of cigarettes, of the odour of men other than himself. She had his pyjamas ready, the blue striped ones he hadn't taken, carefully ironed.

It was a struggle up the stairs. He had to take each step one by one: twelve steps and twelve pauses. She held his arm all the way up and helped him across the landing. His body turned and his legs lead him to the right door. He looked down at their bed, subsided and lay down on the left-hand side where she had slept these last four years. His eyes were closed before his head touched the pillow. He lay on his back and slept in dusty monumentality.

With tears in her eyes Margaret knew that neither he nor she could move him, that neither had the strength to lift him and pull off his clothes. All she could do was pull down the extra eiderdown from the shelf in the cupboard and cover him with it. But there were the boots: they would not come off because she couldn't undo the tightly bound leather laces. She thought of a fork, then a knife, but finally got the nail scissors from her dressing table, the mirror showing her darkly desperate, and cut the laces. Beneath the rough brown boots were pungent khaki socks.

The boots she put for safety in the gap between the cupboard and the dresser. The socks she could not yet face; neither did she have the energy to get herself undressed and into her thick woollen nightdress.

She could do no more than lie, fully dressed, next to him under the blankets and eiderdown, craving his warmth, but knowing that she was going to have to give him what little she had.

Richard slept without moving, a log in the night, while she had to grip, clamp her mind to prevent her turning, twisting her body, shifting position in case her stomach should revolt in instant painful protest and disturb him. She was yet to learn that pain could go, vanish slowly into the substance or string of life; that you'd only notice when it had completely gone, and then by its absence rather than its diminution.

The night was huge. It filled Margaret with enormous spaces where she floated awake, stunned but too weak to be shocked. In the deep recesses of these dimensions she found herself sweating as if with apprehension, or was it fear, foreboding? She tried to make plans, but these were too buoyant, too fugitive to grow coherent in her mind. Instead, questions intruded: what to do tomorrow, then in the days which followed? How to construct some kind of life, because it was the very foundations of this life, in the next few days and weeks, which might put the whole architecture of that life on a strong enough footing to ensure survival. At the same time, she couldn't help herself thinking that the future had been on hold for so long that it could have ceased to exist and become a complete blank. They had been thrust into a vacuum, a nothingness. What should she tell him, what say, what confess? How to tell him of her life, the life that she had never expected to be separated from his? How could she express the darkness of the mental prison in which she'd been living?

Later in the far reaches of the night the questions shifted: how would he be in the morning? Would sleep have - would sleep have given him strength? Would sleep ease his - soul? Because it was this that she knew she feared most - that it was his soul which had fled, had been taken from her. This was so strong that it became like an immutable fact that was part of her. With renewed tears she slowly came to realise that she now believed it because this is what had happened to her. Her soul inactive and trapped in the prison of these four years. If she knew this, would he?

In the intense darkness before the winter dawn she knew that, clothed in this terrible new freedom, she would have to bring back herself, her essence. But infinitely more difficult would be if she had to bring back Richard's too.

Chapter 9

JANUARY 1946

She might find Richard standing alone in a room. As she met his gaze it would be as if she wasn't there. Then he'd come to and smile. A thin smile would be how she'd describe it, a conscious tug at the mouth of the muscles either side, as instructed by his brain. His mouth would move as if he wanted to say something, but usually didn't. To her it seemed that he didn't know what to say, so she would quietly and cheerfully mention the weather, or how she'd kept the room just as it had been before, oh and I must get some more potatoes, custard powder and bread. Once or twice he nodded, looking around the room, object by object, as if reacquainting himself. She'd go up to him and put her arms round him. He'd raise his, and again it was a consciously considered, not a natural reaction, if he put his arms round her. There was no male urgency or strength. He was merely telling his arms what to do so that he could remain detached.

Or she'd find him with a drawer open, carefully examining the contents. For instance, the top drawer of the sideboard in the dining room where she kept the leather cases containing their wedding cutlery. He'd take each vivid scarlet case out, carefully placing it on the dining table. Then, with an expression of great concentration, he'd carefully press the catch so that the released lid would spring up just enough to be comfortably opened by thumb, revealing the cutlery in all its shining glory. Polishing them once a month had been part of her routine, part of her slow procession through memory; a journey which might have finished in a more difficult place than where it had started. She watched him carefully, partly in case he tried to lift something, or drop something - a cup or plate, or the Japanese set he often seemed to stare at for a long time.

Once she saw him seated at the bureau, watched him carefully push up the slatted cover as if he'd never done so before. His hands touched the papers thus revealed and she froze in her now frequent pose - hands on both sides of her face - and knew that he'd found her unposted letters to him. Why, oh why hadn't she taken them out; why oh why hadn't she scrumpled them into the lounge grate and set them alight, just one match and it would have been done.
She watched in horror, that sinking feeling of the stomach which was so familiar. But his gaze at the letters, and his touch which wouldn't riffle through them came to a quick end. He closed the bureau, stood and met her eyes. 'Oh, Richard,' she said, 'I couldn't - .'
But he interrupted. 'But my messages,' he said, and looked as if he wanted to say something else but couldn't find the words.

'It's nearly lunch time,' she whispered.

Time was long and slow. A few weeks had passed in a succession of heavy days, and of nights' black weight only relieved by the balm of oblivious sleep. Richard had spent the first few days in bed, she feeding him with breakfast, lunch and supper. While he ate, she sipped soup, sitting on the side of the bed in her brown overcoat, watching his every move, every change of expression. The bed, the whole room and the landing outside had filled with the smell of sweaty clothes, and of a man's body. His hair was already too long, his beard insistent. 'It's so cold,' he said once. It was. She couldn't remember how long it was since she'd had a fire lit anywhere in the house. The oven had been the warm heart of the house. Open doors throughout the house received a little of this heat even if it were scarcely noticeable.

In those first days she had to help him, shrouded in a blanket, to the toilet. She brought up kettles of hot water for the sink and held his hands in it for warmth, for revival. Otherwise he didn't wash and she had still not prised from his back the reeking khaki of war. While he slept, she made dashes for the shops and bank. These exhausted her and she lay beside him during the day and slept.

There came knocking at the door once, twice, several times a day, but she was either too tired or too afraid to open up to the world; he oblivious. Spied at from the bedroom window it would usually be Elsie, and once a man from the Electricity. The postman had no need to knock when he brought the weekly letter from her mother.

'How is dear Richard? Your father and I are so looking forward to seeing him ....'

She steeled herself to write back, *'Richard is so tired, he sleeps nearly all day. So it'll be some time before we can see you ...'*

It took nearly a week before she could get Richard step by slow step downstairs into the kitchen. She said it was easier for him to manage the egg and bacon, she said it was warmer. But it was a trick, a small deception to achieve a different goal. After two days when she saw that he could do this on his own, she sprang the trap. It was laid at least an hour and a half before Richard surfaced from whatever sleep he swam in, whatever dreams he secretly and silently watched. The kitchen was warmed by the open doored oven sufficient to make the walls and windows stream. She boiled kettle after kettle, saucepan upon filled saucepan.

The day before she'd delved into the garden shed and found what she was looking for: the old zinc bathtub, used in that previous life before baths, and now retired as a store for flowerpots. After dark, which provided the only privacy she could hope for, she dragged it screeching of metal on concrete up the garden path and straight into the kitchen by the back door.

She'd almost forgotten about the Laundry until the steam filled kitchen brought it back: the painful, amusing, unhappy, and boring images of the place. Bettie's red face, and the hating pair, Garner and Savory, who by turns had irritated and frightened her because she thought that they might any day turn against her in terrible alliance. Only Mr Baines seemed to swirl in through the mist with any kind of credit, a nice man she decided to remember. Perhaps like Mr Bailey. 'No side to those two,' her mother might say.

Or shopping. She'd have to leave him for the troubled hour it took her to go shopping, this strong urge for food to nourish him. It was like leaving someone very ill at home. She had to steel herself to get into and out of the town centre as fast as she could. Rations, calculating how much sugar, tea, cheese, butter, bread, lard margarine, meat and milk she'd get: propelled her to the Food Office.

'Ah, your husband's back,' the clerk with the warts on his forehead, and the slow manner, said, 'I'm afraid, Madam, that he needs to present himself here in person, with his identity card, of course, and we'll be able to process him a ration book in no time at all.' He looked at her for a moment and added, 'Er, well it shouldn't take more than a few days. Good day.'

In Woolworths, in Simons the butcher, and in round the wooden supports of Poulton's grocery stall, a few tired paperchains and streamers fidgeted tentatively in the late Autumn breeze. Margaret at first thought of notions of cheerfulness - the War over, the men back - but the notion of Christmas took longer to heave itself over the horizon of her mind which was intent on buying porridge oats, bread and a cabbage. Of course, Christmas.

At first, Richard seemed not to notice the old bath tub steaming quietly in front of the kitchen sink. Margaret had planned it that he'd eat his scrambled eggs, drink three cups of tea, eat slice after slice of toast with marmite and then marmalade spread straight onto the rough brown surface. He'd eaten their weekly ration of butter three days ago, but this didn't appear to matter.

That morning, when he had reached some unknown kind of satisfaction, some feeling of fullness, he began to slow his consumption of toast and glance at the bathtub.

Margaret, watching keenly, pushed up the arm of her jumper, and tested the temperature with her crooked elbow which she knew from her mother is how you test the temperature of water for a baby. She adjusted the temperature with a kettle or two of cold water from the sink, stirred the water with her hand for an even tepidity and then stood, looking at Richard with a resolution which had him meet her eye.

Not knowing how else to put it, she said, 'A nice warm bath!' Her tentative enthusiasm surprised her. She couldn't remember when she'd last raised her voice like this about anything. The tone remained in her mind, but at the same moment her innards twisted inside themselves. Not a bad spasm, but enough to remind her - take care, I'm still here, I can strike at any moment. She paused, then moved slowly and carefully over to Richard where he sat watching. 'Now, love,' she said, 'first the jumper. Arm out.' As she pulled at the sleeve of his raised left arm, she fought the tears which sprang into her eyes. She was talking to a child, wanted to talk to a child, bathe a child, touch a child's body, wash it. As close as this and tugging at the garment, the stench of filth was further released. Richard seemed not to notice but she was having to hold her head back, gasp more distant air, however little. The other arm came out more quickly as if Richard was learning a new skill. Then he tugged the rest of garment over his head without twisting some possibly painful part of his neck or ears.

It was done, and thrown straight into the sink full of warm water, bubbling with soap suds. The first step in anything is always the most difficult. The khaki shirt was more easily taken off, following by the khaki vest. Here she stopped, appalled. His torso was like a skeleton. Bones she recognized theoretically, but had never before seen, stuck out of his body at what looked like unnatural angles. His shoulder blades and ribs looked as if a knock or a rub would reveal their terrible whiteness, or they'd spring out of his body under their own internal tension. And his skin, his poor skin stretched opaque like greaseproof paper - mottled, motley, blodges of brown on a background of white. Weals and half healed boils, and worst of all there were long lines of livid red all over his back somehow supported by the frayed rope of a spine. She had to pause behind Richard because she could feel heaving deep inside her nascent retches which if allowed to come to fruition would tear and contort her stomach in an explosion of pain. She took a deep and sudden breath so that she could stand for a precious few seconds, without breathing, without moving a muscle, willing her insides to calm, to reach back into some kind of repose where she'd get the space to finish what she'd started. Richard, as if noticing for the first time that she had gone quiet, that something was wrong, tried to peer round at her, couldn't twist enough, but began to unbuckle the belt of his trousers. But worse was to come: without his trousers the fullness of his distended stomach was revealed, a cruel parody of pregnancy. Dr Simpson was all she could think. He must come. He must come now.

The moment came for her to help Richard into the bath tub. He sank into it with a sigh, leaning back against the higher side, his legs bent, his hands grasping his exposed, swollen knees to take a little weight off the contact of his back with metal. Margaret had the soap and flannel ready. Tentatively, delicately, as if he were a - she couldn't say, baby, even in her inarticulate depths, she began to wash his body, every inch, every crack and crevasse, the length of every bone, the knotted spine, the creased neck, his stubbly beard and straggly hair, his gnarled hands, his bony arms with their scraffito lacework of white and livid red lines, - the shadows of what endured? Then the legs so thin that they more resembled arms. She couldn't see and didn't wash his genitals; she refused to think about this, but was able to snatch a glimpse of them when she asked him to stand so that she could dry him from the waist down, so that he could step out onto the bath mat, so that she could begin to clothe him in the vestments of their former life, clothes which she had cared for, washed and ironed these four years of unknowing. His genitals, she knew at a glance, were intact, whole, as if his body had concentrated all its meagre resources into this one vital organ, this essence of a man, as if this was the only hope of a body's ultimate survival. She looked up at his face as she knelt and dried him. His eyes were closed. But his face, she dared to hope, was less taut.

'I've got the fire going in the lounge,' she murmured as he allowed himself to be dressed. She'd put out his clothes on the back of her chair, to air in the hot breath of the open oven: a white vest and shirt, his grey slacks, and the pullover with its green rhomboid pattern set in lines interspersed with running patterns in red and a bigger pattern like a split square in blue. The sort of pullover worn by chaps after a cricket match, after tennis, after a ramble in the country. A pullover and a Pimm's in some club house. She'd toiled over this sweater for a year, her mother unpicking and correcting her mistakes week by week. It had been like an apprenticeship, started in childhood, which had led to no further pullovers, sacrificed instead to war effort blanket squares.

There in the Turkish Bath of the kitchen she stood back as if expecting to look at a new Richard: a clean new man down to his dark blue socks and his old brown leather slippers. He stood gazing down at her, his hands hanging at his side, his face immobile, his clothes suspended over his sparse frame as if dangling from a hook behind a door. She'd tried hard, she'd go on trying hard, she couldn't think of anything else to do. She knew she was at an end which she hoped might, instead, be a beginning.

Holding his hand, she led him into the sitting room. What he would actually do in there she had no idea because she had not thought beyond the one enormous task of removing his foul khaki clothing and washing away the smell of four filthy years. This had been like a wall blocking the morrow, and by extension the whole of the future, because living one day at a time was an essential part of what being Margaret had become. Besides, there was another pressing task which was all a part of what she wanted to do that day: she wanted the space of sufficient time to rush upstairs and strip the bed, fling the blankets into the spare bedroom, find fresh ones and plunge the sheets and pillow cases into the same thick, purging soup as she had thrown his army clothes.

Yet, at the same time, she didn't want to abandon Richard in the living room as if he were elderly or infirm. She felt a strong urge to watch him, to seize upon any sign, any indication of the possibility that he could be restored to her Richard, her husband. But even without turning round from helping Richard get comfortable with the settee cushions she knew that the fire she had tried to light had died. The air in the room was as dank and uninviting as it had been for so long.

'Oh no, the fire!'

She saw Richard look at the fireplace. A tiny trailing wisp of smoke rose lazily towards the chimney. The rolled-up paper would not, could not fire the black intensity of the coal. She said, 'I'll fetch a blanket.'

She returned with the travelling blanket: the blue plaid one stored in the spare room, waiting for picnics and hikes that had never happened during these missing years. As she eased it over and round his shoulders so that its ends draped over his legs, she could have wept that everything she touched in their house cried in remembrance of the time before Richard went. That here was another example - the blanket they'd placed on the ground for picnics, the blanket that enveloped them when they swayed through the countryside laughing in Leonard's car - their furtive hands daringly groping each other. But it was Richard who interrupted the procession of these destructive memories.

'Would you mind switching on the wireless? I haven't listened in for ..'

His voice trailed away with the obviousness of what he was saying.

'Oh, yes, of course.' Neither had she. Tentatively, she turned the knob on the bottom left hand side of the set and heard the click of the switch. They both waited for the valves to warm up. But the station display hadn't lit up, neither did turning up the volume help.

Defeated, she turned to look at Richard. Just as he was about to speak, she thought, the plug. She heard him murmur, 'The plu-.' But she was there, reaching behind the set, pushing the two prongs into the socket. 'Ah,' she heard, and looked up to see the stations glowing in the familiar warm amber.

'The Home Service,' he whispered. They waited, holding their breaths, silenced. Seconds, just the few of them required for the valves to collect the broadcast waves, assemble them and pass them out through the large speaker at the top of the set, felt as if they took a little lifetime. Suddenly the voice boomed out into the room, startling them both.

A little laugh, uncontrolled, perhaps uncontrollable, sprang from Margaret's throat. 'Silly me, I forgot the -!' as she grasped the volume knob to turn it right down. She looked over her shoulder at Richard to laugh again, desperate to make this a joke to share with him; but his eyes were far away, fixed on the wireless, listening with an intensity and concentration that she couldn't remember having seen in him before. Silently she closed the door after her and reached for her coat.

Dr Simpson's wife often answered the door, particularly in the morning when there were more patients. Mrs Simpson had the sharp eyes of a woman who could have been a doctor herself, but had not had the opportunity. The way she spoke to you suggested a nursing background. This may have been true but, being the wife of a doctor, she had interested herself in the range of problems with which her husband was routinely involved. She also offered free advice, sympathy and consolation where and when she could.

Margaret knew that Mrs Simpson knew everything about her, and that this didn't matter. She could have been her mother. She spoke quietly to Margaret, to draw out what she'd come for. As Margaret's voice faltered over the suppurating sores and red marks, Mrs Simpson knew exactly if and how she should touch Margaret's arm, then let her hand slip down and hold Margaret's.
'What I'll do, dear,' she said, 'is catch him between patients within the next few minutes and tell him to come and see Richard the first opportunity he gets today.'
Margaret would have liked a pair of arms round her, would have liked to be touched on the face, would have liked to have been given permission to weep. 'Thank you,' she whispered.

Three hours seemed stretched to something like a whole day before she heard the knock on the door. It made her jump. Sitting with Richard in the cold living room she'd held herself in a tight knot of fear and expectancy.

She'd said nothing about Dr Simpson. The slamming of the doctor's car door had seemed detached from her. At least it was not Elsie. She opened the door to a long draught of cold air and Dr Simpson stood huge in the hallway. She murmured, 'The kitchen would be better. Warmer. I'll bring him in.'

Richard was dozing with his head flopped onto one shoulder. He started when she touched his arm. Elgar was playing faintly, scratchily on the radio: *I vow to thee my country.* 'Come on, love,' she whispered. He allowed himself to be helped up and lead into the kitchen.

'Dr Simpson has called by,' she said.

The doctor, she saw, looked Richard keenly up and down, then extended his hand. Richard looked at this as if he'd never before been offered a hand, but rallied and brought his right hand up. They shook hands. As the doctor let go, he raised Richard's hand for a second or two longer, looking at it as if by chance. Margaret helped Richard into his chair. Dr Simpson sat opposite, a huge presence on the chair which Margaret usually occupied. She stood between them to one side.

Dr Simpson cleared his voice of the cool November air and said, 'Good to see you back.' Richard said nothing. 'Just a routine visit, to see how you are.' Richard gazed across the table at him. Margaret thought she saw him try to nod. Dr Simpson paused, looking at Richard. 'May I feel your pulse, please.' Richard didn't move.

Margaret could bear it no more than a couple of seconds before lifting his arm from his side and across the table. She undid the sleeve button and pushed back Richard's shirt and jumper. Dr Simpson felt Richard's pulse, looking at the hand, the bony wrist and glanced more closely at Richard's face. He breathed deeply as he released the wrist and bent over sideways towards his bulging leather bag. Straightening, he put his stethoscope to his ears. 'If you don't mind,' he said, 'chest first.' Again, it was Margaret who had to unbutton Richard's braces in order to pull up his shirt and vest. She saw Richard wince to the cool touch of the stethoscope, but otherwise his eyes gazed vacantly across the kitchen. She had an overwhelming desire to tell the doctor what this man called Richard was like, or had become, was being. That the state of his torso, so plain here and now in this kitchen, was so horrible as she saw it again anew as if through the eyes of a stranger. At the same time enormous inhibitions stood like immovable brick walls in front of her. The doctor must examine, must observe, must decide. From as early as she could remember this was a commandment you could never question, never break. With the open palms of both hands sweaty against both cheeks, Margaret stood and watched the examination.

Dr Simpson stood, moved awkwardly past Margaret to tap and listen to Richard's back. Returning to his seat, he folded the stethoscope and replaced it in his bag. He placed both arms on the table. As if from a distance Margaret heard the doctor say quietly to Richard, 'It was bad, wasn't it?' and waited for a reply. Richard seemed to have offered a minimal twitch of the head as a signal of agreement. But afterwards Margaret couldn't remember if anything else had or hadn't passed between the two men.

When Dr Simpson stood, shook Richard's hand again and walked out of the kitchen, Margaret followed him into the hall, as if she was her own mother hoping to glean diagnostic hints of herself as a child.

Silently Dr Simpson retrieved his black coat from the coat stand by the front door. He put it on, using or occupying even more space with his arms. 'Is he eating well?' he asked. Margaret nodded. 'Good,' he said, reaching for his homburg and allowing it a hint of a pause on its way to his head so that its journey could be taken to include a token doffing. 'Oh,' he added, bending over his bag and searching for something, 'Some ointment. For his back, and anywhere else as yet not completely healed. I'll call again in a week. Keep him warm and rested.'

The compulsion to shop was difficult to resist. Where Margaret had bought a loaf and her butter, cheese and meat rations once a week, with Richard it was more like trying to feed several others, instead of the half person she had become, who needed so little food, who went without, for whom food had little taste. Food ran out every other day. Dashes to the shops were not getting any easier. When she finally managed to walk Richard to the Welfare Office to get him a ration book, once home again the effort made him fall back into bed, silent and immovable. She acknowledged her mistake - he was not ready for such an expedition.

Comment [A]:

Yet when she walked to the High Street she hated the time away from him at the shops, as if their very existence compelled her to leave him for a frantic hour or so, and that when she got home she'd find him gone, vanished into some global turbulence and never to be seen again. 'I'm back!' she'd call, as if that would immediately summon his presence before her. It didn't.

She'd have to stalk the house, room by room, to find him and repeat the obvious words when she found him. Sometimes he'd look up, she thought, as if at a stranger. At other times he'd smile, his eyes scarcely focused upon her; or he'd be asleep because the effort of rising, washing, dressing and breakfasting had tired him. In this way Christmas came and went, marked only by card from her parents, and a card from Elsie.

At some time in the afternoon there came a knocking on the front door. The wireless set played Beethoven, Richard dozed, and Margaret, making out the shape and colour of Elsie's face through the frosted glass of the front door, decided to pretend to be out. It worked, but she had to stop herself worrying about being quizzed by Elsie the next time she was trapped either in the house or on the street.

But a day came in which early sun and diminished wind hinted of better times to come. After the first few weeks when Richard had spent a lot of time either in bed or sitting listening to the wireless in the living room, Margaret decided to get him ready to walk down to the shops with her; or catch a bus, which ever he'd prefer. He stood ready in his overcoat which Margaret could not bring herself to fold up and put somewhere else even though it shrieked of his absence. Richard had found his trilby, the Lincoln green one which had once been fashionable.

They got about half way down the slope of Dickens Close when he stopped and could not go on. After this she left didn't try to take him into town again, but walked him round the garden, then up and down the Close without the terror of having to confront and negotiate shops and people. But it was something she knew she'd have to work on.

It was like a game - she'd mention the bank now and then, and how, soon, he'd come and say hello to Mr Bailey.

He'd nod. 'The bank,' he'd say.

But then came the day when she returned from the shops, unlocked the front door and was hit by the smell of smoke and what was it? Tar? She fell in, horrified that Richard had had some kind of accident.

Bursting into the lounge she found him kneeling before the fire. In both hands he held a sheet of newspaper tightly braced against both sides of the fireplace so that a narrow gap was left at the bottom. The newspaper was lit from behind with a yellow glow, and air rushed like wind through the gap he'd left and pushing licking flames up the chimney.

'Richard!' she called. Glancing stiffly round, he withdrew the sheet of newspaper with a flourish to reveal the fire roaring like the fires of old, flames thrusting themselves up and out through a heaped bed of scraps of wood and chunks of coal. The flames and most of the smoke roared up into the chimney, while remnant lazy curls of smoke drifted back into the room and up over the fireplace lintel.

He said, 'You need wood to start it.' It was enough. Abandoning the fire, he walked slowly back to the settee and sat staring at the glowing, growing and burning image he had created.

In the new way he'd found, Richard progressed round the house. The bedroom where he studied his shirts, vest and pants neatly folded in the two bottom drawers of the chest of drawers. Next his suits, jackets and trousers in the wardrobe, fingering them, testing the texture and feel of the fabric. The waiting shoes at the bottom of the cupboard he took out and turned over: the brown brogues, the formal black ones, the light and extra shiny black pair which he stopped to think about for a long time until his mind told him that these went with the black evening suit hanging above them. He tried to see himself wearing the suit with the dancing shoes, where he was, what he was doing, who else was there. But again, as with the wedding cutlery, or Margaret's rings which she took off at night, it brought forth no image, no memory, no sequence of events, faces, places. He knew that these things had taken place, but they were shadowy, remote, illusive and would not speak to him.

It was when he opened the bureau, pulling down the sloping lid, and remembering to pull out the two supporting brackets, that he came across envelopes clearly thrown in and abandoned. These were stamped and franked, but unopened. Furthermore, they were all addressed in typewritten script to Mr and Mrs R. Ward, 12 Dickens Close. He found the silver paper knife waiting in the desk and slit open the top envelope. It contained a folded foolscap sheet which unfolded, revealed it to be the bank's account sheet, together with a little bundle of used cheques, the ones which Margaret had used for drawing cash, the same amount each week (from the dates), two pounds and twelve shillings.

Each cheque cashed was recorded next to its number and amount. Amounts paid in on the opposite side were from the Ministry of Defence. He opened another, then another, until he had all the sheets in a pile before him, and all the expended cheques to one side. The pass sheet at the top was dated January 1946.

It may have been up to an hour, the hour of Margaret's sortie to the bank and shops, that Richard stared at, then riffled through the pass sheets and the chronologically ordered cheques. Here was a record, of sorts, of the whole of his time away from Margaret, away from this house, this town, this sceptred isle. Some notion of the enormity of this chronology hovered round him, a huge fog in which he sought memory, sequence and consequence.

From the front door came clicks and rustling noises, followed by the grating complaint of its hinges. Margaret sought him out first - was he all right, had she been out too long? In the few seconds it took her to find him in the dining room, Richard had on impulse closed the lid to the bureau. She found him sitting staring at the shiny surface of the lid, himself a dark, indistinct reflection in it.

'Cup of tea?' she asked breathlessly, tugging to remove her coat. He usually scarcely reacted, and she brought him one anyway. He usually drank it. This time he nodded. 'In the lounge,' she said, 'where it's warmer round your fire.' Not only had he found wood in the shed suitable for kindling, but he'd remembered how to damp the fire down at night by shovelling sifted ash from the grate onto the glowing coals. On his knees before the fire morning, noon and night; the one thing he could do.

Richard had to wait two days for Margaret to go to the shops again. During that time, he wandered about the house with new, vague but huge notions wafting in, around and out of his mind. There was a swirling sense of loss, but he was getting used to that. Inside this was another notion which was more insistent, centred round money, cheques, payments for -? This lead him again and again to think of the bureau. But each time he went back to the desk he found there a dangerous dark fog like a wall surrounding the notion. But this slowly refined itself into a realisation that he'd have to wait until Margaret went out so that he could return to the bureau and secretly examine the pass sheets and used cheques even more thoroughly.

The opportunity duly arrives. He finds a pencil and starts at the beginning ticking off each cheque drawn from its stub with each corresponding entry and date on the pass sheet. The dates and amounts all match exactly, but did she pay for electricity and gas by cheque? This would have to wait. He is meticulously careful that the cheques and the ticked pass sheets remain in order, a shallow pile of time. Memory jogs him, but is reluctant to reveal all so soon. He turns over the bundle of cheques so that their reverses are revealed. He stares at each one and then turns it back the right way up. His sees that his hands have started to shake, that he's feeling what - apprehensive, almost frightened? Each cheque for the whole of the four years of his absence is blank on its reverse. There is nothing written there. They are all signed by Margaret. It gradually sinks in that his cheques from Burma have been honoured but are not included with the ones Margaret has used for cash.

Out of the mishmash of impressions that masquerade as memory, there is one of him writing something - not much, in pencil on something small, something as small as a - cheque. At the precise moment that he sees a brown face in the jungle he hears the front door hinges, he hears Margaret's sigh signalling that the sortie is at an end, she's survived, tired, but glad to be home. She finds him immediately and says, 'Oh, there you are again - ' He says, 'The cheques. Where are the ones with writing on the back of them?'
He sees her face go blank; she doesn't understand. There is an odd sensation in the pit of his stomach. It's like anger. He raises his voice, 'The cheques,' he repeats, 'written on the back.'

Margaret's pulling off her head scarf. She shakes her head to feel her hair fall out of the tight shape of its silk constraints.

'Richard,' she says, 'what cheques, what writing? I don't under - .'

Something else hits him. 'Please get me my kit bag,' he says.

'Kit bag?' she says, and adds, 'Oh, the one your brought home, that one.
Now where did I put it?' She stops to think with her coat off one shoulder.

Richard finds himself breathing deeply, his heart beating heavily, insistently.
'Find it,' he says, 'you must find it!' His voice has risen, his mouth is set tight, his eyes wide. He wants to shout, but knows that it'll be a howl, that he doesn't, in any case, have the strength.

'All right, Richard' she says, 'it's all right. I think I know where it is.' Shrugging her coat fully on, she goes through into the hall. A few moments later she is back with the faded yellow canvas bag. She remembers that she was going to throw it away with the disgusting army clothing she couldn't get clean, as if in getting rid of the clothes of the past she might usher in a new, better present. But she'd forgotten the kit bag hanging up in the dark of the under-stairs cupboard where she'd hidden during the bombing after she couldn't face going into Elsie's shelter.
Margaret hands him the bag, holding it out in front of herself almost as a shield, so that it keeps a distance between them. Her eyes are wide with anxiety. Richard takes the bag with trembling hands. He pulls at the straps snaked through their restraining brass buckles.

They're stiff and unwilling, and he makes impatient noises. Margaret doesn't know whether to leave him to work out how to open it, and hang up her coat and put away the shopping. But he gets it open, and he's scrabbling with one hand in the bag. With a snort of impatience, he turns the bag upside down and shakes it so that its contents fall out onto the floor: an envelope, a dirty handkerchief, a label, a few foreign brass coins and, ah, what he's looking for. He sighs as he reaches down for the chequebook stubs. For a moment it looks as if he's going to unbalance and fall off the chair.

As if already shocked, but not knowing why, Margaret watches him.

He's got the stapled wad of stubs in both hands. His fingers prise it open at random, then allow the individual leaves to flick by one or two and three at a time where moisture or damp has tried to stick them to each other. He raises the wad nearer to his eyes and peers the individual stubs. Then he looks back at the pile of dead cheques and the neat ticks on the pass sheets - and sees that there are still no gaps which could be filled by the cheque numbers and amounts displayed on his stubs. His eyes lose focus and tears stream down his face.

Margaret leans to put her arm round his shoulders. She makes cooing noises of comfort even though she has no idea why he's so quickly changed from anger to grief. She searches in her coat pocket, finds a handkerchief and dabs at his cheeks. Seeing him cry makes tears well up in her as well. Weeping together, they remain like this for long minutes at the desk in the dining room of this house in Dicksons Close.

Later they have soup in the kitchen.

Richard has slept on the settee in the lounge. He's woken from a sleep into which he feels he has sunk to great depths; he's swum in deep, dark caverns, from which he's had to clamber, panting and sweating to haul himself out into the light of consciousness. Somehow, he's emerged with a tiny bit of knowledge, something he can tell Margaret. In between sipping the soup and eating slices of bread and margarine, he tries to tell her. Twice he gives up.

When he's finished the soup, he sits up straight, takes a deep breath and says, 'It's taken me a long time to remember, but now I have. I've got there.' This is longest string of words he has assembled since getting back. He pulls the cheque stubs out of his trouser pocket and put them on the table between them.

'Not the first few,' he says, tapping the stubs, 'but perhaps a dozen of them - .'
'The cheques?' she says.

He nods. 'Ashin would come and I could give him a cheque. He'd get me extra food, cigarettes, almost anything.'

'Oh.'

He pauses and thinks, his face withdrawn in concentration. 'Yes,' he says, 'we couldn't receive any letters or send any out. But the cheques seemed to get through. Or else Ashin wouldn't give me the stuff. So, I wrote to you on the backs of the cheques. Ashin got his money. But where are the cheques?'

Margaret tried to understand. She murmured, 'Cheques?'

He nodded again.

'Oh,' she said, because it was beginning to sink in, 'could another bank, I mean a bank somewhere else. India's near Burma, isn't it?'

Richard shook his head. 'I don't know if that's possible. None of us had a bank in India. We had our money paid in at home for our families. Cheques have to be cleared in the bank accounts they were drawn on.' He fetched the bank pass sheets from the dining room and showed her all the ticks. 'These are cheques you used. Mine aren't here.

'Oh.'

Implications are hard to reach and slippery to hold. He was moving along a line of deduction faster than her. Even so, Margaret could see that this effort had exhausted him, so that when the bread and soup were finished, he hauled himself up and told her what she expected: 'I must turn in.' She nodded; she'd not be long either. Perhaps he'd forget this thing about cheques; the war had ended, he was back. This was sufficient for her, even if he was lost or stuck in some vast landscape of the present which others might call the future.

Chapter 10.

FEBRUARY 1946

Richard finds kindling in the garden where the apple and pear trees, their blossom already starting to swell for bud burst in April, have shrugged off rotten, burdensome branches and twigs. There is other wood, planed for projects he cannot remember, or un-planed lengths to repair a fence all lying about on the bench in the shed, or propped up in a corner. He lifts the larger gleaned garden wood piece by piece onto the bench and clamps each length so that he can use both arms to saw it into eight-inch lengths. These he upends on the bench so that he can split them down the seams with his billhook to make more usable kindling.

On good days he can lift and swing the rediscovered tool on four or five cut lengths. After that he has to pause and sit on the wooden chair whose very existence and usefulness, until now, he had been totally ignorant. Its provenance was a mystery to him; it just seemed as if it had merely waited for him to chop wood and become weary. Sitting on the chair, he finds that his hands have found the sharpening stone and draws this along the length of the bill hook blade until it is razor sharp.

He's now scrubbed and polished daily because he's rediscovered the routine of washing and dressing. In addition to this he now keeps the kitchen boiler and the fire in the lounge going day and night: coke in the kitchen, but coal for the living room. This means that there's once more hot water in the kitchen and for the bath all the time, and the reborn airing cupboard in the bathroom keeps newly washed clothes comfortingly warm and dry. Indeed, the bathroom itself takes on a new lease of life because of the heat drifting out of the airing cupboard; stripped off to have a bath is nearly a pleasure.

There's a deep rhythm to the night time damping down and the morning revival of this source of heat. Monday mornings when Margaret assumes a business-like air and assembles all the clothes she needs to wash, and when Richard knows that the fire needs its thorough rake of clinker and ash so that it can once more take big gulps of air and, thus resuscitated, reinvigorate the room. He's then able to sit in the lounge watching his fire, dozing in its comforting heat, finely gauging its performance and need for more coal or some other small attention: adjusting the air flow of the front grill, maintaining the glowing coals at an angle of about forty-five degrees to maximise the heat output into the room. He lets the brittle clinker and powdery ash cool in a bucket before tipping it into the dustbin. He shovels into the copper-hod coal from the concrete bunker, just enough for each day. Then he rests from his labours before looking again at the bank pass sheets and the stubs of the apparently unpresented cheques which had paradoxically done their business and allowed him food and cigarettes. Ashin would have known if they hadn't got through, and wouldn't have done business with him.

Having Richard in smart clothes: today his acceptable dark tweed suit and a tie of diagonal stripes of red, blue and deep green, is part of Margaret's plan. She's mentioned church in passing once or twice on Saturday.

She has memories of herself as the new wife walking down Dicksons Close, along Whorple Road, through the wide alleyway beside the old Georgian house and out onto the Downs Road; by which time it's nearly eleven o'clock and the church bells batter the sun filled air, and lift the street with a sense of occasion.

The occasion is Margaret going to church for the first time in, what, four or five years?

Richard's still walking slowly, as if he has time to spare, as if he's not bothered about being late. Beside him, holding his arm, Margaret frets but the bells still toll and other people with the same intentions in their step, their bearing, their clothes, are only a little ahead. She's dressed to blend in with Richard: her deep blue skirt and jacket, lightened with a cream blouse. 'I can feel the sun on my face,' she says, as an excuse for looking up at Richard. He's looking ahead, his stride is measured, studied, perhaps laboured. But he's making the effort. There and back will be the furthest he's walked so far. To them both it's like a test, or a measure of improvement. Even so she'll be careful not to make too much of it. Praise has its place, she thinks, but there's a danger that it could be seen as the goal or achievement beyond which not much more need be done. She's hiding her apprehension, she's making the best of things, bringing her husband out in public like this. She knows she's got used to seeing him as a tired man, prematurely aged, that his new everyday presence has begun to distance, but not wiped out, his former appearance. If this is him now, how will others react? What will she see in their faces?

This preoccupation intensifies as the church comes into sight on the main road. But a counter-notion flexes objections: would anyone at church actually remember them, would they, Richard and Margaret, actually recognise anyone themselves?

Crossing the street, looking across at the paved area just below the wide steps which lead to another terrace before the final steps leading to the big open doors, Margaret feels she's looking anew at the place she hasn't visited for years. She works out that it was shortly after the letter. That first letter. Or rather, it was after she had finally steeled herself to open it. That can't have been four years ago. There was no conscious decision of any kind: going to church was a concept which simply vanished from her mental horizon along with a jumble of other things - engulfed in a miasma of confusion, ensnared in the loss of a sense of days, months, years. Those parts of herself which were dragged away from her one by one when Richard was missing, when the world outside as well as the hidden one inside her head had become fraught and dark places.

As close as this the bells are too insistent, too damaging. She looks up at Richard. His face has drawn in upon itself, is closing down. She grips his arm harder and speeds him into the cool and holy air of St Martin's. Inside, the bells are muted by the heavy medieval masonry but still powerful. Their clanging stops just before Margaret has located the pew where they had used to sit - half way up the nave aisle on the right. Yet it was as if she felt awkward about this, to slot back at every turn, take every opportunity, fit into exactly the same niche. Was she trying too hard to recreate their former lives, their old selves? As if the world had not changed, as if this huge thing called The War had not occurred, as if Richard had not been taken to the other side of the world, imprisoned there, suffered the lord only knows what, had returned a broken man, yes, she'd have to say that now if only to herself. And how much can anyone be repaired so that you can look at him or her and marvel that they had once been damaged, nearly destroyed, but now look whole as they used to be? Her hesitation could have disturbed Richard. She had no way of knowing if he'd even remember this pew in this position inthis church. She couldn't ask, she couldn't say brightly, 'Shall we sit here, then?' She'd already seen the effect on him of being asked, 'Would you prefer your egg fried or scrambled?', 'The sun's shining, shall we walk round the garden?'

His face would be blank, his lips tense. Don't ask me he could be thinking. Just give me some food, just take me here or there. Just let me be.

It came as a shock when she stopped and looked. There were already five people on *their* pew. Confused, she looked behind and in front of this pew. The church was almost full, except for the first three pews at the front. To try and give the impression that she was as confident as anyone else she quickly led Richard forward and eased herself into the third pew and he followed, as she knew he would. But here, nearly at the front of the nave, she felt exposed and on show. In order to hide, she knelt forward to pray, as she had been taught to do, as she had for years before the War, when looking back, she had nothing much in particular to pray about. The bouts of mother-directed praying at bedtime seemed somehow to have eluded her.

Hidden in the pew like this, Margaret finds a curious and unexpected ease and detachment which she knows is so difficult to find at home, or on the street, or in the bank and shops. It's a double-edged sword. Whereas, in the before time she'd kneel and her mind would drift away around shopping lists, cleaning the house, then her mother, social events at the tennis club, the picture house, what she'd wear.

Now, in contrast, she had only one thing filling her mind, and this was so huge, so overpowering and the gates of her mind were so rusted up - Richard, Richard, the Richard she wanted back. She wanted a man who was healed and full of their shared memories. A man with an easy smile and manner, a man with energy and ideas and - and she wanted forgiveness for what she hadn't done and which wasn't her fault - she wanted someone, God would do, to tell her that destroying a child was for the best, that her life with Richard was something worth preserving, that otherwise the risks, the dangers were too horrible to contemplate.

On her knees on the scarlet hassock, leaning against the back of the pew in front, she thinks how prayer is something that she's completely forgotten. As if the prayers of childhood, the bedroom floor she knelt on, the soft bed serving as the hard pew had vanished like some sloughed off part of her. '*Pity mice and plicity,*' she'd pray, rehearsing the words alongside her mother who never caught her unintentional version of the words, '*Pity my simplicity.*'

The sound of people shuffling to their feet suddenly fills the church. The organist has been toying with chords trotted out in a harmonic and convincing sequence which will allow him to stop at any time without being caught out half way through a piece of Bach or Vaughan Williams. Margaret pushes herself back onto the pew seat and lightly prods Richard as she stands. He pulls himself up and stares as the priest passes them on the way to his station in the depths of the chancel. The vicar stops in front of the altar rail, bows his head and makes the sign of the cross. A late couple creep into the pew in front of Margaret and Richard from the side aisle walkway. Margaret heaves a sigh of relief: Richard will see when they stand, sit or kneel. She won't have to risk prompting him in the full public gaze of those sitting behind them.

The vicar has turned to face the congregation. He is revealed as a thin man, earnestly bespectacled and with an ashen face. He spreads his arms a little so that his palms are opened to embrace his flock and says in a ritual voice that veers towards a chant,

Repent ye; for the Kingdom of heaven is at hand. We will begin our service with hymn number ...

The organ powerfully introduces the tune embedded in its full harmonic
backing. Margaret is aware of Richard flinching. She passes him her hymn
book open at the right number and surreptitiously takes his from the wooden shelf at waist level below him.

Richard is stunned by the acoustics. The organ in front of him and the voices behind raised in song bulks and fills the huge vault above where the sound seems to be both magnified and contained. He can't join in because he knows that no sound will come from his throat. At the end of the hymn they sit and he accepts the prayer book, open at the right place, that Margaret hands him. He reads the words that the vicar is intoning,

Dearly beloved brethren…

He knows the words, but follows several sentences until his eyes want to close the better to hear them.

… saying after me: Almighty and most merciful Father.

Richard closes his eyes again and confesses his collective sins by heart, his lips moving, not knowing whether or not in the blur of noise dominated by the bass of the men present he is making any sound at all. It's all in the book, the one he had out there which he had to read after the padre died. Where is it now?

He looks along memory's jagged, twisting line to locate this loss, but can find nothing, no clue. This, in turn, induces an anxiety he's too familiar with and which crashes down onto him at any time or place. He's only just learned a strategy to deal with this - he reminds himself that he has the stubs. That they are the link, the vital connection to himself in his life away from Margaret, evidence not only that he existed then, but that it all happened to him, because so much of it seemed to happen to someone else outside his own flesh and blood. Blood, yes, shed blood somewhere, everywhere. His hands bloody but, oh God please, not guilty.

Nevertheless, he and the whole congregation are pardoned and granted forgiveness. In the gap between the absolution and the next part of the service Richard tries, and fails, to relate this to his life. It is as if he is trapped in a present where sin does not exist, where past sinning is terrible but too remote and indistinct to even be summoned for examination, let alone forgiveness.
Then the simplicity of the Lord Prayer penetrates: he thinks he's joining in, but it's still difficult to hear his own voice within the weight and welter of the vocal congregation. A hymn follows whose tune is so unpredictable that he cannot follow its intricacies or indeed fit the words into it. He wants to sit down and stay sitting so that he can hold himself together and endure to the end of the service.

The vicar walks slowly down from the chancel and climbs the steps of the dark oak pulpit. Richard feels Margaret's hand on his arm as the vicar begins,

I take as my text this morning those revelatory verses of Paul from his letter to the - .

Richard tries to listen, but it is too much. He cannot follow the tangled weave of the disciple's doctrine, admonition and advice. He wants to close his mind to the vicar's cadences, his tone of voice, his insistence. He retreats into himself and lets his mind drift where it will. And it does: God does not speak to this old man, it tells him. Robed, he stands and speaks at us, but has not seen circles of light glow round the heads of dying men.

This man, Richard thinks, with the beautifully well-modulated tones of ether, has no notion of flowers in the wilderness, yet above him soar the heavenward arches of inspiration. The words in his own mind, he thinks, are so much easier, so weightless compared with the ones forced out of a moderating, trained tongue.

Suddenly, the organ blares and thumps out the first bars of the next hymn. A huge muscular spasm shoots through Richard's body, making him leap to his feet. These same feet turn left and take him bodily from the pew onto the aisle where, oblivious of the interested eyes of the congregation, he walks as quickly as he can towards the main door lit from above by the huge stained glass window at the back of the nave where St Martin hugely cuts his cloak in two for the beggar at the side of the path. The saint's halo glows, while his horse, impatient, eyes widened, wants to continue the journey. The beggar is trying to hide his surprise behind a smirk of gratitude. He is bald and half naked in the cold, but decently and acceptably muscular and clean.

This is not the end. Margaret, it seems, can accommodate it. She hurries after Richard. He's walking faster than usual and she expects him to head down Worlple Road in the direction of home. But he's not. He's walking as purposefully as he can manage down Church Street in the direction of the town centre. Half way down he stops and stares at a large building on the right and it all becomes clear to Margaret - the factory where he used to work. The notion or memory of work and its connection with Richard has not yet been reached, had not lumbered up over the horizon of recovery. Nailer & Warburton Engineering..

There is too much which he does not want to place on the table in full view of them both: Church and his former workplace. He knows that something thus exhibited would not go away, and would surely fester and swell. Besides, he realises, unexpected light seemed to fill the flint and stone fabric of the church. Sometimes this light played about some broken soul in the congregation and he knew that he was not alone.

But despite this, Richard accompanies her each Sunday and endures, so that he will not have to say, will not have to try to explain anything he is incapable of expressing. And after the service his steps still take him briefly back to his former place of work where, as chief engineer he oversaw the maintenance and repair of all those machines pressing out all those new-fangled plastic containers. Before the Army took him, before the War, before - .

One Sunday he says, 'I'll go and see them tomorrow morning.'

Because walking to church and back on Sundays seems to be working, Margaret plans a bus trip to take Richard, belatedly, to see her parents. Her guarded and brief letters to her parents have been slyly optimistic about Richard's health, but stress that he's very weak. However, that visits may soon be possible. The implication being that they will come and see her parents, not the other way round.

Finally, she chooses a Sunday afternoon because she remembers that's when it always used to be. She writes,

'We'll catch the twenty- five past three bus which should reach Stoneleigh at about ten minutes to four. Richard is able to walk a little faster now and with more assurance than before, so I'm confident that the walk up the road to you will be manageable for him.'

This is to prevent the possibility of her parents initiating a set of complicated negotiations and arrangements with Tom-next-door and his car. She wants to have total control of the visit, at least as far as the journey both ways is concerned. It also obviates the time-consuming likelihood of a series of letters both ways, which would further delay the outing. Even so, one arrives by return of post: 'It will be wonderful, dear, to welcome Richard. We're so thrilled. I'll unroll the red carpet! Lots of love, Mummy.' Although Margaret had begun to use the word, 'mother'. it already seemed to her that the epithet has little chance of sticking.

'Daddy' is more difficult, entwined as it might be with other notions more difficult to disentangle. Father, Pater, Dad, Daddy?
Richard, fed with a tiny piece of leg of lamb, roast potatoes and spring greens, and well rested, is led out clean and smartly dressed as he is now used to.

The wait at the bus stop is minimal, with Richard able to sit on the bench by the stop, together with two old ladies for whom this was an opportunity to talk to each other and anyone else in earshot about the terrible state of things generally, particularly rationing and the shortage of things like bananas and oranges. Long training with Elsie had left Margaret adept at making the right noise at the right time. Richard, as usual, seemed oblivious - either in a world of his own or from some capacity to switch off invasive noise, despite the continuing theme of the day moving on to money and the cost and extent of the operations they offered each other and the world in direct competition, each one worse than the previous one.

The greeting in the gloom of the hallway had been awkward. Richard, behind Margaret while she kissed her parents, was a silent presence round whom Margaret had to edge to release him into the space thus freed to greet his in-laws.

'Richard, at last, dear,' Rose had inclined herself towards Richard for whom it was so intimate a movement as to have him not so much recoil as hold back and instinctively offer his right hand. Rose took it, but held on hard enough to pull Richard to her. She raised her other hand to the nape of his neck and pulled herself up to his cheek. 'Thank the Lord, you're back!' she murmured into his ear and kissed his cheek. She releasing him immediately, perhaps feeling his taut stance, his strained face. It was easier when Frank stepped forward. Two men can offer each other a brief handshake and then step back, duty done, extraneous words firmly suppressed.

'Oh, come in, please do come in,' Rose cooed, leading them into the living room, demonstrating by bustling, plumping up cushions and murmuring about cups of tea so that she wouldn't stay and endure the silence which followed Richard into the room. Moments later Rose returned with the tray crammed with tea things, but to a room devoid of conversation. All four sat and drank their tea, careful to avoid any slurping noises, while Margaret's Sunday afternoon parents respected the silence which served to deflect the fact that communication had always been difficult when Richard had been present, although this did not detract from their affection for him or their gratitude that he had married their daughter.

'You wait for real tea,' Rose intoned brightly as if to children, 'I've got a surprise for you!' She was adept at producing words that passed as conversation and filled huge gaps. There being little reaction, she added, 'There's no knowing, these days, what you'll find in the shops. A few things are getting through which were always so scarce during the war. Love or money wouldn't -.'

Action being a great salvation for awkwardness, Frank suggested that he and Richard take a quiet turn round the garden. Richard stood, spilling a little of his tea on his trousers.

'I'm so sorry,' Frank said, 'when you're ready, when you've finished.' Rose stood to fetch a cloth but Margaret beat her to it with a handkerchief stored up the sleeve of her blouse. The crisis was quickly and quietly resolved. Richard finished his tea and the two men stood, readying themselves for the expedition.

The garden is the back garden, the front being assumed to be of less importance since its function was partly to allow the house to stand back from uncomfortable proximity with the road and thus glean a modicum of privacy. Despite this, it not only had to be kept tidy, but was, crucially a statement of the gardening skill of the home owner for all the road to behold. A back garden, on the other hand, is where you can sit out, read the paper, drink tea in the afternoon on a clement day, and have your being in the setting up of secret and rare hobbies in sheds or green houses - potting on dahlias, sowing seeds in boxes, keeping chickens or guinea pigs.

On a calm, sunny afternoon in late February the sun can sometimes warm your face and you wonder why you're buttoned into a thick coat. Father in law and son in law took a turn, inspecting the daffodil spears which this year Frank claimed were more advanced than usual.

Indeed, they were strong and healthy, their tight flower buds just becoming visible. 'And not a slug in sight, yet,' Frank added. Richard had seen daffodils at this stage in his garden and in gardens along the way. But it was here, where they were even triumphantly signalling an eventual end to winter, that they penetrated his consciousness sufficiently to provoke a memory of a memory when each day, even each minute of each hour, he had to hold hard to the rock and sanity of images of home. During his captivity, daffodils in Spring had been one of his most compelling and powerful day dreams: Margaret among daffodils. Tears sprang to his eyes. He found his handkerchief and blew his nose, dabbing at his eyes, concealing his lack of composure.

This was when his hand sought his jacket pocket: the little book, the revelation of St. John, which he'd forgotten he'd put in the pocket; and had forgotten why. While Frank's attention was diverted towards his early Spring flowers, Richard held the small, old booklet, peering at it as if he'd not seen it before. In the new light of this Spring day in England he saw how worn and dirty it had become, how it had warped into the shape of his thigh in its hiding place - the pocket of his tattered army shorts. He wondered if it would open, if its leaves would unfurl to reveal anything now, or whether its pages would be fused by hot sweat and prison filth and torrential rain when they were making new roads. But this was not all - he had one last thing to do with the booklet.

When they reached the cuttings pile in one corner Frank stopped. He muttered, 'I must burn this when it's dry enough and the wind is in the right direction.' He was about to say something else when he turned fully back to his son-in-law. But saw instead Richard's hand extended towards him. What was more, the hand held something out for him to take. Frank took and examined it closely as if he didn't know what it was. Richard caught a sniff, and when Frank glanced up at him caught the tears in his father-in-law's eyes. Frank seemed to move slightly towards Richard who gently recoiled. But Frank checked himself and put the book into his trouser pocket and the alarming moment between the two men was over.

Words, though, it seems were permitted and, as if it followed logically, Frank added in a whisper lest neighbours or family might hear, 'Er, was it bad out there, old boy?' His voice, so quiet, was gentle and sympathetic. From the safe distance which Richard had established between himself and Frank he looked down at his father-in-law. The question surprised him, if only because it was the first time it had arisen or been asked of him, apart from Dr Simpson. He nodded. Frank took this as a tactful indication that further queries would not be appropriate, and was relieved.

A little later the two men re-joined the women in a silence made more profound by the confidences briefly shared by mother and daughter about Richard in his absence and in the short time of his repatriation. But the subsequent relief of the announcement of tea, proper tea time, brought deliverance to them all. For it was all laid and ready in the dining room. 'And the surprise is - ,' Rose paused for dramatic effect, ' - a Swiss roll! Real cream and real chocolate!' And there it lay in all its glory, as the centre-place of the table, on the treasured baroque patterned plate standing on the triumphantly embroidered table cloth stitched by Rose when she was expecting Margaret.
Somehow the prospect of a slice of the Swiss roll and the special spam sandwiches to be followed by strawberry jam sandwiches, the strawberry jam being another 'find', enlivened or invigorated Frank. Or it may have been the relief of having survived this visit thus far, as well as the end being plainly in sight not too long after tea.

'I say,' Frank said to no one in particular as they all sat down at the table, 'dashed awful, these camps, y'know. Only reading about it today in the paper. There's far more coming out than before.' He paused and found what he thought was an eager audience, happy for someone else to fill the void. 'Apparently they were all over Germany and Poland. Thousands, thousands of people were gassed or shot. Like prisons, the poor beggars had to work like slaves. Well, they were slaves I suppose, and at the same time put up with every sort of brutality and harsh treatment. Died like flies. All coming out now - y'know, these trials of the Nazis at, at ,- New - something like New-ring-burg.'

The only reaction to this speech was a discrete cough by Rose to indicate that no more should be said about P.O.W. camps. Frank's face reddened as he tried to work out if what he'd said was or was not an indiscretion. In the quiet which followed, barely audible chewing was the only thing that could be heard.

Another Friday has been reached, but it's a special one because Margaret thinks that Richard will be able to cope with coming with her and even visiting the Bank.

'The Bank,' he mutters several times. Because he often mutters Margaret has switched off her mind to this, being more preoccupied with her own thoughts: thoughts of how she's managing Richard's recovery, his turns of unreasonableness, his turns of switching off his mind to all around him. Besides which he hasn't again mentioned the whatever it was to do with cheques in Burma.

Mr Bailey is smiling. 'How good to see you back, Mr Ward. So glad you're here.'

Richard is aware of faces peering over the wooden screen behind Mr Bailey, popping up and down like seaside Punch and Judy characters. Margaret pushes her weekly cheque across the shining wood surface. She doesn't notice Richard pulling out the stubs. Mr Bailey stamps the cheque and pulls open his wide wooden draw for the cash. From time to time he looks up from his concentration over the correct number of pounds, shillings and pence, his face showing the satisfaction of what he's doing, his voice the while filling an otherwise awkward silence, 'So glad, so glad.'

When Margaret collects the money and packs it carefully into her purse, Richard holds up the stubs in front of Mr Bailey.

He breathes heavily and says, 'I drew these cheques - .' He pauses. 'In the Far East. And as far as I can tell ..'

Looking up at him, Margaret clutches his arm. 'It's all right,' he murmurs and turns back to Mr Bailey, 'The cheques got through, in due process. And I received the goods.'

Mr Bailey is staring at him.

'But on the bank sheets sent by the bank to my wife there is no record of these transactions. A dozen or more cheques and no record.'

Very carefully, as if about to touch something dangerous, Mr Bailey puts his hand forward to take the stubs. Richard pulls them back, checks himself and then surrenders them to Mr Bailey. The clerk flicks through them.

'I'm afraid, Mr Ward,' he says, 'I am not competent to comment on this. If you'd care to make an appointment with Mr Long.'

Richard looks at Mr Bailey and then slowly extends his hand for the stubs. With the stubs retrieved, he says, 'I want to see him now.' He hears an intake of breath from Margaret like a sigh.

Mr Bailey replies in a quiet voice, 'I'm afraid he's not here at the moment. Second Wednesdays of the month he has a meeting elsewhere, I believe. Er, London.'

Richard stares at him. He feels Margaret's hand on his sleeve. Aware that if he jerks his arm away from her this will be a rejection and he doesn't want her to think this, he pulls himself away slowly, carefully.

Thus, detached and moving to his left, he suddenly quickens his pace and reaches Mr Long's office door before she can say anything. It's locked. He peers at the glass panelling and sees that it's dark inside the room. As he turns back, defeated, faces peer again over the oak screen and duck down quickly out of sight as if struck by Mr Punch. He passes Mr Bailey whose face has closed up in defence against whatever violation was intended but couldn't be consummated. Margaret whispers, 'Sorry,' to him and hurries after Richard who has already reached the huge door where Mr Long used to linger, purely by chance, in an attempt to detain her.

Outside the bank Richard finds that he's used up most of the energy his body is willing to allocate on a daily basis. He leans against the greying white sandstone of the bank, his face drawn and pale. He whispers, 'Is there a seat somewhere?' Margaret leads him slowly past Wilkinson's the gentleman's outfitter and into Riddlington's.
Riddlington's is where you meet your mother, as Margaret used to, or where you take your aging aunt or grandparents. The waitresses wear black dresses and starched white lace collars and cuffs. The tablecloths are

immaculate and the dark wood panelled walls are relieved by Constable reproductions with the odd stag at bay thrown in. There's a hush in the place as profound and reverent as in a library or church. It's the kind of place which Elsie will often mention, insisting that it has 'class'. Indeed, there she is with a crony, sitting in a commanding position centre stage a little to the back. She sees Richard and Margaret enter and raises her floral face like an unavoidable beacon in order that they shall acknowledge her, in order that she can tell her friend all she knows about them, dramatizing the narrative, bringing in the whole war as a sub-plot, and emphasising her vital role in the story.

Margaret, however, being bound up in a troublesome world of her own, and even more than usually affected by that sense of panic and self-preservation that those entering public places routinely feel, does not see her. She wants to sit Richard at a table for two, so as not to risk the calamity of total strangers excusing themselves and sitting with them.

They are immediately approached by a waitress who leads them, with apologies to a table with four seats. No two-seaters are available. Despite this, Margaret agrees with the woman that they'll have tea. Richard is already sitting, slumped.

The waitress mentions the possibility of morning scones being served, or perhaps modest chocolate or vanilla buns. Margaret is thrown by the choice. She's not been to Riddlington's since - notions of her mother, sandwiches and summer dresses invade. 'Scones, if you please,' she says, then agrees with the waitress who asks if the scones should be accompanied by strawberry jam. 'Yes, yes,' she says with impatience, trying to concentrate on sitting opposite Richard so that she can monitor his condition, check his every move and expression.

It's becoming clearer to her what his obsession, or obsessions, might be. At first, she was in a situation with him that she would describe, if she had to, as panic. She was trying to cope with a man whose state of mind and health seemed impenetrable. She had assumed, unquestioningly, the huge burden of reconstructing both him and she soon realised, herself. A double task which she had to force herself not to think about because if she did the weight and significance of it would become so immense as to crush her.

She reaches to touch his hand, and withdraws as soon as she knows he won't resist, isn't angry. He has closed his eyes, and his breathing is more settled and even. As they wait for their order, he opens his eyes and gazes round the restaurant. She has the unexpected but distinct feeling that, removed from the tight mental constrictions and atmosphere of home, she might be able to broach a subject which might otherwise be rejected, refused. Above all, she instinctively feels that she must not criticize his behaviour in the bank.

'These cheques - this was in Burma?' She tries to speak quietly so that no one in the hushed room will hear. He neither nods nor shakes his head. 'You say you wrote something on the back of them?' This time he nods. 'And this was a message for me?' Richard shifts his gaze back at her. His eyes are magnified by tears which he wipes away with his hand. Again, he nods. She says, 'Oh, Richard, so many things happen - in war time – things are destroyed, lost, never arrive.' She looks past Richard as if her eyes are drawn to the florid features of Elsie who immediately and reasonably discreetly waves a gloved hand. But Richard is shaking his head.

'It's not the same,' he whispers, then more loudly, 'it's not the same. You should have got them. I want to know why not. I must know.' He's now staring at her with an intensity which alarms her.

While it might be clearer to her what this obsession of his might be, it doesn't help. All it does is confirms that it's not something that'll go away. There's a surge inside her which tells her that this is an obsession which threatens them both, which is a barrier standing in the way of Richard's and possibly her recovery. But this surge has words of its own: 'Richard, you never got my letters, did you? I wrote every week and you never got a single one. Even though they said you were missing, I still wrote to you. How do you think that makes me feel?' She's left out how her words on paper became jumbled and unfocused; how, after Richard returned (in those first few terrible days) she threw them into the lounge fire grate and struck match after match until they curled up and died in briefly blue and then yellow flames. Now she feels there's more to come pouring out, and is frightened and appalled. But he's staring at her, he looks as if he doesn't know what to say, as if so often, like her, too many emotions fight for words at the same time and clog up speech. She feels deep panic at the thought that he might raise his voice, even shout, in this quiet and sedate place.

To confirm her fear, he takes a deep breath as if he's found a way through, but the waitress is looming over them with the tray, a dark and irresistible shape which says, 'Excuse me, sir, madam,' and from whom a hand descends bearing one after the other a gleaming stainless-steel teapot together with accompanying milk jug and sugar lump bowl, cups, saucers and side plates in sober blue willow pattern, and of course the plate holding two scones, accompanied by their set of tiny strawberry pots. She says, 'Will there be anything else, madam?' Margaret shakes her head. There'll probably be no more: what she and Richard have said to each other is probably enough for now. It's as near a quarrel as she'll allow. Both tried to reach each other during their separation. They both failed through no fault of their own. It seemed plain to her something that could and should be put to one side. After all, she could have said to him, You're here. Many never got back. Mrs Miller's son, and Mr Wilson further down the road. Unaware of parody, she thinks, 'Be thankful for great mercies.'

When Margaret and Richard's mouths are full of scone, butter and strawberry jam, Elsie and her friend rise and pick their way between the tables; she towards Margaret and Richard, her friend towards the exit. When she reaches Margaret and Richard's table she pauses and comments on the weather, adding, 'And so nice to see you two out and about.'

Elsie, Margaret knows, has to balance and reconcile a number of things: Margaret and Richard are trapped and fair game. But Elsie's friend is waiting, hovering at a discreet distance, perhaps not wishing to intrude on the subjects of Elsie's monologue which had started immediately the victims had appeared. Elsie must somehow balance her lust for information with the discretion she should be seen to exercise in public, if not in Dicksons Close. Margaret watches how Elsie's face reflects these rapid mental calculations, sees Elsie winning and losing hidden internal battles and, mercifully, appear to judge it unnecessary to call her friend back and make introductions. 'Ta, ta,' she says with a wave of a glove, turning like a ship changing course and sweeping her friend out of the hush and swish of Riddlingtons into the realities of the high street outside.

Richard, Margaret noticed, had looked up briefly, had tried to rise in the presence of a lady, may even have tried to say hello, but his expression did not change from his one of habitual preoccupation.

They reach home after a slow walk and a stop for Richard to sit on a bench looking over the green algae of the park pond where, before the war they used to pause and watch children floating model sailing boats and little clockwork racing boats.

Once he helped a crying boy whose little boat had run out of spring and was out of reach. Richard had taken off his shoes and socks, rolled up his trousers and, laughing, had waded into the green depths to retrieve the boat. The strong sun shone and in minutes had dried out his trouser turnups. She chided him in such a way that he knew she approved.

Home from this first expedition, he shuffles into the living room and lies on the sofa. Margaret stoops to pick up the envelope on the hall door mat. It's buff and HMSO. She tears in open, partially ripping the letter inside, and shredding the shoddy brown envelope. There can be no more prevarication now. The typewritten words, as before, swim about in the panic they induced in her mind, before assembling themselves to inform Richard that he is to report to Carshalton Barracks when his period of leave has expired.

Chapter 11

APRIL 1946

Richard's hands had not yet sought hers. Once or twice, he'd touched her on the arm; once or twice passed an arm round her waist and rested a hand fleetingly on her hip. One day, early in the morning when she knew he often lay awake, still and immobile until drowsiness returned, without warning, and without preparing the way with a word or caress, he had rolled over to her and pulled at the hem of her night dress. It would not move until she was sufficiently awake to pull it up, away from its constriction beneath her.

'Oh,' was conceived as, 'Oh!' strangled in its moment of creation as she instinctively suppressed both shock and surprise at his penetration. But even these were immediately cast aside by the overwhelming assault of pain. She held her breath until the holding of it submerged any sense of mind and body. Like a drowning woman she fought for breath, fought against suffocation while he lay on her. How many breaths? She would never know because she could not recall the moment of his cessation, the moment of the mute spilling of sperm. Only the release from on top of her of his weight, his pressure. Then this wooden man lay on his back again beside her as if nothing had happened, no hand seeking hers, no sigh of pleasure, just silence and the resumption of his regular breathing. She lay awake, trying to understand, searching for significance; trying to discover where this lay along the slow path of recovery. Was this forward or back? Above all was this newly awakened pain to remain part of her?

Later, in the early brightness of this clement April morning, Margaret had to force herself to think back to the early morning - had this really happened? Or had it been one of those waking dreams where what is real and what is delusion merge into each other and are indistinguishable?

And now Richard lying beside her, unstirring, his breathing regular, almost intrusive. Wide awake, she had to get up, and had to stir herself into the daily activity of life.

Sitting on the toilet she knew from the odours rising from her before she washed that it had happened. Here was either another dimension to life, or merely another piece to a fragmented jigsaw; a puzzle which had no picture on its lid as guide. Or here was something which had happened once and might not happen again.
When she went back into the bedroom Richard was still asleep. She collected the clothes she had worn the day before and took them back into warmed sanctuary of the bathroom.

In the kitchen she prepared breakfast: porridge, scrambled eggs, toast, expecting to hear the distant creak and thump of activity from above. None came. For a moment she panicked and crept upstairs to peer through the crack left by the partly open door, but no, she could see the blanket rising and falling to the rhythm of his breathing. She stopped cooking and busied herself with this new found time on her own - some cleaning? It was almost like a new concept, like something not yet invented. Yet she chided herself for not thinking of this in the days and weeks after her mother had swept, cleaned, and scoured the house. Already fatty deposits were smudging the oven and hob, grime discolouring the white enamel of the draining board, staining the enamel of the iron sink. She found and wielded the Harpic. When she'd nearly finished this she crept up to peer at Richard again because his absence was worrying her. She wanted him awake, wanted to get the day started so that she might glean some hint as to how he felt about the love, if she could call it that, somewhere around dawn. The half-cooked breakfast fidgeted her. How can a day proceed without the physical, symbolic and ritual aspect of breakfast? She tiptoed upstairs again and peered through the crack in the door. Richard had turned over so that he was facing the door. His eyes were open. One hand reached up from under the bedclothes and rubbed them. She went into the bedroom and sat on the bed, looking down at him, awaiting his emergence. Her weight disturbed the bed so that he stretched and turned his head and looked up at her. His mouth moved a little, trying to make a smile.

She said, 'Tired?'

He nodded.

'I've just thought,' she said, 'stay there and I'll bring up breakfast.'

As she reheated the scrambled egg, and found a tray from the dining room, she wondered why she hadn't thought of this before. But this was countered by a fear that he might get used to this and want to stay in bed all day. People spoke of a relative or neighbour who stayed in bed, gradually extending the time until they didn't get up at all. An aunt, was it Mabel? had done this for years even though the doctor couldn't find anything wrong with her. Her mother had called it *seeking attention*, in a tone of voice asserting that this was not a good thing.

Dr Simpson was breathing harder. It may be that Margaret hadn't noticed before. When he came to see Richard for what, the second or third time? She told herself that it didn't matter, that what was important was that he had responded again to her urgent request. How could a man like this be expected to report for duty at such and such a barracks? She was filled with the so familiar sense of dread which had inhabited her every waking moment while Richard was away. With Richard back this feeling of nagging worry had slipped unobtrusively from her mind, like a pain whose precise moment of cessation you cannot recall. It was the one thing that had been relegated to the past in face of the overwhelming problem of Richard. She'd got him back physically, but his mind was still away, fixed on preoccupations ground into him in captivity. Small things like the fire in the living room he kept so expertly alight, or the small repairs he carried out: tap washers, the front door lock; or walking down to the shops with her, except for his obsession with the bank, might be celebrated as evidence of progress towards his former self. But these things were so slow in coming and, in the face of the complete Richard that she wanted back, insignificant.

And now she was faced with losing Richard a second time. Her stomach, as if in sympathy, began to ache again. She reverted to a foetal position in bed and let silent tears dampen her pillow. Beside her Richard slept, apparently oblivious, occasionally turning over with a great churning of himself and the bed covers, occasionally flinging an arm over her body where she let it lie in fear of waking him.

It may have been that the day was quiet; not much weather today, someone might comment. Such a detail might be remarked on, but was not of sufficient significance to be slotted into memory. Nevertheless, the sun shone on the vigorous spears of the daffodils in the front garden, even if there was no wind to hum in the telegraph wires along the road or agitate the twigs of spring buds in bushes and trees in nearby gardens.

The good doctor may just have been rushed off his feet, and this may have caused him to be short of breath. The examination, as before, took place in the lounge. Margaret noticed Dr Simpson sniff approvingly at the warmth. Richard lay out on the settee and the doctor went through his routine of listening, tapping and examining. 'Healing well,' he said, after having Richard turn to face the back of the settee to make an examination of his back possible. Margaret had brought in the tube of ointment to show that it was nearly all used.

It was at this moment that a thought struck her: she'd not paid Dr Simpson a penny. The treatment she'd had before Richard had come back, this treatment now. The doctor had not presented her with a single bill. She'd have to ask. She'd have to make herself, no, force herself to mention this. She had no idea if they could afford what would surely be a terrifying accumulation of bills. Why hadn't she thought of this before?

'How are you feeling?' Dr Simpson asked when Richard's examination was over.

Richard looked at him for such a long time that Margaret was about to answer for him when he said, 'Feeling.' As if the word were so new, rare or unexpected that he'd have to mull over its meaning. Again, Margaret was about to speak when Richard added, 'I'd like to walk in the country. I'd like to stop feeling tired - .'

Margaret, sitting opposite was stunned.

Dr Simpson cleared his voice, 'Er, I have colleagues who have been treating former prisoners of war. We all agreed that it may take what will seem a long time, but, believe me, I can see that you are already better than when I last saw you, what, only a week ago.'

But before she could fully take in what he'd said, Dr Simpson turned to Margaret and said, 'Now, if you don't mind, we'll swap you and Richard over so that I can see how you are.'

As she stood, Margaret could see dark lumps, and feel sombre heaviness just above her eyes, and her strength wasting away. There was terror mixed in with this - that she'd be revealed, that the doctor would inadvertently say something. At the same time, she knew that to refuse to be examined would be as bad, would expose herself to suspicion.

Later, she could remember very little of the examination itself, only of subsiding, then lying on the settee. When it was over, she glanced across the room at Richard, now slumped in the Parker Knoll. He had his eyes shut, and his arms folded defensively across his chest.

'Thank you,' Dr Simpson said, 'that should be all.' He put away his stethoscope and stood. Margaret followed him into the hall, closing the door behind her. She was again the mother awaiting the verdict.

'Any further pain?' Dr Simpson asked quietly.

She said, 'Only a little, from time to time.'
He nodded and murmured, 'A good recovery.' At first, she thought he was referring to Richard. But the doctor added, 'But not so far for your husband. His sores are slowly healing, but the recovery from his trauma may take longer, may be a long haul for him. How long I can't say.' He paused, cleared his throat and added, 'Er, things of the mind often take longer - .'

But Margaret hardly heard this, had steeled herself to whisper, 'The bill, you haven't sent me a bill, er, bills.'

Dr Simpson looked at her closely. He was breathing heavily again. He said, 'Have you got the letter you mentioned, to hand?'

Margaret stared back at the doctor. 'Oh, yes, it's - .' She opened the door to the dining room to fetch the letter.

'May I take it, please?'

She gave it to him like a child handing over a ball in the playground. He folded it, careful to reuse the creases it arrived in and slotted it into his top inside jacket pocket.

'He is not to leave this house,' he said, 'I don't mean going to the shops, seeing other people and that sort of thing. I mean, he is not to report to anywhere until such time as I say he's fit enough, even if it is to be examined by Army doctors. As I said, things of the mind. They might not understand.'

Margaret nodded because she knew that was demanded of her. The bill, the bills, were still hovering there in the space between them. 'But the bills,' she said.

The doctor was putting on his coat. With his back to her he said, 'You are not to be concerned about them. They've been taken care of.'

She may have tried to question this, but in the panic of incomprehension she could not recall exactly what he'd said. In any case, the doctor, half turning towards her added, 'Goodbye, Mrs Ward,' firmly pushing onto his head, with an air of unassailable finality, the black homburg of his profession, thus unambiguously indicating that the visit and any possible further conversation were at an end. She watched him from the doorway as he made ponderous progress up the garden path to his waiting car - a pillar, a rock upon which she leant, relied. But in the nature of rocks; unmoving, immutable.

Richard had gone back to the settee. He'd just switched on the wireless because as Margaret went to sit next to him the music of Mantovani burst out. She leaned over and turned the volume down. 'He said you're much better,' she said. Richard nodded. She could detect nothing from his face. "And me, too,' she added, 'I didn't feed myself very well - .' Richard nodded, not looking at her. Suddenly, where before there was a blackness oppressing her from above, there now appeared a heat, red, like a burning cloud in front of her. She wanted to shake him, really shake him, shout at him, 'Come on, snap out of it! I really cannot stand this for much longer!' Instead, she said, 'I'll get some lunch. Oh, and this afternoon, if we walked up Ashtead Road, we could get on to the Heath. It's no further than the shops. And - .'

Oh God, she'd not thought: it was near the Laundry, not far from the Canadian Camp, now deserted. I'm blurting, she thought, babbling. But it was said: the notion, this activity was created and stood up in full view in the few feet of room between them. She'd have to brave it out. It would be difficult, but it was the beginning of the countryside, and she tried to hope that it might be a beginning for Richard too. So many 'mights', so many 'perhaps', so little change.

The walk, predictably, exhausted Richard. But this was nothing new. They reached the far side of the Heath where the land fell away into a shallow valley of green fields and clumps of woodland. The grass had thrown off its winter grey and the hedges had almost become swathes of salad green below trees that still clung cautiously to patterns of winter grey and black. Paths ran hither and thither among the autumnal brown of last year's bracken. She didn't say anything about the Laundry, no more than glancing at it as it steamed away with its usual quiet self- absorption. She found that in her mind Savory and Garner had receded, as had Mr Barnes, and even if Betty had suddenly rushed out, she'd have waved a wave of finality and led Richard pointedly away towards the countryside where he wanted to ramble.

At one point he nodded towards the deserted Canadian Nissan huts the other side of the Heath near the main road. To Margaret they were unimportant, grey, as if still subsisting on winter. But she answered, saying she didn't really know - they might have been something to do with the war; and walked on, carefully avoiding haphazard paths that wandered towards them. She found her heart pounding. Lying was not something that came easily - and could easily become a burden which grew heavier: one lie leading to another. And now the doctor's fees.

Who? Who could have paid them? A moment of panic assailed her – Mr Long? Some attempt to make amends for how he'd treated her, some residual attempt to have power over her? It took half the Heath to dispel that one: he couldn't have known. No, he definitely could not have known. Such a ridiculous notion, she knew, could be damaging. She sensed how one destructive idea might follow another in some terrible descent down the slope of destruction.

The next weeks in the house which Margaret forced herself to keep clean would have merged with others if this new thing in bed had not appeared. She had had no idea whether or not it would happen again. When it did, she was surprised, remembering the only thing her mother had said to her the night before her wedding day. 'Richard is a good man, my dear. So's your dad. But remember, love, men are men. They have certain needs.' There was a pause as Rose adjusted the wedding dress on the ironing board the better to iron its hem. Either she'd gone far enough, or there was more to say which required further careful consideration. She sighed and concluded, with a certain air of resignation which Margaret picked up but could not fully understand, 'And wives, dear, have their duties to perform, as well.' She nodded, as if mostly to herself as she turned the dress round, affirming that her last remark must be seen in the context of her previous one.

So, she would do her duty. But as the pain began to lessen, she began to see it as something else that Richard had returned to. That each thing he rediscovered might lead to - . She had to rein back broken thoughts, fanciful conclusions which leapt ahead towards a beckoning promised land, but which might materialise as desert. She had to return time and time again to shouting, insisting in her mind, One step at a time, only one, only one, no more! Slowly, pleasure began to slip back, quietly, unbidden, though assailed sometimes by what she hid from the world, the ravage of war which everyone had shared, each in his or her own different way. If this happened in the middle of the night she fought the past, Out of my mind, out, out! The repetition, the silent chant that this became would eventually let her slip into sleep. How long it lasted at night she couldn't fathom. The one thing that she must do, she knew, was to hold on to the possibility of pleasure as something that might continue to re-emerge: meaning the spasms. Yes, she found the memory, biding its time: soon after the honeymoon when the soreness had subsided. That time long ago when she looked at Richard as he walked across the room to her to put his arms round her because they had not touched for a few unendurably long moments when he seemed to be saying, *Tonight or in the morning, we will make love.*

Make love again. More love. At first, she had no idea what the spasms, as she called them, were. Even though she didn't know if this was right, or even acceptable behaviour, she learned to press Richard to her in such a way that the potential for a spasm was increased. One of the first times this spasm hit her, surged through her like a wave she couldn't resist the cry of pleasure; the only way she could describe it to herself, but she felt Richard rear up, staring down at her with an expression somewhere between worry and alarm. He quickly rolled off her, his arms still holding her shoulders, 'Are you all right, love, was I hurting you?'

She had to think quickly, had to say something convincing, 'It's happiness,' she'd said, 'just happiness.'

Even so, because she didn't know what it was, this pleasure, when it happened after this, she coped by clenching her teeth, refusing to allow pleasure to have a sound, or a voice. If it happened twice, as she found it sometimes could, if Richard stayed inside her long enough, she'd have to fight the spasm twice, hide it twice, only make a noise of pleasure when he came so as to give him all her pleasure as well.

Gradually, she discovered a reconciliation between pleasure and ignorance, in that surely what gave such deep pleasure, even if it had to be kept secret, could not be bad, could not possibly be evil, could not be something which you should not allow to happen. But at times, irritation and anxiety rose within her: there was no one she could speak to about this: neither her mother, a close woman friend (if she had one), her sister-in-law, or Dr Simpson.

Now, bringing up the breakfast on the tray only before used to carry in and out Sunday lunch or the tea things (if they ever got round to inviting her parents) she worried because it seemed to exhaust Richard. Energy and recovery, she thought of as mutually dependent. Yet she couldn't stop him when he *rose*, her secret word for it, because this is what a man did, and this is what a wife should receive. Needs, duties, pleasure linked and entwined. It was an instinctively felt and inviolable rule that a good wife did not refuse her husband this ease and pleasure, this what was it, release? For it was a release. Richard would then smile, his face flushed with exertion, wanting to touch her more, speak to her more: about the garden, of going for a walk, of buying some new shoes. It seemed a way forward - she had no idea what was going on inside his mind but for her, at least, it was like the opening of an important door, however fragile and creaking, onto their former life, the reconstruction or repairing of their illusive but light-filled memories of fun from that magic time before the black shades of war darkened and smothered all existence.

At breakfast a few days later Richard said, 'The cheques. Mr Long.' Margaret didn't have time to think through the spasm of panic that this announcement provoked. But Richard had already shuffled into the hall, and lifted his coat from its hook. In her panic, Margaret had to decide: was she going to go with him, or as far as the bank but not into Mr Long's office where his presence would repel her. Or wait outside and leave Richard to do the whole thing by himself?

Watching Richard from the kitchen, while still in the middle of washing up the breakfast things, she somehow settled for some indication from Richard himself. As he put on his hat, would he turn and look to see if she were following, getting herself ready to accompany him? But he didn't. Without a backward glance, without another word, he completed the motions of a man assembling himself in order to go out. The front door clicked quietly shut, leaving Margaret with the washing up cloth in one hand, staring up the hallway with half a mind to throw on her coat and run down the hill after him.

But another part of her mind prevailed: it was his decision - he's actually decided to do something. He was actually not waiting for her to prompt him. But, despite this, the cost to her was tears over the drying up of the breakfast plates and cutlery, and the scouring out of the frying pan which had contained his one egg and slice of bacon. The thought of her mother presented itself to her, of seeing a restful face, an unhurried presence, a calm and ordered life.

Her mother had advanced safely through more than sixty years - two Great Wars, and The Depression of which Margaret could remember little; cocooned as she was in one of the brave new houses which seemed to have weathered all this with little to show for it, with no desperate or destroyed people living out their last days behind thick curtains, no houses had collapsing with neglect, no houses bombed.

Only a father here, a son there, the majority either too old, too young or secure within the embrace of reserved occupations. Even Mrs Stokes' husband, whatever his name was, who was in insurance before the War - he'd spent the whole war assessing war damage. 'Reparations,' people used to say, 'after the war's over. When we've won and the Germans will have to pay.'

This meandering of the mind was immediately contrasted with her image of herself: a woman in tears, as if this was the only impression she could summon. A state of tears which might not include streams and drops and wet handkerchiefs, but which nevertheless remained a weeping state of mind, the weight of unending distress, enduring unhappiness. Added to this was a slackness of the body, a difficulty with thinking anything through or being decisive, like just now with

Richard. Yes, and like Richard, a lack of energy, perhaps like him an absence of hope. Perhaps like him diminished by the loss of the lives they had before the war. Not so much actual loss but the lack of a positive feeling of comfort in memory, a lack of being bolstered by remembering the fun, the life she had, the person she used to be, the person he used to be before the world had been plunged into this terrible war.

The kitchen drawer to the left of the sink was stuck. It had been reluctant to open for some time, a minor irritation marking out a pattern to the day in a tussle with it, morning, noon and night. It would usually give in, but had become a chafing of mind and muscle which was so insignificant in the grand order of things as to be instantly forgettable. And yet in the grand order of things this drawer had decided that this was the moment to assert itself: it was not going to slide open. The least it would concede was half an inch. This did not go so far as to create a dark slit into which, as a temporary expedient, the breakfast cutlery could be slotted. Even the strength of two arms and a back would not shift it. To make this worse, she hadn't added it to the mental list of things that Richard could do, or had she, and he'd forgotten? But one last, desperate tug had the drawer wrenched out, crashing onto the kitchen floor. Staring from the drawer to the cutlery scattered on the drawing board, Margaret felt herself freeze. It felt as if her chest had become a solid piece of flesh and bone, as if her ribs and spine were no longer separate entities with different roles. She leant over the sink, dish cloth in hand, as if stuck in this pose. Although her face outwardly stared through the kitchen window onto the green blur of the back lawn and the light points of the swelling buds of apple blossom, she saw nothing. The world had become a blank, containing no thought, no mental reflection, no movement.

How long she remained suspended over the sink she'd probably never be able to calculate. The next thing she was aware of was walking out of the kitchen up the hallway, grabbing her coat and the felt hat which you were supposed to pin at an angle, but which she crammed onto her head. Automatically she slipped the long strap of her bag over her shoulder; and when she next had some conscious realisation of where she was, she found her quick steps taking her past the first shops of the High Street. The bank was still some way off, but there seemed to her to be no urgency in visiting it and finding if Richard was still there. Before this was the bus stop. As she reached it a bus lumbered alongside and stopped. Several people descended and an old woman mounted the back platform. Margaret simply followed her as if this had been her intention. 'Hold tight, dear,' the conductor said to the old woman.

Margaret sat alone on the lengthways side seat nearest the back. Her mother had once had to grab her when as a child she was about to be propelled into the gangway by the sudden swerving of whichever bus it was. The incident was repeated a number of times at the table and to neighbours, how Margaret was nearly thrown out of the bus.

Her mother.

'Any more fares, please.'

The conductor held out a hand. Margaret scrabbled for her purse in her bag. The fingers of the hand just below her face twitched as if it had many fares to collect. She handed over the tuppence required and took the ticket which had been cheerfully cancelled with a ting. Ten minutes or so later, when the familiar little shopping arcade curving round the roundabout appeared, she got out.

'Mind the step, love,' the conductor said, looking the other way.

Her feet knew the way.

Minutes later; it felt as if it was longer than usual, and had the air of a working day, lacking both sunshine and weekend front garden activity when neighbours would sometimes acknowledge each other's existence.

'Margaret!' Rose was both pleased and concerned, holding onto the door as if it would give her some reassurance, wiping back a few loose strands of hair while she was thus exposed to the road in her pinny. 'But come in, dear, sorry, do come straight in. How nice to see you.'

Frank hovered down the hallway, 'Let me take your coat, my dear,' he said. 'This is so nice.'

As Frank took Margaret's coat, he tried to hide his downward glance, but Rose could not stop herself asking, 'But why the slippers, dear?'

Richard had reached the bank and had to lean against the counter to wait for Mr Bailey to finish issuing an elderly customer with a new cheque book. This transaction was a laboured affair. There was some small difference in the layout of the cheques which threatened the existence of the older man. Richard, drooping on the counter, heard Mr Bailey say, 'It's perfectly simple, Mr Aitchison, you write the date and amount in the same place, it just looks further down, but it is scarcely more than an eighth of an inch different.' Mr Bailey carefully enclosed the cheque book in an envelope. 'But if you have any difficulties, please do not hesitate - .'

The old man fiercely fingered his bowler hat which lay on the counter beside him before detaching one hand to take the envelope. His rattly intake of breath signified that he wasn't best pleased. With relief Mr Bailey bade him good day. Glancing up, he was about to greet Richard but was cut short.

'I wish to see Mr Long,' Richard said. He, too, was breathing deeply.

'Ah, Mr Ward, how -, er, do you have an appointment, sir?'

Richard shook his head, still leaning for support on the counter.

'Ah,' Mr Bailey hesitated, 'er, I'll just check with Miss Hurst.' As he turned towards the partition behind him several faces ducked down. Standing, Mr Bailey could see over it to the clerks' stations behind. 'Miss Hurst, if you please,' he summoned, his voice discretely subdued. Sheila's face appeared, wearing a blank expression of denial that she'd been spying. She raised her eyebrows. 'Yes, Mr Bailey,' she said. Mr Bailey turned back to include Richard in agreeing a mutually suited day and time for an appointment, but he'd gone.

Mr Long looked up from his desk with an expression of studied surprise and annoyance at this intrusion. 'Do you have an appointment?' he said. The omission of Richard's name and title was deliberate. But Richard had already sat down in the customer's chair opposite Mr Long who reacted by admitting that Richard's name had not evaded him.

'Mr Ward, I see customers strictly by appointment. I do not wish to waste people's time by -.'

He stopped and stared at the cheque book stubs that Richard had placed before him on the shiny desk, next to the one sheet of paper which served as evidence that work had been taking place.

Richard leant forward. In the moment of reflection allowed him by Mr Long's surprise he was able to register how the manager had aged, how his face had thinned and lengthened, how his bald dome was sagging and appeared lower and less prominent, giving him the appeared of diminished authority. At the same time Mr Long recoiled before the advance of Richard's hands pushing what looked like a book of cheque stubs across the desk towards him, before rallying his managerial forces to deal with this intrusion, this unexpected situation. As an aid to this, but in an unprecedented reaction, he reached for his paperknife.

Richard said, 'These are cheque stubs.'

Mr Long expected but didn't get a qualifier, *as you can see*. He found that he had instinctively drawn the knife defensively towards himself. Two things struck him simultaneously as he tried to rally himself: he was not dealing with a man who was completely normal, and he must retrieve the situation by asserting his authority.

'Mr Ward,' he said with appropriate emphasis, ' I - .'

The door opened for a second time. It was Sheila, red in the face. 'So sorry, sir,' she said, 'it's Mr Henderson, sir. For his appointment at a quarter to eleven.'

It appeared that Richard had neither heard Mr Long nor Miss Hurst.

'These cheques,' he said, 'were all drawn up by me - .'

Sheila, even redder, interrupted, 'Sorry, sir, shall I ask Mr Henderson if he could kindly wait a moment?'

Again distracted, Mr Long needed a moment to consider. He now clasped the blade of his knife in one hand, while continuing to hold the handle with the other. Both hands were relegated to a defensive position in front of his stomach.

As if still unaware of the presence of Miss Hurst, Richard continued, 'Drawn up by me and must have been honoured because I received all the - .'

'Mr Ward.' Mr Long had at last recovered himself. 'As you hear, I have a client, an important client, waiting to see me. He has an appointment and cannot be further delayed - .'

Richard, to Mr Long's surprise, didn't appear to hear this either. ' - have all been honoured but have not appeared on - .'

Sheila was still waiting, all ears, and puce with compensatory embarrassment.

The door opened further to a large dark shape that had appeared in the frosted glass. A man with a bloated red face peered round the door over Sheila's shoulder. His hand holding the door also clutched a black homburg of obviously serious intent. 'Look here, Long,' the man said, 'I'm a busy - .'

' - on the bank statements.' Richard said. At the same moment he caught sight of the Japanese paper knife in Mr Long's hands. Suddenly it felt as if a lead weight had filled his stomach. Almost simultaneously a hot, familiar but unidentifiable smell filled his nostrils and he had to find air, had to escape from this sombre, constricting room. Above all he had to lie down. Pushing up and across the small office he blundered first into Sheila and then into the large man blocking the doorway.

'I say, do be careful, old man!' the man said.

But Richard was past him and the floor in the small concourse appeared to rise slowly up at him. He just managed to protect his face, instinctively pulling up his arms to break the force of the floor's impact, but not once letting go of the cheque stubs.

'That's quite all right, dear.' Rose twittered, her voice singing her discomfort and insecurity in the face of her daughter's unexpected visit. The possibility of Margaret staying for some lunch had been suggested by her in the flurry of the initial greeting. The idea that their daughter might stay to lunch was not a deliberate ploy on the part of a mother to detain the daughter she saw too little of and was in a state of continual worry about. It might also have been to cover up or partly hide the untimely question about Margaret's slippers. 'Of course, dear, lunch will easily stretch to three.' Rose turned and looked back towards Frank who still stood by the kitchen door trying to make sense of the sudden and unexpected arrival of his daughter. As if startled to be included in some conspiracy, he nodded and muttered, 'Of course, of course.' Adding, 'My dear, how nice,' and kissing her cheek in his usual awkward way. He ushered her into the living room. Rose, with greater legitimacy than Frank, was able to flee to the kitchen in order to stretch lunch from two to three, and wonder upon this unexpected visit.

The slippers, possessing as high a profile as lunch, were carefully not commented on or glanced at again. They were in an altogether different league; one below which lurked dark and dangerous depths. Frank, after commenting that milder weather was at last prevailing, had a sudden brainwave which allowed him, too, to escape: a pre-lunch drink. 'I won't be a moment, my dear,' he said, almost allowing himself another glance at her slippers.

Alone, Margaret sat on the easy chair she had usually occupied, except with Richard when she was expected to sit on the settee with him. At first it seemed to her as if she was experiencing quiet for the first time for as long as she could remember. The paradox was there, hovering and not fully apparent, because the days, months, and years of her solitude had been compressed into a black barrier shoved somewhere into a seldom visited attic of her mind. Though there were discrete and barely audible movements from elsewhere in the house, the tranquillity here enabled a ringing in her ears to become more apparent. This was a hum, not of a motor or of voices heard from another room, but more like the verbal machinations or workings of her own mind.

Half notions began to assemble themselves: that this noise was the trickling of unhappiness, the dripping of distress, the flowing debris of uncertainty. All these things captured in a drone that was forever trapped in a single, unending note. What were now habitual tears flowed down her cheek, soundlessly articulating her anguish.

Frank opened the lounge door with the uncertainty of a man carrying something he didn't want to spill. 'Rose!' he called back as he entered with the little round papier-mache tray only ever used for the purpose of safely conveying from the dining-room the slim stemmed glasses half full of carefully hoarded sherry. Rose bustled in behind him with a giggle before either of them noticed their daughter sitting bolt upright with tears coursing down her face. But both knew they had a choice to make: to either ignore the tears or to attempt to be involved and to share some burden of which they knew nothing. Rose sat on the settee, and Frank leant forward, courteously offering her the tray. He then moved towards Margaret, carefully lifting the second sherry glass and handing it to her as if her state precluded her from taking it herself.

Rose took a minute sip. 'Oh, Frank, how long is it - ?' But checked herself. Frank raised his glass. He looked as if he wanted to say something. In the silence that followed Rose's words, to cover up the fact that she'd tasted a nearly forbidden fruit before allowing for the possibility that her husband might say something, and might have said something to lighten or relieve whatever was the matter, she felt she had to say something.

'So nice to see you, dear, er - unexpectedly like th - .' She covered up the tired and incomplete words by sipping from the glass as if this was her first taste ever of sherry.

Margaret's hand shook a little, but was not yet in danger of spilling the sherry. At the same time, she leant forward, holding the glass away from herself. With a half suppressed habitual groan Frank rose, putting down his glass on the tray which waited on the small carved occasional table next to him. He carefully took Margaret's glass from her and replaced it on the tray. Then, equally carefully, under the full gaze of Rose, fetched another tiny table from its accustomed place to the left of the fireplace and repositioned it next to Margaret's right knee.

The whole operation was completed by his replacing her glass onto this small table. Then he carefully pulled out the handkerchief from his top jacket pocket and handed it to Margaret. Without a further word he sank back into his habitual seat and rewarded himself with a larger sip than his first. Both parents watched their daughter dabbing at her eyes and cheeks with the handkerchief.

'I'm so sorry,' Margaret said. She sniffed, blew her nose on the handkerchief and gazed at these her parents through watery eyes. She looked as if at any moment she could weep again. 'It's just that I have been so worried - .'

'Has Dr Simpson called again, dear?'

Frank looked at his wife, as if alarmed by such a direct question. Margaret nodded. 'About once a week,' she said, 'The expense - .'

There was a pause during which Rose looked at her husband.

Frank cleared his throat. 'Er, my dear,' he said, addressing Margaret, 'now look here, you're not to worry in the least about that, er, about the doctor's account. We've, taken care of that. And that's quite all right. Absolutely all right.'

As if to reinforce and underline the certainty and immutability of what he had just said, he tipped the remainder of his sherry into his mouth in one final and almost reckless swig.

'Well, dear,' Rose said brightly, downing her sherry in the same spirit of abandon, anxious the draw a line under this serious and potentially embarrassing moment spent surveying the murky depths of the unknown, 'I'm sure lunch must be ready. Let's all move into the - ,' she reeled a little as she stood and tried to take a step. 'Oh, my giddy aunt, the effect of the, sh -', and giggled discreetly all the way to the kitchen.

It was Dr Simpson who brought Richard back from the bank and who had to cope with the encounter with Elsie. 'Hello, again, Mrs Hipperson,' he said briskly. Elsie was forced to both control her innate narrative flow and to describe herself by name as a neighbour, being daring or assertive enough to add the words, *and friend*. She desperately wanted to remind him of the drama of Margaret's collapse in her hallway.

Perhaps the good doctor knew this, and knew well how to stifle such a time-wasting possible second re-enactment of this scene.

Dr Simpson had tried the Wards' kitchen door as well as the front door and it was clear that no one was in. By which time this woman with the florid face of one consumed with inquisitiveness had launched herself down the short front garden path, imposing upon him both news and speculation about seeing Margaret and Richard hurrying off separately down the road, undoubtedly going to the shops, and should have been back by now because she or they usually didn't take this long. In fact, she hardly ever did, not since she'd stopped working, but Mr Ward was welcome to stay with her until his wife returned.

During this monologue Richard was propped against the front door with his eyes, and probably his ears, closed.

The list of visits already badly delayed spurred Dr Simpson to some speedy resolution of the problem. 'Thank you, Mrs Hipperson; that's very kind of you. I'm sure Mr Ward will be very comfortable with you while awaiting his wife's return.' He assumed his closed, unassailable features: thus far and no further, useful with overzealous and garrulous patients. Taking an arm each, they walked Richard the short way round to Elsie's house, got him into the lounge where he flopped onto Elsie's settee. 'Will you be all right now?' the Doctor asked walking briskly away, aware that this would apply to more to Elsie than to Richard.

Tom waited in the car while Rose climbed out with Margaret. 'I'll just see you in, dear,' she said. Margaret took too long finding her keys because her eyes were still watering. She hadn't the strength, nor the words to go with it, to become involved in the whole rigmarole of refusing this most basic, even if loaded, offer: the, *No, no, it's quite all right, mother, I'm sure Tom will want to - , we mustn't keep him - .*

So Rose was able to follow Margaret in. In the moments that it took Margaret to flit from room to room, and haul herself upstairs, she knew that the house was possessed of its former emptiness, its former silence. She had no idea if Richard even had a key. But there was no time to speculate on anything because Elsie's strident voice was already filling the hallway where Rose waited. It was a voice raised several notches in volume, stimulated by the extraordinary events taking place before her very eyes that day: Margaret and Richard leaving the house separately, the one not returning until just this moment in someone's car well after the appointed time for lunch and the other having been brought back earlier from somewhere by the doctor. By the time Margaret was back down the stairs, Elsie had got to, '... it's all right - he's fast asleep now. I really didn't want to wake him, poor man, he's fast asleep on the settee. Exhausted, I'd say.' She paused for breath, looking carefully round, peering down the hall into the kitchen, as well as into the living room to the right of where she held her ground.

'Where he'd been, gawd only knows,' she added, reddening further as her cheeks reacted quickly to her innate tendency to veer uncontrollably into the dangerous territory of prying and speculation she so loved.

Elsie, having decided that a woman nearer her age might be more receptive to and understanding of odd things, leant forward towards Rose. Her voice sank to the secret and conspiratorial. 'He babbled about blood. On and on. There was too much of it -. Then he went to sleep.' She drew herself back to indicate that, being a tactful and compassionate sort of woman, she'd say no more because it was not only beyond her but that she shouldn't interfere, and besides for decency's sake she should make out that it wasn't anything to do with her. Then she turned to Margaret. 'Now, dear, what do you want to do? You're very welcome to leave him with me until he wakes up, but it's entirely up to you, it really won't matter in the least to me.' She smiled, apparently satisfied with her generosity and greatness of heart. Her hidden intention was obvious: the longer I keep him, the more I'll find out, the more I'll participate in this drama.

'You're very kind,' Rose said, 'so good of you.' As if Elsie had picked up something she'd dropped in the street.

Margaret stood on the threshold of the kitchen, as if unable to decide where she belonged, as if to distance herself from what was passing between her mother and Elsie, as if to hold them both away from her at several arm's length. She felt that her whole life was sinking into a heaving, boiling mire, that one thing would compound with another to conceive worse problems that she'd have no control over whatever new mixture would arise. Actual or possible scenarios of Richard and the bank, Dr Simpson and her parents, of Elsie who knew or did not know anything or everything. And now, blood. But even if that was how she saw it, her immediate and urgent need was to get Elsie out, bring Richard back and urge her mother back to the car and the patient Tom. 'I'll come and see Richard,' she said, 'and poor Tom's still waiting.'

The three women walked out of the house and made their way up the short front garden path, Elsie leading because the baton, however much smaller than she hoped, had been passed to her. Margaret saw her mother go round to the car, and assumed that she'd get in. Followed by Margaret, Elsie unlocked her front door and crept in, her shoulders slightly hunched to give Margaret the signal that they must both proceed quietly and with the utmost care.

Richard was revealed to be asleep on the settee in Elsie's lounge with one arm flung onto the loud carpet, undisturbed by Elsie's whispered reprise of the events leading up to her helping him into her house. She omitted further mention of blood. It would have made no difference to Margaret.

'Thank you,' Margaret said. Elsie screwed up her face as if Margaret had just broken wind in the presence of the king himself. But Margaret hadn't intended her words to be so loud; she hadn't planned this to be so, it had just happened whether or not Richard was asleep.

But it worked. Richard stirred slightly, and opened his eyes. The fingers of the arm drooped over the side of the settee twitched and rose to rub his eyes. Even though his face remained immobile his eyes sought and found Margaret's almost immediately, as if they had known which way to look. Elsie followed Margaret and Richard home with the simple but effective excuse that he would need two hands to help him back. He did.

Margaret could feel when his legs began to buckle and they had to stop to let him recover. Tom's car, she noted, was not there. It struck her that she'd swapped her mother for Elsie; that the immediate problem now would be how to get rid of Elsie so that she could start to think about how to get her head above her life's mire, claw her way back to somewhere near where she was when this day dawned and before Richard had said he was going to the bank. But how? Her mind refused to tell her anything, refused to supply her with a strategy or plan to persuade Elsie to vanish immediately they'd got Richard in.

Fortunately, the front door was still open, so Margaret didn't have to help hold up Richard and struggle at the same time with the key.

'Thank you,' she said again, intending to imply that she'd be all right now. She didn't get as far as this because she was startled to hear the voice of her mother say, 'Thank you so much, Mrs Hipperson. We will be quite all right now, thank you.'

Rose had already taken Richard's other arm, leaving Elsie without prop or support with which to justify her continued presence in Margaret's house.

Chapter 12.

APRIL 1946

Rose had already started cleaning before Richard was brought back from Elsie's. It was only after settling him back onto the settee and mentally progressing as far as the concept of a cup of tea that Margaret smelled something caustic wafting down the hall into the living room. That she didn't at first recognise the pungent and powerful smell did not occur to her. Yet at the same time it was an aroma reeking of the security of the past, of a past bound up with her mother. And there was Rose in the kitchen, wielding the magic of Harpic over the kitchen sink, the draining board, and the tiles of the back window-sill.

Within minutes she'd rubbed the grime of war years off the kitchen table so that it shone with a maturity approaching polished mahogany. But above all she had heaped Harpic onto the hob and liberally applied it to the oven below where its smell had already begun to combine with that of the congealed, baked grease inside. 'How is he?' Rose asked, turning from the sink, her face already blotchy red from her assault on germs and filth.

'Woozy,' Margaret said. Behind them the sound of soothing music drifted from the wireless which she'd switched on.

'Has he had his lunch yet?'

Margaret shook her head. Richard and lunch was a connection she had not made. She reeled under implications she had not noticed before: his lunch, his entitlement, her wifely duty.

'What's he going to have?' Rose persisted, wiping the sink dry with short, brutal strokes.

Margaret looked at her mother's back busily bent over her task. She tried to speak, but her stomach suddenly lurched and the sob she wasn't prepared for burst into her throat, to be instantly stifled. Had she intended to go shopping? Had she thought in terms of food for Richard, her husband? Could she bear to admit these shortcomings? She could, however, retreat, so she fled back up the hall in case her mother should turn and witness the next sob racking her.
The door to the living room was open, and Richard was still lying on the settee.
'Richard,' she sobbed quietly, kneeling before him, 'are you hungry?'

He opened his eyes first and, not finding her somewhere above him, began to look lazily round the room until he found her.

'Are you hungry?' she repeated, 'Would you like any lunch?' Imperceptibly shaking his head, he closed his eyes to allow the music of Chopin to wash over him.

Back in the kitchen she said to her mother's back, 'He's not hungry.'

Rose, now crouched and scraping at the inside of the oven with an old knife, sniffed. 'A man needs feeding,' she said, in a tone of finality. She stood and added, 'When I'm finished in here, I'll get the bus home for your Dad's supper. Then I'll be round in the morning.' Her face wore the tight lips of a woman who will not be deflected from a decision once made. With a sigh which could be interpreted as resignation or accusation she turned to wash her hands in the sink before removing Margaret's pinny from her resolute midriff.

Rose had come and continued to clean on the Tuesday, Wednesday and Thursday, long enough for it almost to have become an established routine - arriving at ten and working through the day. So that, come Friday, if the house was prepared for the bustling and moving of furniture, it now became quiet and empty without it. Richard said nothing, but Margaret had to cope with an ambush of feelings that were so overwhelming and contradictory that she was able to ignore them, the one cancelling out the other: the power of a mother to take such drastic action, versus her intense feelings of guilt that she'd neglected cleaning and dusting for as long as she could remember, and her inability to organise the appropriate food at the appropriate time.

Rose left on the Thursday afternoon with a face already beginning to assume the ashen hues of exhaustion. Mother and daughter embraced in the hall, Margaret trying and only partly succeeding in whispering, 'Thank you.' Rose turned back half way up the front garden path, 'Oh, and say good bye to Richard for me, dear,' as if in the ferocity of the purging of the house she'd forgotten about him. No arrangements for future visits were mentioned. It's up to you now, dear, was the message writ large between them which Margaret was expected to receive and understand.

Saturday. Margaret woke with notions of food and shopping. Over breakfast in the germ-free kitchen she spoke of the shops. Richard looked up from his boiled egg; a drop of saffron yolk had stuck to his chin, coalescing and gathering as if becoming a piece of fading amber. She knew he'd probably come, and couldn't discourage this because it had taken so long to get him to walk that far, take an interest, to return to this small part of the hum and drum of everyday existence. She took a deep breath. 'I still have most of the money from last week, so we don't - .' Richard nodded. 'This afternoon,' he said, 'another walk on the Heath.' Even if she couldn't summon the energy at least he wasn't hell bent on going to the bank.

A day, any day impresses itself upon the volatility of life in unpredictable, random ways, despite the workings of the mind of Bureaucracy or the multifarious organisation of government and institutions. Somewhere someone has your name on a list; somewhere someone is going to communicate with you. Unpredictable it is, random it isn't.

The visit of the postman was still rare. Apart from Rose, who was there to write to them? The phone had been reconnected, and Margaret could phone anyone she knew, even if she didn't ever think of doing so. It was as if the act and art of speaking to someone whose face she could not see had been lost to her. For Richard, it seemed to her, it was easy, the phone simply did not exist.

At this random moment in time it is eleven o'clock in the morning; this is the time of the second fixture in the day, one that Richard looks forward to: a cup of tea. A brief moment together, a break in the activity of Margaret's day, a halt in the daily maintenance of their lives because she's established in her mind a routine of cleaning the house, changing the bed and washing clothes; soon after to hang out the pregnant spinnakers of sheets, the wind-handled puppetry of dancing shirts and trousers, the erotic swaying of skirts and dresses, and the busy perambulation of socks.

The click of the garden gate had them both glance round: the postman. A different one now; John something or other Elsie called him when she spoke of him, omitting what she'd tell him about the neighbours. An older man, comfortable in his postman's uniform, suggesting long stretches of a life spent in uniform, but not in this war, except perhaps as a fire warden. A man soon to cease wearing any uniform, unless he has reserves at home ready for the paradoxical uniformity of civilian life. Cup and saucer in hand, Margaret and Richard mark the progress of the letter to their letter box - light brown and official looking, already held in front of the postman's ample stomach. They listen to the plip of the envelope on the door mat: a small expletive which might nevertheless alter the course of the world. Margaret could see Richard glance round to see where to put down his cup and saucer. She felt her usual dread of the new, the unexpected. This was Tuesday and her mother's letter, if there was to be one, usually arrived on Thursday or Friday.

'Let's leave it until we've finished,' she says. Adding to herself notions of living this particular moment just a minute or two longer before confronting whatever it was that the world would demand of them.

Richard said nothing, but drew the saucer closer to him, lifting the cup and sipping the hot tea. The postman walked slowly back up the front garden and carefully closed the gate behind him. Watching him progress along the street to the left, Margaret caught through the increased width of vision provided by the bay window, a glimpse of Elsie wandering up to her gate to swap news with John, whether or not she was to be rewarded with a letter.

A letter cannot be put off for ever; delay makes the receiver becomes impatient to know his fate. Margaret had already guessed that the buff envelope which John bore could not be good news. To hope that Richard would be set free from the harness that war had buckled tight round him was far too much to expect. Even several months later life didn't work like that, wasn't as uncomplicated as that. As she bent down to pick it up the letter had conspired to conceal its identity for the last few desperate seconds, hiding OHMS underneath itself. Margaret wanted to tear it open there and then on the doormat, to know what it said, what it demanded, how it would change their lives. The fear, the terror of the letters received when Richard was away could plainly burst the fragile dam of memory and engulf her again. But it was addressed to him; she must do the correct thing.

Richard began to open the letter carefully, slowly, as if similarly motivated to put off the evil moment. But Margaret could see this was merely part of his old systematic approach to solving things - by careful thought and manipulation. But the envelope's flap was too well stuck, so that with a small sigh of irritation he had to rip his way in and allow to fall the wreck of the buff envelope while retaining the creased letter itself.

Watching a person read a letter further prolongs the agony of waiting. Margaret wanted to spring up and peer over Richard's shoulder. From the other side of the room she held her face with both hands as if it would otherwise break out in some way she'd regret. His mouth formed the words, one by one, in a parody of the slow motion you sometimes see at the picture houses. But she could not read his slow, deliberate mouth at all. She said, suddenly breathless, 'What, tell me please, love, what does it say?' Richard continued to mouth the words of the letter. Eventually he lowered it onto his lap. His face refused to give her a clue. She stood and scuttled across the room as he offered it up to her.

He said, 'I, I think they want me to –'
Standing in front of Richard who is slumped on the settee, Margaret tries to read the letter torn from the buff OHMS envelope but the words lose focus, then regain it, but refuse to relinquish their meaning. Her tears, falling short of the letter, do not smudge the words, do not try to alter their earnestness. Without a word she pushes the letter back to Richard as if were infected, imbued with some evil she must refuse. He took it back and mutely scanned it again. After a while he let it drop onto his lap and raised his eyes to her. With Margaret

standing looking down at him on this particular day in April 1946, their eyes are locked together for what may have been a long or a very short time, because it was like time frozen. Indeed, the clock when they next looked at it had stopped for lack of winding, and they couldn't have told anyone whether it had stopped at a quarter to twelve that morning, last night, a week, or a month ago, because winding it up each day had not yet become once again a part of their daily life.

But the world does not stop with the arrival of another possibly world-changing event because no one had wound up the front door bell either. The stern, almost authoritative knock shocked them both out of their trance-like state of trying to make sense of the small typewritten words on the OHMS letter. Both stared outside for a clue, Richard craning his neck, Margaret already facing the window. A car stood in the road near the open garden gate. In panic Margaret stepped forward towards Richard and leant over him to peer to the right from the bay window. It was Dr Simpson who waited, facing the door, lightly stamping his feet to restore the blood circulation to his legs and feet after being crammed in his car.

'Dr Simpson,' she whispered, as if to confirm the summoning of a genie. As she walked quickly to open the door her mind leapt, somersaulted with confusion; so much so that it tried to tell her that the letter and Dr Simpson were connected - that he was here to reinforce the authority of the letter. How else could two almost simultaneous events be explained?

The doctor stepped into the hall wreathed in rehearsed words of justified apology: '- and had meant to come last week or the one before - the usual things - so many home visits for the usual Spring epidemics, - and these things hang on, as you know - .' He swept past Margaret with an 'If I may,' as if knowing Richard was waiting for an appointment in the same room at the same time as before. His bustle had a kind of momentum to it. So much so that he failed at first to absorb anything of the shocked atmosphere into which he had stumbled. It was only when he saw Richard's blank eyes that the doctor turned to Margaret who stood once more with her hands pressed on her cheeks and appeared unable explain or volunteer information, that Dr Simpson brought himself to a halt and began to look and feel his way more carefully. Richard, meanwhile, held the letter up to the doctor who quickly took it. Dr Simpson's reading of it was far more rapid than either Richard or Margaret's. 'Ah,' he said, 'a post war reorganization of the Royal Engineers - .'

'I see,' he said, putting the letter down on the stool near the fireplace. He bent down to open his medical case. Then he coughed, playing for time. 'Well, let's have a look. If you could pull up your shirt and vest, please.' Bending over Richard he listened and tapped in his customary and comforting way, occasionally murmuring on a breath *good* or *right- ho*. Emerging from this, he straightened and turned to Margaret who stood waiting as if in shock. Richard sat up, his face blank and uninvolved with what was going on. 'A word with you, please, my dear,' the doctor said, first leaning to pick up the letter, then making for the door. Margaret followed, surprised that the doctor marched purposefully down the hallway into the kitchen. Once inside, he closed the door and invited her to sit down. He sat at the kitchen table where Margaret usually sat, so that she had to sit in Richard's place.

Drawing a deep breath, Dr Simpson said in a low voice as if Richard might be listening the other side of the door, 'First of all I'm going to reply to this letter. Your husband, in my professional opinion is not fit for a resumption of military service. In fact, I doubt very much that he will ever be fit enough. This is not to say that he cannot resume his pre-war work. That is totally different from military service.' He paused to let this sink in. Then he sighed in that way he had when about to add something more difficult.

'My dear, I'm going to have to do something difficult for you both. But you're not to worry - it's a new treatment from the United States. Your husband greatly needs to be helped in order to recover so that he can resume his work, er, live a normal life as he did before the war, now that he'll be de-mobbed. But he does need help.' He paused to try to gauge her reaction. Wide-eyed, she knew she would do anything he said. She was one of his *first-born*, she trusted him as if he were her own father.

'What I'm going to do,' the good doctor continued, 'is take him to the hospital - probably overnight - where he'll have this new procedure - then come home. If the procedure is successful, and I have every reason to believe it will be, it will enable me to certify that he is fit enough to work -.' His voice trailed away because he saw from her shocked gaze that the removal of Richard was the only thing she'd been able to hear, that the doorways to understanding and therefore hearing were rapidly slamming and that, in due course, he knew he'd have to repeat what he'd just said. And he did, this time adding, 'The treatment at the hospital is usually spread out over a few weeks, depending on how the patient reacts. But I have every confidence in your husband's ability to benefit from this new procedure. And just to reassure you I'll take you both to the hospital for his first appointment.' Then he went on to explain, in the simplest of words and shortest of sentences how it would be difficult for them both, but if Richard went into hospital for this help he, the Doctor, would be able to convince them very quickly that Richard wouldn't be able to resume military service.

Margaret tried to follow what he said, nodding agreement, or at least compliance, because she trusted him, because he was a doctor, their doctor, and because she knew that he of all people must know best.

The Doctor's silence which followed allowed Margaret to take this in.

When saw that her eyes had focused again onto his he said, 'And you, one more thing - are your monthly periods still back to normal? I meant to ask you last time - .' He watched her reaction: it was almost as if she didn't know what he was talking about. Then she, too, focused on his question, dragging herself away from what he had said about Richard. Monthly periods. Her face closed up, withdrawing to consider. She tried to remember the last time she'd washed out the soiled towelling, hanging them out on the line in the back garden, almost a parody of displaying a baby's nappies to whoever might glance over the fence. There was a faint memory of doing this; a memory of the smell of the old towelling which could make her gag as she washed them in the sink. It was something she'd often put off, ashamed that she had, glad when she'd got to the rinsing stage where the odour was fast disappearing down the drain, where the smell of carbolic had begun to assert itself, or the pungent smell of bleach for a particularly resistant stain. Then the cathartic wrenching and wringing, the hanging out of the damp towelling as a final act, a conclusion or closure on another month got through. But also, an admission of failure.

'Er, - I think so, yes,' she said. It was an easier option than admitting ignorance. She'd have to think back later, try to count the days or weeks, try to reconstruct memory of period pains, of washing the towelling. Yes, she must have. Yes, Richard had once stood in the garden staring at the drying towelling. But when had that been. 'No,' she said, 'I don't think so - I can't remember.' She paused and he watched how she struggled. But the wait worked. Margaret took deep breath and sat up straight. 'No,' she said, 'I haven't, I haven't had a period for a few months.' And sat stunned as if someone else had told her this.

Dr Simpson nodded. He, too, needed to absorb this. Air could be heard expelled from his nose with just the hint of a sigh. 'Please come into the front room,' he murmured.

The good doctor indicated the settee, glancing at Richard who was slumped in sleep on one of the easy chairs. 'Please pull down the waistband of your skirt.'

While Margaret did this, he fumbled with his bag to retrieve his trusty stethoscope. This he lay on Margaret's stomach, here, there and back to here again. Then he put the instrument down and pressed two fingers on several places on her stomach. Margaret heard his breathing almost falter, become irregular, as if it were trying to tell him something. She watched the doctor reach for his stethoscope, fold it and put it away in the waiting leather bag, as if to allow for his breathing to catch up with its usual regular self. 'My dear,' he whispered, glancing round at Richard who slept on, 'it's early days, but I think you may be expecting.'

Margaret's gasp woke Richard. The waking jolt had him stare at her, try to sit up but lacking the energy. Dr Simpson, with both his self and his bag reassembled, reached for his hat and said, 'I'll try and call next week. Good day.' And walked out in his usual brusque and assured manner.

It wasn't a long ride. Margaret had had no idea that this hospital was on the other side of the town; she had no idea that such a place existed.

The hospital mentioned by most people was not far from where her parents lived: where difficult births, difficult deaths and in between the two extremes were the innumerable operations and illnesses which people talked about in fear that they would one day have to undergo, or boasted about having survived. Above all, it was the place where you went to die if you could afford the luxury of not dying at home. But this unknown hospital was different, not like this. It was a silent place and prompted no memory of itself in her mind.

Dr Simpson drove up on the morning he said he would. There was a misunderstanding about the clothes that Richard should take. Only a small suitcase was needed, little more than a change of vest, underpants and socks, if required. Richard stood ready in the hallway. He, too, compliant or at least resigned. He knew he should be getting better, but wasn't. He, too, trusted and believed in Doctor Simpson.

Under the circumstances it was reasonable enough to expect the drive to the hospital to be conducted in silence.

Anyone could have been fooled into expecting the long, curved, tree lined driveway to lead to a country house. It had once. The imposing facade dominated the view once the drive had the house in sight: Victorian brick gothic with little turrets and imposing windows framed in cut limestone, steep roofs soaring above the large columns guarding the substantial entrance of oak double doors. Someone had to say something, and it fell to Dr Simpson to attempt to ease Richard into this new world. 'Here we are,' he said, gruffly, as if grudgingly maintaining professionalism. Neither Richard nor Margaret said anything: new places, new situations absorb or swallow words rather than produce them.

Dr Simpson didn't seem familiar with the place in the way that might be expected: doctors knowing everything about anything. He bumbled while trying to sustain a sense of confidence in both himself and his patient. In this way they walked down a corridor too far, leaving behind a carpeted foyer warmed by a coal stove and graced with prints of English pastoral scenes. Several easy chairs and an antique table holding a few copies of Country Life magazines completed an unthreatening interior. Instead, the corridor they found themselves in was bare of all embellishment, a black line along both sides at waist height, opaque windows giving very little light. Here a man blocked their way. He had before him a bucket full of a soapy substance, and in one hand a large scrubbing brush. His posture kneeling on a folded cloth was what made Margaret stare: the man had rolled up his trouser legs so that the pallid white of his lower legs was visible as he vigorously drew the brush left and right, forward and back over the polished brick floor. Immediately behind him, like the preening tail feathers of a bird, the man held his bare lower legs vertically, the soles of his shoes pointing at the ceiling. Seeing people approach, he made no effort to move.

Instead, he strained his head upwards to give them a wide leer. In a high-pitched voice he said, 'Got t'keep scrubbin' and cleanin', ain't we?' The doctor held Margaret and Richard, steering them round, back the way they'd come. 'So sorry,' he murmured, adding, 'they may have changed the layout.' Back in the country house foyer, Dr Simpson peered around himself carefully,
'Ah,' he said, 'this way,' and knocked on a side door, opening it impatiently. Inside, a heavy man rose from behind a desk.

'Do come in,' he said, waving one arm. Since there were only two chairs for visitors, the doctor indicated that Margaret and Richard occupy them. The man behind the desk seemed to hesitate, as if he thought this odd or inappropriate. But Doctor Simpson ignored this and introduced Mr and Mrs Ward. The man nodded, making no attempt to leave his position of authority to shake hands. He wore a dark blue suit and tie of such plainness that Margaret at first mistook it for a uniform. The only embellishment he wore was a tiny circular badge containing a tiny white cross on his left lapel. Since he was not, apparently, going to introduce himself Dr Simpson did. 'This is Mr Thurrock,' he said.

Margaret nodded; Richard looked.

'Mr Thurrock,' the doctor continued, 'is in charge here.'

A silence followed which seemed difficult for anyone to break. Mr Thurrock sat and drew a piece of paper to himself. Margaret had already decided that she didn't like the man, that if it were she who had been brought here she would find him and the whole place frightening. She found distasteful the fleshy pink of his face, the fat nose, the ears sticking out from a skull of very short cropped hair - like a German she thought - what is it, a crew cut? Richard, she saw, merely gazed, his reaction impossible to guess. But the Doctor Simpson broke the uneasy silence.

His cleared his throat and said, 'Er, perhaps, sir, you could outline for Mr and Mrs Ward, brief details of the treatment here.'

Mr Thurrock roused himself, staring at the piece of paper as if for guidance. As an official preliminary he coughed, looked up and said, 'There will be an initial period of examination and diagnosis.' His words were hoarse, forced, as if he had some permanent constriction in his throat. Margaret couldn't take in a word he said.

'A day or so,' Dr Simpson interpreted.

Mr Thurrock nodded.

Margaret thought, What, a day or a few days?

'And then,' Mr Thurrock added, 'as the Americans say, we'll take it from there.' He consulted the paper again. 'Now,' to Dr Simpson, 'if I could have your signature.' The doctor signed, ponderously, as if such a favour had to be wrung out of him. Margaret became aware that tears were beginning to threaten, that in the well of her stomach the familiar weight that dragged her down had reappeared. Mr Thurrock stood and coughed. The interview was at an end. He stood and picked up Richard's small black case, as he might a dog's lead, and walked to the door. Not even glancing at Margaret or Dr Simpson, Richard followed. The logic of a man following his small, black case.

The car door wouldn't close. She tried again and it still would not *clank-click* shut properly. Margaret felt inadequate, so familiar a sensation. Dr Simpson had to climb out of the driver's seat again, walk round and close it himself. Although a man of few words, his movements, his heavy breathing, the fixed set of his jaw told her that he had had enough, that he wanted to retrieve his normal world of patients seen one by one in the comfort of his own home.

When he stopped outside her home, Margaret managed a *Thank you, Dr Simpson,* turned and fled down her short front garden path to the embrace and security of her own cruel sanctuary. She sat at the kitchen table with one hand on her belly, cradling her chin in her other hand. What was it the doctor had said? She knew she must focus on this as if on a lifeline thrown to her. Expecting. Expecting Richard to get better? No, no, the other meaning of the word. A baby. Richard's. Mine.

Even though Dr Simpson had tried to reassure her that he'd fetch Richard himself the next day, she paced the house, as if to check that Richard was there, that the whole thing had been a dream, that somehow he must still be here, if only she could find him. In the kitchen the two breakfast plates, unwashed in the sink, under greasy cutlery could have given her some hope. But she'd reached this last: the stairs had been first where she ran up with some temporary energy of desperation, the cold air of the empty upstairs bedrooms and bathroom hitting her in the face, then the sitting room where the fire had gone out, the dining room shiny, clean and clinical, and finally the kitchen once more. It was done.

She stood in the hallway with both hands pressed to her head, still wearing her coat and beret, allowing tears to flow freely, copiously. There was nowhere else to go, nothing left to do, nothing she could do. Richard had gone and she didn't know when he'd be back.

A buff envelope could fall through the letterbox any time day or night and tell her that he was missing. Or another would float down onto the doormat and tell her that he'd never existed, that in any case, he'd never been her husband. Yet another could crash onto the mat and tell her that she was evil, immoral, had committed adultery, had murdered a child and would be sent to prison, that the whole thing, her life and his absence was all her fault. There was nothing in her life that she could see, could touch, could embrace which she could unreservedly see as good or worthy. Nothing she could feel proud of, no solid structure on which she could stand and feel that she'd achieved something. Where once she could remember the fun, now the fun had receded so far as to be irretrievable, therefore as good as forgotten, as good as never having existed.

The telephone rang. Its compelling tone exploded inside Margaret's head. It tore into her in relentless pulses, on and on, a deliberate ringing torture. She couldn't shift herself the two paces required to reach the phone, nor release her hands from her head. In any case, her eyes were blinded with tears, and she had lost her sense of direction which way the instrument lay, and the noise came at her from all sides, from inside as well as outside her head. Behind this lay the certainty that she wouldn't be capable of speaking to the unknown person the other end of the line. It would be someone intent on heaping upon her further indignity, further cruelty.

Chapter 13.

A nurse is pushing a mobile bed which clatters and crashes when she uses it to push open the door to the room where Richard waits. The man on the mobile bed is trying to say something to her. He's a tired man, defined by weary worry lines on his face, and pallid, sagging cheeks. His words are slurred and his hands are tight fists. Richard sees that the nurse is looking closely at him, her next patient, as if assessing his height and weight, whether or not he might make a fuss.

Richard feels rising again that sense of panic, that sense of the inevitability of things:

Me next, me next. Thunk.

The nurse has to pause in her pushing because, being an old building, there's a step the other side of the waiting room. She has to first open the door and then find a piece of wood which will act as a smaller step, halving the height of the permanent one. During this window of adjustment, the man on the bed assembles himself sufficiently to groan as an aid to attracting Richard's attention.

'It knocks you out, mate,' he whispers, 'Honest, pal, I wouldn't have agreed. I'd have said no.'

Richard watches as the man closes his eyes, as if pretending he'd said nothing, as if he can relax. But there's something about the man which is uncomfortable: his chin looks pushed too close to his nose. Ah, Richard thinks, a fellow prisoner - the toothless men he'd been used to.

The nurse trying to lift the front of the bed up over the step says, 'Now, come along Mr Hodge.' Cool air pours in through the open door.

The man's head is almost level with Richard's when he whispers, 'It knocks you out mate, it knocks you clean out.'

The nurse is panting with the effort of lifting the back end of the mobile bed when she says, 'Now, now, Mr Hodge, it's not as bad as that!' Then the bed is through the door and clattering over the red earthenware tiles of the corridor.
Moments later the nurse is back, the clattering lighter, and she has with her another nurse. 'Just sit on the bed here if you please, Mr Cooper. Then please lie down with your head on the pillow.'

So, Richard lay, as if felled, on the bed, as if having submitted to the sword, and is wheeled away. He hears the second nurse sighing as if it is the end of the world when the bed will not obey the order to remain trundling down the middle of the echoey corridor, until the first nurse corrects the sideways impetus with a jerk reinforced by an intake of breath. A door is opened and Richard feels the bed slow and swerve into a side room.

This was a small room, like an incidental store room, but which now held a chair and small table on which lay a wooden box with several dials and switches. Black coated wire stretches from the box to a pair of headphones. Rising from the chair a man in a white coat said, 'Right- ho', and 'Good morning, sir,' as if meeting by chance at the entrance to somewhere important. He indicated the space where the bed should go as if the nurses might have forgotten where to position his patient; which was with his head next to the control box and chair where the doctor stood. The nurses sat quietly on a small bench to one side. The only sound in the room was the heavy breathing of the second nurse, and the whisper of the Doctor's white coat as he stood and leaned over his patient.

'Jolly good,' the man whispered because he was a man who evidently distrusted silence.

Richard felt something, he presumed headphones, being pushed over his head and positioned above his ears, instead of on them.

'This won't take long,' the doctor murmured, 'please lie at ease.'

Words Richard never heard in his Army days. Instead, the words migrated into a fantasy from the past:

Please kneel at ease while your head is cut off.

He heard an intake of breath from one or both of the nurses.

What happened next Richard couldn't afterwards remember. In the sense that he'd remember a detail, say, like a man whose neck needed an extra one or two cuts, or a headless body that twitched longer than usual. All he could tell himself afterwards was that it was like being hit, punched, or knocked on the head by a giant wielding a mallet. The next thing was waking and wondering where he was in a bed with what looked like black smudges smearing his eyes and the weight of a headache the thumping pain of which he'd never before experienced.

Glancing painfully round, he saw that the nurses had gone, and another man was lying in another bed next to his and vague memories of the man's lined features.

When Richard rubbed his face, it was because of the tears which cascaded down his face. Not the tears of sorrow and loss but the tears he'd suppressed when the camp was a place of execution and he had what he could only express as an excess of experience, an excess of terror.

But a voice forced itself through to him. 'Say you've got a bad headache, mate,' the man in the next bed was saying, 'keep telling them and they'll carry on with the aspirins. The longer you keep that up the longer you can put off the next one.'

Richard tried to turn his head to see if this was the Mr Hodge who had spoken to him earlier, but the pain in his head prevented this. Although he had a blanket over him, he was cold, and getting colder. But another feeling rose: a sense of exasperation, of asking why am I like this? Yet at the same time he was surprised that he should be thinking this, that he should say to himself that he was a man battered by things others did, not by anything he'd done to himself.

But the man in the next bed hadn't finished. 'This is the second, or bugger it, the third time and I don't think it done me no good.'

This time Richard, by working out how to first swivel his hips, then his legs, followed by his torso, was able to turn and, fighting the assault of his headache, see the man, to try to gauge what he was like, or how he, Richard, might be like him.

What he saw was what he thought might be a wizened old man: the cheeks fallen in furrowed rows, the forehead flattened out of the uprightness of younger days, the bushy eyebrows of age, and the pale eyes which squinted through sketched, stretched lines. At the same time Richard brought both hands to his own cheeks and forehead to feel and gently probe his own head and face but was unable to find age or exhaustion in the same measure as the man with whom he now shared this small room. All he was left with was some compelling idea that he shouldn't be here, that he wanted, with all his soul, to get away, to return to his home burrow and think through some idea of who he was and what he should do. At the same time, he felt that this notion, vague and swimming somewhere just above his head, was something that had not sprung into his mind before. What was more, behind this feeling, but permeating it was the thought that he'd been forced to abandon Margaret for a second time. Inside himself he found that some new compulsion was suddenly clinging on to him - that this was a resolve, a steely promise that he'd never again do this. No, not even if Dr Simpson said he should. He swung his legs off the bed and sat up.

His head hurt, but he knew what he'd have to do.

Half way home, past the long stately drive to the hospital, past the Common this side of the town, down the long slope to the outskirts of the town, skirting the top of the High Street, through the park with the pond where fathers, uncles and grandfathers launched their sons', nephews' and grandsons' sailboats, up the alley way past the walled-in secret Georgian mansions, and out onto the main road and into the brave new England of brick-built semis and detached houses up cul-de-sacs; then past the new general hospital until he strode up Dicksons Drive, still a man with a purpose, with an energy he willed with all his strength to last him out until he reached the very head of the drive – and Margaret.

Seconds later, he sees her surprise, her worry, her incomprehension and as he takes her in his arms, he knows he can wipe out all three.

Standing in the hall, Richard sees that Dr Simpson is at his most serious, and tries to think of a joke about him which might amuse Margaret later on. But the good doctor is not pleased.

Richard forces himself to speak first. Even so, there just a hint in his mind of a realisation that he is in charge, that he knows what he wants, and that this does not include new-fangled treatments as brutal as the one the doctor imposed upon him. 'I refused further treatment,' he says. 'I'm not having that again. It's two days ago and I slept a lot more than usual and feel much better.

and consider that I don't need any more of this kind of treatment.'

Margaret holds her breath, as if this would in some way end this scene, or better remove it altogether from this room, and then from memory. She has to resist the urge to clasp her head with both hands, and like a child think she can hide from these two men who have been and are her prop and security.

'Can we sit down?' Doctor Simpson says quietly, and automatically heads from the hallway and his early morning breath into the lounge, and moves one of the two easy chairs round so that it's facing the settee. Margaret and Richard sit on the settee to await, like two naughty children, whatever the doctor is going to say, whatever punishment he is about to inflict.

Dr Simpson coughs. 'Mr Ward,' he says, ' this is your decision. While I might not agree with it, and if you're certain that you will refuse further ECG treatment, I will have to go along with it.'

There's a silence in the room which no one wants to break: Margaret because she's shocked by this exchange between her husband and the Doctor, and because she's wondering why Dr Simpson wasn't more assertive.

But the good doctor wants to press on, time being of the essence in his professional life. Looking at Margaret he says, 'I've had the tests back,' and, 'they are all right but I think that I would feel happier if you had the birth in the hospital.' He lets this sink in, watching for a reaction from Margaret and Richard. They glance at each other, but that is all.

The ball still being in the doctor's court, he clears his throat again. 'But you must appreciate that this is in the nature of a precaution, not because I or they think something's wrong. Er –.' He knows he's in danger of making things too complicated, 'Current medical thinking,' he continues, 'is moving away from child-bearing at home towards hospital births. So that, in the unlikely event of there being any problems, the resources and knowledge of that institution are readily and quickly available. And, of course, the few days of post-natal care which follow can be very useful to both mother and baby in establishing ..'

There was more, but Margaret could not hear it through the clamour of thoughts about the hospital, of not being at home, of not having Richard there with her all the time - hospital looming as some kind of exile, separation. But then childhood memories kicked back in. Dr Simpson - his writ wrote large as her mother might say - for so long the saviour of the family, if you forget him taking Richard to that awful hospital. You place yourself entirely at the feet of a saviour, you do what such a person says. You obey. Looking at Richard, she nodded for both him and herself. Richard himself, she saw, hardly reacted, was not going to object, but touched her hand, and saw that the doctor accepted that this was their way of agreeing. He let out a half-suppressed breath and drew his bag of tricks onto his lap. 'And now,' he said, looking at Richard, 'if you don't mind, a brief examination to see that all's going well, even though I have no reason to think otherwise.'

Looking at Richard, he added, 'A routine check-up. We'll go into the kitchen, if you don't mind.'

Margaret watched Richard rouse himself, and haul himself up off the settee to walked slowly out into the kitchen, to the place where the doctor has chosen to examine him. She hears the kitchen door quietly close.

Dr Simpson sits on what he now knows is Margaret's chair, Richard on the chair he sat on before he went to war. 'Just raise your shirt,' the doctor murmurs, pushing forward his stethoscope, directing and prodding it on Richard's chest. 'Turn around, please,' he mutters and wields the instrument at points across Richard's back. 'Thank you,' he says.

Richard tucks his shirt back into his trousers and awaits the diagnosis. This comes in the form of a nod, the hint of an affirmatory grunt, the muttering of a single word, 'Good', and a rapid departure.

It was a day after this that, before breakfast, Richard put on his brown suit at told Margaret that he was going to Warburton and Nailors's. She hadn't expected him to go immediately; and his rapid departure left her with that unwelcome sense of abandonment she knew so well, where time was either on hold or ran away with itself so that a morning or afternoon vanished into an ether of forgetfulness. This had her wander about the house as if looking for him, expecting to find him still there.

In between these bouts of uncertainty, she forced herself to wash up and put away the breakfast things, sweep the kitchen floor, make their bed, wash and hang out in the garden a kitchen cloth and several knickers. Lunch then became an automatic thing to think about. She looked into the kitchen cupboard and found potatoes and the half of last week's cabbage. But it was the notion of sausages which sprang into her mind - a quick dash, bearing all before her, to the High Street.

Coincidences happen and when they do, they often have ascribed to them notion of fate, or of a divinity overseeing what happens. So it was that she encountered Richard after the secret Georgian pathway and just across the park - a tall figure marching towards her, oblivious to the world, snug or trapped in his own preoccupations. She giggled as she touched his arm and saw how he stopped and stared down at her in something like a moment of anxiety.

'Ah,' he said, I'm starting back there on Monday. 'They lost several men in the war, and were surprised to see me.' and adds, 'Part time to start with, until orders build up -.'

Margaret has to think through thoughts which flood in: Richard away all day, she left alone with this weight, this swollen belly in front of her, of no longer able to watch Richard all the time in case he should unaccountably revert to a silent self, a huge presence in a silent home, and which excluded her.

A couple or three weeks pass before the good doctor comes to see Margaret and almost smiles that all's well. It's one of the days Richard is not at work.

'And how's your job going?' Dr Simpson asks, 'How long is it now?'

Richard thinks for a moment, contemplates the uneven passage of time and eventually replies, 'Nearly two weeks, I think.'

The doctor nods and his face closes in with the weight of the next appointment, and the ones after that. Richard follows the doctor to the door, opens it and finds that Dr Simpson is waving to him to follow him out into the front garden and then beckons him up the garden path.

'I've got a date with the hospital,' he says quietly. 'If she hasn't presented by this Friday, I'll take her in as a matter of some urgency - you're not to tell your wife that. I'll come again in two days' time, if I haven't heard from you. Good day to you.'

The first time Richard touched her bulging stomach which the flowing maternity dress failed to hide Margaret was surprised. Because at first, though knowing she was expecting, Richard had done that thing which she knew men do - take in the knowledge and then don't mention it again. The next time, when was it? As they were getting ready to go to the High Street, he smiled when he touched her. A discreet smile, almost hidden, but there because their eyes met as if in confirmation that this was a smile, not a grimace, as he opened the front door and touched her shoulder as if to guide her in the right direction.

When a time of panic occurs, it feels as if life before was all sweet and lightness, but what might happen next is so unpredictable and frightening as to be scarcely imaginable. Although there was a plan to get Margaret to the hospital as quickly as possible, when it happened it was different. It was 2 o'clock in the morning and she said her waters had broken. He didn't know what she meant, even though she must have told him this would happen. He phoned but no taxi replied to his calls. He'd got Margaret downstairs into the lounge where he could now hear her groaning - a deeper and more urgent sound than he'd ever heard before.

'I'll be straight back,' he called.

Knocking on Elsie's door seemed to take a long time before it opened to a drowsy but suspicious neighbour, taking in at one gaze his grey dressing gown. But Richard delivered his message just as Elsie's delighted and surprised face appeared behind her husband's.

'Could you please – come now, it's urgent?'

While her husband stood there mute, as if he needed more words, more information; Elsie had the car keys off the hook by the telephone and jangled them in her his face.

Suddenly he understood. 'Ah, yes, of course.' And to Richard, 'Get her ready and I'll bring the car round immediately!' And like a man of action he ran out of the house, the hem of his own dressing gown flying out behind him.

How Richard forced himself into the delivery room he couldn't afterwards remember. What remained of the memory of this time was Margaret screaming, 'Richard, Richard!' Lying on the delivery bed with nurses rushing hither and thither, her voice was so urgent, so pitiful that nothing else existed for him but to be with her. Crouched by the head of the bed he held onto her hands and would not be moved despite the mid-wife calling for reinforcements in the form of a doctor and several more nurses. They were white with fury and embarrassment, called on him to pull himself together, but were powerless to prise apart this man and woman because a birth was about to happen, and the world itself dictated that this, above all other considerations, would have to be done first.

Clutching Margaret, Richard watched in an almost detached way as he remembered it later, how he'd never seen her face so red with effort, how she pushed with the seeming strength of a wrestler, how she panted when they said she had to, when she pushed again and again to their urging, straining as if she had run a mile, she filled the room with a wild mixture of scream and moan and the timbre of her throat made the cellulite lamp shades crackle.

It was a long and difficult birth before the baby was launched into the world on a tide of blood and mucus which shot off the bed and spread over the pristine linoleum floor and the baby lay for a few seconds of blurry-eyed contemplation of this new, lit world of faces peering at it, and then opened its mouth and shrieked the place down with the shock and discomfort of being born.

'It's a girl!' someone said which, later, Richard was sure was his own voice.
Hands made a grab for the baby and it was carried across the room by the doctor, thrust onto a small bed,

and bundled into a tiny blanket by a nurse. Richard saw this, but what he heard was worse: Margaret screaming, 'No, no! Give her to me!'

Richard moved faster than anyone else across the delivery room and snatched up the baby. Half way across the room he was met by the doctor and a nurse. These he dodged, as if on the rugby field of long ago. At the same time the other two nurses launched themselves across the room towards him but immediately slipped on the blood and mucus on the floor, colliding with the doctor and nurse who were on their way back across the room. The four of them lay dazed and entangled for the few moments Richard needed to give the baby back to Margaret, and to grasp her round the shoulders, the three of them united and immutable.

How Margaret and Richard found laughter deep down in some mysterious workings of their minds and bodies they would never know. But it came from a profound well or spring for so long suppressed.

Laugh they did and somewhere a bell rang and rang as if the whole world should be awakened and made witness to what had happened.

Not long after this both mother and baby slept and were wheeled into a small hospital room. Richard may have remembered a voice, possibly the doctor's saying something like, 'Come along, Mr Ward, you'll need some sleep as well. They'll give you the visiting hours at the desk as you leave.' A firm voice, but no longer one of outrage.

Outside, in the cool night air of moderation, Richard stopped and considered: why am I not exhausted? Two policemen bustled past him and into the hospital, bothered and irritated. An owl hooted somewhere opposite the hospital where the green stretches out along the main road and past the ancient pond before reaching Dicksons Rise. Filled with a huge need to go and tell someone Richard turned left towards the High Street. In the moonlit park he found he wanted to skip. And did, surprising himself that it felt so easy.

By the time he reached the High Street a vague glow had forced its way into night, and human life: early traffic and the busy feet of workers, began to suggest notions of an approaching day. He told a hurrying postman that his daughter had just been born, he told a busy milkman, he told a large man in tough trousers and huge scarf, carrying a bag of tools. But, at last, on the dusky high street a light falling across the pavement from the all-night cafe had him stop. People, an audience were inside, and this is what he wanted. When he told the blousy lady who took the tuppence for mug of all-night tea she announced the good news to the whole cafe. The tramps, the down-and-outs, the shift workers and the insomniacs stood, clapped and cheered. A large, motherly woman hugged him, saying in a raucous voice, 'It's a marvel, love.' And someone else shouted, 'Or more like a bloody miracle!' And someone else yelled, 'And we need lots more of them after this bloody war!'

Later, Richard pulled himself up Dicksons Rise. Although light filled the Rise, day had not yet started because light lingered behind drawn curtains and the locked doors where patient bottles of milk stood at attention. At the top of the drive where the seldom seen car or van does a complete circle to beat a retreat from the Rise, Richard stops. He wants to shout something, but can't think what. Perhaps he stood thinking about this for a vital few seconds too long because a figure wreathed in a long, grey dressing gown and a headscarf which barely conceals her curlers, emerges like a latter-day wraith. Her face is so animated, so urgent, so tell me, so what is it? He finds he cannot run, hide, recoil from Elsie who seems so full of the thrill which fills him; so filled with Margaret, and with the baby, that he cannot pretend he has not seen her. Even his face, grinning, compels him to engage with her, so that to his astonishment he flings his arms round her and says, 'It's a girl. It's all right, they're all right!'

'How wonderful, dear, and what's her name going to be?'

Richard steps out of his embrace of Elsie, to consider, to look down the line of Margaret's pregnancy, but finds no discussion of possible names for a boy or a girl. But Elsie is standing there, her eyes locked onto his and must be answered. The name "Sally" leaps into his mind. Yes, in a few hours' time he'll go back to the hospital and plead a special dispensation because visiting hours are only in the afternoon and say *Sally* and watch how Margaret reacts. Dimly, he hears Elsie make a noise or noises of approval, and this is when a sudden chill of exhaustion hits him. He turns and stumbles down his driveway, fumbles for his keys, and hardly hears what Elsie is trying to say, but it could have been about breakfast. But he was past that, past anything but sleep.

The day came, a Saturday, when Richard and Margaret were to make a public appearance with the baby in the new second hand pram that Rose had found advertised on a card in one of the tobacconists on the High Street: a large pram, a limousine of prams with its great curled springs, one for each of the four big wheels. Tom had somehow got the wheels off so that it could be taken the few miles to Dicksons Drive; and somehow got Rose as well into the old Ford. Looking like an abandoned waif, rescued into luxury, Sally slept or gazed at nothing with dreamy dark eyes. Old ladies smiled at them in a way that was new, and felt empowered to glance into the pram and coo.

So it was that an old man stopped and peered. Mr Bailey from the Bank, who leant heavily on a stick. 'Wonderful', he said, peering more closely. 'I do congratulate you both. I am so delighted for you.'

Tears of sympathy sprang into Margaret's eyes because Mr Bailey had to blow his nose and wipe his eyes. Margaret sees how retirement has bent him so soon into old age, and lightened his eyes as if old age does not require the sharpness of earlier days.

'All change at the bank,' he murmurs, 'New manager, new broom, - . But I'm happy to have put all that behind me - . As you may or may not know, I lost my wife a few months ago. So, the days are long - .'

Long. Mr Long.

'And the manager, Mr Long?' Richard asked.

' Ah, he has also left - .' and it seemed at first that he deliberately stopped himself adding something. But he rallied, drew breath and glanced up and down the High Street.

'Irregularities,' Mr Bailey whispered, staring past them, as if to disassociate himself from what he added. 'And a, er, certain illness, I do believe.' Then sighed, to indicate that he would say no more, that he was a man unaccustomed to passing on gossip, particularly as that gossip had included the word, syphilis, which the Manager had caught in the West End.

Mr Bailey peered once more into the pram, touched the brim of his hat and whispered, 'So wonderful,' smiled, and touching his hat again, turned and walked slowly away, scarcely having to rely on his old man's walking stick.

Chapter 14.

DEPARTURE

AUGUST 2000

Sal has to clear the house. It's the first and last time she'll ever have to do this. The relief on Phil's face when she said she wanted to go alone to see the extent of the job was palpable. She sees how death can lend embarrassment to routine things, rendering negotiation between family members fraught with difficulty. Not least of all that this preference is code for other things which wash around in her mind: some kind of more personal goodbye to her parents, incomplete after the funeral; perhaps a goodbye to parts of her former self; perhaps the beginning of a new look at these two people from her side of the great divide between life and death. Something she feels she wants to do alone. At least, at this stage, this is how she thinks of it. Phil is needed, but later.

So first she's going to walk round the silent house. She wants to find, as she looks into each room, what thoughts will spill into her mind, or flow into it from the aura of the place, from the contemplation of her parents' death, from the fact that she's never been alone in this house since she left home for goodness knows what, thirty-five, forty years ago? Here it is that she was conceived, grew up and from whence she went forth into the world, *and multiplied*, Phil would have added.

There was one thing, though, that she's brought with her through the front door, struggling with the yale key which had never fitted properly. This was the regret which didn't so often surface now, but had strongly at the run-up to and the actual funeral, that she didn't have a brother(s) and/or sister(s) - her thoughts usually included brackets and slashes - not only to share the weight of death and a funeral, but also to distribute in lesser loads the daunting weight of memory enshrined in this, the family home, and delve for others from the collective gene pool of a sibling or siblings.

Wandering about like this, trying to retrieve other, illusive memories not only of her own but of her parents, she has no one outside her immediate family to consult, ask, and compare memories. She has no brother or sister, no old or close friend, either, to share this with in a way which would spark forgotten memories she wants to recall. Do you remember the time when - ?, from the dark flint of the past. This burden seems unfair, but it also seemed unjust that she should still see it like this because she's lived with it for so long. What else could she expect? After walking round her parents' house several times, she told herself that she'd have to do what came next on her own: dispersing, throwing away, packing up the lives of her parents. And in the process tampering with her own memories, adjusting, and reappraising them on her own. Some she'd be able to share with Phil. But even he, she knew, would or could only take so much, and would weary of this burden. Indeed, she had to acknowledge that she'd been like this when his mother died in her nineties: someone else's spontaneously retrieved memories have to be rationed, gently tendered and then put away for a better day.

Of course, she'd often looked at the old, nearly antique furniture, the faded and tired old-fashioned wallpaper, and the knickknacks: the mug from the Isle of Wight, the little box from Skegness, the tiny wooden bagpipe from Scotland: the destinations of a forgotten age. To her the 40s and 50s seem little more than a hangover from the 20s and 30s, (for god's sake, it was nearly sixty years ago) interrupted by WW2 which the National Curriculum demanded she do with her Year Sixes.

Was she getting the idea, the concept, of how the forties was the 'pivotal' decade of the twentieth century, and how WW2 and the atom bombs on Japan were the 'hinge' events of the last century? Did they, would they understand this and internalize it? Would this influence them in the mists of the future?

When the topic came up on the curriculum, she'd phone her parents for first-hand knowledge; 'Mum, where did you get milk, what shape were the bottles? Remind me about pounds, shillings and pence, and ration books. Oh, and air raid shelters, where was yours? Were you evacuated? And did you remember to carry your gas mask all the time?' On the other end of the line, she'd wait for the pause as her mother delved and retrieved memory - a silence that always seems so much longer when you have no body language to fill the gap. Sal would be impatient; she'd think of all the jobs she could take a rush at during those few seconds: wipe the electric hob, unload the dishwasher, add sugar and honey to the shopping list. But then the thin, querulous voice of her mother would creep back on the breath of a sigh, 'Well, dear, it was a long time ago, but I think -.'

And now that Sal can't ask, the questions she wants answered rise like new roadside hoardings overnight: did everyone pull together, could you get soap, what about the food that wasn't rationed, where did you get your ration book from, were eggs easy to get, were there shortages of something most weeks, what happened to people whose houses were bombed flat while they survived in air raid shelters? These lost, never-to-be settled questions loom large; their answers unconceived, never to live, never to become part of her.

So where do you start? she thinks, because she's still standing in the hallway where daylight is filtered by the stained-glass window set into the top third of the front door. Ah, memory: the distorted face of Len the postman, changing from red to green and back again as he stooped to deliver. Oh, and that strange look on her mother's face when official looking envelopes slapped onto the doormat. Her trembling fingers.

What was that all about? Just a letter from the council about the rates, or an income tax form or changes to the rubbish collection. The harmless buff envelope then left on the living room mantle-piece for her father to open, to deal with. Which he'd often forget for days.

But this brief recollection allows a plan to be realised: she'd start upstairs and work her way down. Last of all would be the sitting room - *the lounge, dear.* This way a pattern could be imposed on what otherwise might deteriorate into a random and therefore less acceptable attempt to think out how she'd do this thing called clearing out.

At the top of the stairs she's puffing. This both surprises her and has her think about her parents who were thirty or more years older - they'd managed these stairs up to the end. The deep green carpet with the brass stair rods, *oh god, it's raining stair rods,* which used to be taken up for the spring clean. The rods brassoed and gleaming; the carpet hung out along the washing line for an airing, then whacked with the carpet-beater to spruce and fluff it up. It even leant a fresh spring to your step as you went upstairs on the spick and span carpet and gleaming stair rods. She could almost feel that sense of renewal and accomplishment that her mother had clearly enjoyed: the whole house Spring Cleaned. Even - something for the Y6s - mother beating the carpets from each room over the line in the back garden with the kind of willow-wove beater they still use in places like Rumania and Bulgaria.

There's a choice on the landing: her room, her parents' room, the box room, or the bathroom. Sal's footsteps take her into the back bedroom, her room. The room where she grew up, where she had chicken pox, measles, whooping cough, the flu (why *the*?), tonsillitis and innumerable colds, her mother sighing over the handkerchiefs before assaulting them with bleach and elbow grease in the kitchen sink. And the times when the bed was moved into the middle of the room so that her quarantined self could tricycle round and round the room until the germs were judged to be gone, the scabs no longer infectious, and feeling well all the time stole back like a stranger. And like a stranger - of course, Dr what-was-his-name? Simonds, Sampson - Simpson! Who seemed like a giant and she was terrified of him with his heavy moustache and bulky presence and the way her mother ushered him into the house as if he were a celebrity. Later, her mother's hushed report to her father about the doctor's diagnosis, every word he said, every piece of advice about medication, length of time in bed, how long to convalesce before being allowed back at school. Then, later, at some indeterminate point in her childhood when she got what they called the 'Asian' flu, she remembers how ghastly she felt and of course calling the doctor appeared to be on the cards - how her mother burst into tears because she couldn't call Dr Simpson. And how she, Sal, had forgotten her mother's tears how long before this? When the good doctor had died and her mother mourned, and her parents went to his funeral and told her that he'd become very old and this is what happened to very old people. And you could tell from the hundreds of people who'd been at the funeral how good and much loved a doctor he'd been.

But *her room* was now a room from which her childhood had been excised. Instead, it preserved a teenage decor - posters of pop stars and film stars gleaned from magazines. Sal finds both sentimentality in looking back at her teen self and a mixture of embarrassment and regret that at this age she took her parents so much by surprise, while all the time she took them completely for granted. How her life and development knocked too many assumptions out of their world-view. It destroyed too many ideas of how a young woman should behave, develop, what it was appropriate for her to wear; yet she and they survived. But now she thinks, at what cost to these two people who got really old, who had somehow to survive a world where everything they knew seemed to be knocked down one by one, turned upside down, changed or discarded? But certainly disregarded, outdated, forgotten. Except by her age group. Except at a time like this.

As she's about to push open her parents' bedroom door, Sal's surprised by a sense of violating their privacy - as if they're still there, merely hadn't got up this morning, were lying in, perhaps too old to make the effort of staggering into the bathroom, washing and then facing the difficult task of choosing clothing appropriate to whatever the weather might be doing that particular day.

'Ah,' Dad had once said, 'It's an effort, Sal, you have to fight your body from the moment you wake up.' Just that and no more though, because he'd smiled that way he had where he pulled his lips into a grimace denied by the rest of his face.

'Smile properly, Dad, smile properly,' she'd wished she could say. She wanted to hug him, squeeze it out of him, but he'd already, as he did, turned away, embarrassed by the burden of an unwilling confession, the slipping of the mask. Revelations were not permitted; a thing Sal realises that she'd never accepted. Poor Phil, to put up with her furrowed anxieties and regrets, her rushes of tears-stained words.

The bedroom's as tidy as it always was. Why should this be a surprise? She'd blundered in after Dad died, trying to help Mum with something or other, 'Oh, do fetch my scarf, dear. Even though it's May, there's a bit of a nip in the air.' On autopilot, *What's that, dear?* Sal walks past the two single beds and pulls open the heavy, dusty smelling curtains. How long did they used to be kept drawn after death anyhow? Oh, and the black band Dad used to wear when one of his British Legion pals went. Things change and you hardly notice until they're put to the test.

Sal looks back at the twin beds. What would she feel, she wonders, if she was looking down at her parents' double bed which she and Phil got·rid of ten or more years ago? It had been a crisis, almost worse than any she, Sal, had had to cope with. Would her parents have to occupy separate rooms?

It's his muttering, dear, your father - talks in his sleep and keeps turning over, sometimes shouts about blood and heads and a sword.

But when Sal had prodded and pushed the mattress, she wondered how anyone could have derived any comfort from the spread of lumps and twists of old springs, apart from the deep slope from both sides which must have propelled them both into the middle. But the pale, shocked faces when Sal suggested separate bedrooms. Their faces when they considered the full horror of such a divorce as sleeping in separate rooms. Her mother's tears, her father's silence, when all they had to do was say, No. It was Phil who thought of the twin beds. To her great relief he volunteered the tricky task of suggesting this compromise.

'In the car taking them home,' he said, 'I think they've agreed, because they didn't actually object. In fact, they said nothing, though I'm certain your Mum nodded. It's a half- way house, a compromise. We'll try that. It might work.'
Dad on the left-hand side, Mum on the right. The same way round as in the old double bed, the same sides but now in twin beds. She looks down at her father's bed. Her mother had led her by the hand, like her childhood regained, and they had both stood side by side looking down at the shape the drawn-up sheet made of the husband and father.

There's a brief moment when Sal sees that her mother's breathing suggests that she wants to say something.

And she does: 'I brought him up his usual cup of tea,' she says, 'and I thought something was wrong.'

Sal watches her mother fight for words.

' - and he'd gone, gone in his sleep. I don't know, don't know when ....and the doctor, the new one said it was difficult to say.'

But she hadn't finished and Sal was still trying to take all this in when, her mother pulls the sheet back as she might have uncovered a piece of stored furniture, revealing this new father and husband as if he were still peacefully sleeping. But then her mother did something which shocked Sal: bending over stiffly she brought her lips onto her husband's, quickly stood upright again, and then with an almost impatient gesture flicked the sheet back over his head.

Standing there, Sal is still shocked by that image. It's still the last one she thinks of before fitful sleep, and it's still with her in the morning.

Sal thought they'd stand there a while longer this last time with her father, but the ticking of a diesel engine, followed by a heavy, official sounding knock at the door announced that the world knew, and knew exactly how to deal with it, and had come to do so in the guise of Alders Undertakers.

Although it's mid to late summer, the chill of the abandoned house brings out the goose flesh on Sal's arms. She shivers and tries to justify the coolness of this situation, refuses to see it as death drawing warmth out of the walls and the floors. As if prompted by this chill, she tugs at the top drawer of the chest of drawers - the one which all these years didn't like the idea of opening. But it now reveals that it had sheltered, all these years, her mother's other cardigans, the floppy button up ones.

Her hands pull out the top one - ah yes, that dark blue one, a kind of weary navy blue - which Sal can just about remember 'borrowing' for some solitary game. Her hands continue to complete a plan they had - to envelope her in the thumb-sucking comfort of her mother's cardigan. To be enveloped like this will be the only way she can manage to complete this mental appraisal of her parents' house, their belongings, their lives.

Behind this, too, there's a lurking sense of guilt. She'd been on the internet looking for ancestors. She's found her grandparents, Rose and Frank, who lived about quarter of an hour's drive from Dicksons Close. These shadowy, half remembered figures from her childhood. Phil said, 'We don't know anything about our grandparents, they're too often a complete blank to us'. Then he went to the life writing course at night school where they wrote things down about themselves and what they knew of their families: where they worked and the people they worked with, funny things, sad things. But not, as far as she could see, diving under the surface. Like what he felt when he, Phil, first met her; like what he felt when first Rachel, then Penny, then Oliver arrived. Or what he felt about himself, his hopes and fears, his ambitions, what it was like to be a man, a father, and a son in the twentieth and start of the twenty-first century. All this. She'd like to know. So would his grandchildren, if they had any from a generation intent on enjoyment, determined not to be so uncool as to marry, or have children, and in so doing to be or do anything like their parents.

Sal's careful down the steep stairs, reaches the dining room and is gazing at the glass fronted wooden cabinet where the exquisite but deeply unfashionable Japanese porcelain tea set is displayed. She remembers being allowed to hold up a cup to the light, pleased and interested in how the white porcelain with its dreamy Geisha delicately holding their umbrellas translucently glowing over their beautifully curved feminine poses.

So intricate, so civilised, so cultivated. Then the feather-light saucers and plates proclaiming a landscape of delicately suggested Impressionist trees, snow-capped mountains and the occasional picaresque, pointy little wooden house. The whole under a sky of gentle blue, where pink tinged clouds floated as pure decoration, threatening neither rain nor storm.

'Only one plate slightly chipped, dear,' she can hear her mother saying – a verdict on a lifetime of caring for the objects making of her wedding in the 30's, the central event of her life. 'Well, the cup - ,' she would add, a painful admission. She'd phoned Sal in tears after she'd dropped and smashed one of the cups. Phil had superglued it, taking hours of care, as if repairing a life. The cracks were scarcely visible, and he had demonstrated how it could still be used. Margaret's face, pale and tearful, unconvinced that something broken after sixty or more years could ever be whole again; convinced that she had broken, or at least damaged a part of herself and Richard. But she allowed the cup to re-join its fellows in the museum of her life, prompting her valedictory words, 'And we were careful to hardly ever use them.'
And Dad? He must have known all about it, but remained in Sal's memory of the incident somewhere in the background, shadowy, offering neither comfort nor condemnation. She has a moment of insight: was there something in her father, so broken, so fractured, that a broken Japanese cup was nothing, an external thing so small and insignificant compared to the huge themes of his life - the War when he was away - so silent a part of him - and separated for so long from her mother. Context, she thinks, the thousands of other husbands

and wives who were similarly separated; the thousands of men who never returned. Why make nothing of it? Why not celebrate the release from whatever prison, mental or physical, he'd been in? But he hadn't, or didn't, or couldn't.

On the glass shelf above the porcelain tea set is a small inscribed silver plaque leaning back onto a dark plastic support: Nailor & Warburton Engineering, in embellished gothic script at the top.

Underneath this in a more readable copperplate style: *'Presented to Richard Ward on the occasion of his retirement on the 7th of July 1979 after 38 years of dedicated service to the company'*.

She trawls back thirty-eight years from her father's retirement. This makes it 1941 when he started. There's something wrong here, she thinks, the War, he wasn't here. She shrugs, this is not the time for maths. I'll tell Phil later; he likes numerical mysteries.

Another thought wings in and grasps her in its talons: I've been doing genealogy at night school trying to find out about my husband and my grandparents but never bothered with my own parents. Why? Do I already know enough? Has the familiarity of fifty-nine years bred a subtle indifference? Some sense that they've always been here and I can ask all the questions I want at any time; so, there's no rush, no urgency. If I can just get through this particularly busy and fraught part of my life and emerge at the other end in one piece, I'll have the time and leisure to put all that right. This is, of course, the shining goal, the gateway to a new life next year when she retires. The other glittering goal is two years after that when Phil retires because he wants to go on to sixty-five. He explains about his pension being so much better if he does, and the Government wants everyone to work longer. After that he wants them to travel all round the world, wants them to go to all the places his grandchildren (if they have any) won't be able to reach because the oil will have run out, and the world being what it is, he says, there'll be a long gap before new fuel technologies catch up with the shrinking conditions of the emerging world situation.

This stew of grief and guilt for the lost lives of her parents and the lost opportunities of getting closer to them before the end is beginning to engulf Sal. And here it comes - the tears that drift, scarcely noticed at first, irresistibly down her cheeks, fuelled by this notion that she's missed out, she's been trying to find out more about her grandparents these last months when she should have been mining her parents for the details, achievements, missed opportunities and hopes in their lives. The grandparent generation exists solely in a few cold dates and addresses, her parents so much closer, surrounded by the eloquent but silent objects of their lives in this house, but so close, so familiar as to be ignored or unnoticed until it is too late.

Among the tears, it's as if Sal speaks to her hands which clasp and unclasp themselves, work together as if washing out so much dirt: I've allowed myself to be brought up in a museum instead of insisting on learning about these two vanished lives which could have told me so much. All these years I've treated them as if they've been ghosts, yesterday's people. People you're sort of responsible for, who need you, who'll phone up and need you to sort something out when you're rushing about in the middle of your crazy working life. Like that time half way through the OFSTED inspection when Phil was in Australia with his water heaters. What was that one? Oh, god the boiler packing up.

Tears for the boiler? And that time she made it all worse, at Phil's instigation, by giving them a mobile phone, which they could barely use, and mostly avoided taking it anywhere with them.

Sal turns, as if looking for something else to ease or distract her tears. Ah, the writing cabinet. As always unlocked, but seldom before an object of curiosity. She pulls up the slatted, curved cover, watches as it curls back into the top of the cabinet, revealing the writing surface watched over by the series of little drawers and the dark interiors of small partitioned shelves. The desk top is a jumble of papers, letters, bills and notices which spill out of crammed drawers, are stuffed into the little alcoves, are piled high on the writing surface. How could she have missed these in her search for overlooked, unpaid bills, debts, overdrafts, unanswered letters? But on further inspection the desk in the dining room appears to hold clutter resembling more a stratum revealed after an archaeological dig: papers that are tired, curling and brittle with age.

Carefully and at random she lifts one, her fingers delicately trowelling: *17th November 1947, 'Dear Sir - Yours faithfully, M. L. Burrell, Manager'*.

Her eyes blur again until she wipes her away tears.

'The matter has been exhaustively investigated and certain irregularities have been discovered. Do please make an appointment to see me. I took up my post as Manager in September and will be very pleased to meet my clients, particularly long-standing ones such as yourself.'

There's more, but more of nothing that means anything to her. The South Eastern Bank - was this taken over by - ? She delves deeper; it's all the same. The cabinet appears to have been closed at some time in 1947/8 and never reopened. Its place taken by? Of course, the kitchen table. The kitchen table, oddly, seemed to have become a sufficient depository for all subsequent missives where it was easy to find all that a reduced household economy might be involved in: the gas, electricity, the coke and coal, yes coal, even in the twenty-first century.

Of course, the post had to be opened on the kitchen table. Because it usually arrived by breakfast time, it was an early morning ritual she remembers her parents obeying before she, Sal, dashed out for the school bus, before Dad went off to work, walking in his measured way, swinging the walking stick he didn't need. She'd sit there while her father, who was the fetcher of the post, sorted through the envelopes in the unlikely event that one was not for him. Random letters from her eighty something year old grandmother, always addressed to her mother, might interrupt this ritual - or a post card from Margate, Littlehampton or the Isle of Wight from a friend. They would both study the postcard first, and make a game of guessing who had sent it and where it was, with a thumb over the name of the place. She wants to laugh over this game because they both needed strong glasses and couldn't cheat.

Until the genesis of unsolicited mail *What, dear?* most days there was no post, a kind of unspoken emptiness or absence. Nevertheless, the kitchen table became or replaced the desk - all bills and letters being placed on the side which rested against the kitchen wall, next to the toaster which was operated by her father because it had its own eccentricities and ways of doing things. This technical problem was long ago relegated to her father - it had to be pressed down slightly sideways, and the little lever adjusted which controlled the length of time a piece of bread needed, depending on the kind and thickness of the slice. Ah, yes, and sometimes any letters and bills which they needed to discuss were taken into the front room where decisions were jointly made on the sofa.

And after that? She presumes they were either thrown away, or had a long retirement among the growing jumble of ageing papers. She thinks of the meticulous way Phil stores all paid bills, accounts and letters under the umbrella of the you-never-know- when-rule. Well, presumably her parents never did need to search for lost documents, unanswered letters, as if living some kind of charmed life. But no, she thinks, was it instead a life so reduced, so limited that they avoided much of life's routine mistakes, periodic cock-ups, forgotten communications in the context of the mushrooming info of the computer age. Was this their way of coping with the late twentieth century, and which had somehow endured into the twenty-first? It's OK, Dad, where is

says fill in your bank details , address and so on, you don't need to.
It's only when you pay by credit card. You can still send a cheque - oh look, method of payment: tick this little box.

His watery blue eyes gazing into hers - *'What is a credit card, what are direct debits? Everything's out of focus - where are my glasses?'*

What else? Of course, the dining room table with its entourage of six chairs. A seventh which had to be brought in when they all sat down to Sunday tea - Oliver smouldering and resentful because he, as the youngest had to sit on the kitchen chair which was slightly lower as well as being different, having to sit on an exhausted dark red coated canvas which made it stand out as inferior to the heavier stained oak of the dining room suite. The chair which, immediately after tea, had to be taken back to the kitchen as if its incongruity offended the decorum and order of the dining room. But this was not all. The extensions at either end of the table had always to be pushed back so as to restore the table to its smaller, squarer shape and allow free movement round the room, and *Close the French windows please, dear, it's getting a bit -* .

Two chairs, the senior high-backed ones had, of course, to be moved away at the same time because in its smaller incarnation the table could only accommodate two ordinary backed chairs. Finally, the high-backed chairs had to be placed at an angle proprietorially either side of the French the windows. The dining room was thus restored to its customary state to await the disturbance of the next family meal.

And then, only then, all this having been done, could the washing up routine take place. The routine of Phil washing up the cups and saucers, the best plates and special cutlery; and of grandchildren drying everything with the tired dish cloths *Be careful with the plates, love, we've had them for more than sixty years,* while Mother and Father restored all the tea-'things' to their time-sanctioned allotted places - the cutlery at leisure in their special, cushioned boxes with the two catches, together with the best plates on discreet display in the glass-fronted dining room cabinet.

Sal stands in the small kitchen with both hands on her cheeks, and brushing away new tears gazes at the crowded presence of the hopper fed anthracite boiler - 1950s?, the gas cooker 1960s?, the fridge 1970s?, and the kitchen table against the wall which only sat three, as if this placed a limit on the size of the family. The floor to ceiling cupboard, very modern in the '30s, had a vent to the wild outside with a hit-and- miss open and close cover. In front of this Sal's mother kept the butter in its rural bliss dish and cover of honey suckle, lambs and calves to the end of her life.

Well, dear, it gets so hard in the fridge.

Sal pulls open the door of the kitchen cupboard to remind herself of the frugality she grew up in: small packets and bottles, always a small marmite, small tins of baked beans, small packets of flour. All these sparsely dotted about the shelves which were not used for the kitchen set of crockery.

Sal can't stop herself hearing repeated discussions, Mum, if you buy the big tins and packets, they last longer than two or three small ones.

Yes, dear, but things do go off so quickly, particularly in the summer.

You could keep them in the fridge.

Oh, no, dear, things dry out so quickly in refrigerators. Now pass me the gravy powder, would you.

Nothing superfluous, everything used up before replacement, a war time austerity carefully preserved. Sal compares this with her own overflowing cupboards with their choices of salad dressings, array of breakfast cereals, sugars, choice of teas, *What is organic tea, love?* coffee and soups, tins of everything - assembled from all over the world, offered on shelf after shelf in supermarkets, stored on shelf after shelf at home, often so hidden behind rivals that they pass their sell-by date and precipitate guilty thoughts about an over-indulgent waste of money, a guilty affluence compared to the Third World.

And Phil. Sal sees her husband at the sink which was finally changed in the 80s, bent over with the intense preoccupation of perfect washing up so as to escape for as long as he could from sitting in the front room with his in-laws, before the agonised drawing out of the farewell process: they, Sal and Phil desperately wanting to go and get on with the rest of their lives. Oh god, the lesson preparation, the charts and displays to think through, yet another policy to draft, and her parents embarrassed with having to cope with the awkwardness of separation. Nothing stated, nothing said. And in the car Phil barely suppressing a sigh of relief as he drives off aggressively, silenced, numbed. He would tell people that his own parents had relocated, as they say these days, to Spain; evacuated, as he called it. On a bad day when he needed a break, he called this the Great Escape because they were not around for urgent grandparent duties. Oh, of course, but that was when the children were small. Like yesterday.

In the front room *the lounge, dear,* Sal smiles as she runs her fingers over the rounded ogee of the old wind-up clock which she couldn't remember having worked recently. Had it always been twenty past five? No, it couldn't have. Her childhood was filled with glances at this clock - time for the school bus, time for Guides, time to go to a friend's birthday party, time to go to a disco, time to go to college, time to get ready for the wedding. So, when had it stopped? And why? With a forgotten, but automatic manual response, she pulls the clock forward on the shelf of the mantelpiece and feels behind it, immediately finding the key. As if she'd done so through her childhood years, every few days as regular as well, er, clockwork.

That Sal's scarcely remembered sequence so quickly reasserts itself, she thinks, must be because at one time it was her special job, along with bringing in a hod of coal for the lounge fire, washing up several times a week, all to earn her the one pound, or whatever it was, pocket money. Yes, you have to press the catch to allow the retaining glass over the hands to swing open on its tiny brass hinges, and insert the key into the keyhole just below the central point from where the hands radiate. Then wind it up, clockwise, just short of the tightest click, a matter of fine judgement, to avoid overstraining the spring.

Then, if necessary, carefully nudge the hands to reset the hour and minute to the correct time which is now twenty-three minutes past eleven. The clock then imposes or resumes its comfortable, comforting tick and tock of time in the silent room as if nothing has happened, as if its future, its very existence is not threatened. Oh, and during how in the hustle and bustle of the day you could hardly ever hear its discreet ticking. But at night, once the radio, *Oh, do turn off the wireless, Sally, that raucous music!* was switched off, the clock reasserted itself as if the keeping of time was a nocturnal preoccupation which could be safely abandoned during daylight hours. There were times when even with her bedroom door shut at night, Sal fancied she could just hear the reassuring mechanism of the night securely pass, safely measured in a constant mechanical heartbeat of life.

But all this comforting revisiting of childhood is almost immediately shattered because already eleven twenty-three has not passed, unmeasured, into history. The clock is silent. A wound up, dead clock. Is there anyone who can repair clockwork now?
Sally stands back to look at the silent clock from the middle of the room just below the burgundy tassels of the light shade.

From here she's aware for the first time how she's looking not at the nerve centre of the house but at its social and relaxational centre: to the left of the fireplace, in its recess, the bookcase harbours several rows of books which have not changed, titles which have not been replaced by newer ones as if the world stock of narrative is limited to these few strands and a defining date, and then there is the factual - a gardening book, the wedding of Princess Elizabeth and her later coronation, which have endured a lifetime's preoccupation by her parents as if they had needed no more than this. Then there is the shelf which presents the objects, trinkets and ornaments cataloguing a lifetime spent together by these two people, her parents, Margaret and Richard.

In the recess on the other side of the mantelpiece there's the shelf put up about twenty-five years ago by Phil to support the tired television which Sal knows her parents only used for watching the news and the weather forecast: BBC One on which, of course, they reverently watched the Queen on the afternoon of each Christmas Day, hanging on Her every word as it would inform and subtly guide them through the next year. It was as if they couldn't conceive of the existence of other channels - or were unaware or had rejected them.
Underneath the set and its shelf there's the rural style stool, the bulging turned legs, on which has rested, she thinks, from before her birth, the old wireless clothed in its tireless, reassuring Bakelite, awaiting the twist and click of its on/off and volume control knob to warm up its valves and fill the room with its mature and considered tone.

From the sofa on the right at an angle to the rake of the bay window, her parents sat in lengthy and easy proximity listening to the reassuring tone of The Home Service and concerts on The Third Programme, and the Light Programme, long after these were renamed and over-familiar voices chit-chatted rather than informed. And the names on the different wave bands, the long wave, short wave: Hilversum, Paris, Motala, Vienna, Kalundborg – a strange mixture of the familiar and unfamiliar.

Was it for Christmas, one of their birthdays, or a wedding anniversary when Sal and Phil had given her parents a miniaturized battery solid state transistor radio - words which perplexed them? This could be carried round the house, more truly wireless, than the old one in the lounge bound by its umbilical wire to its wall socket. But the mobile radio was left in the kitchen as if it, too, must be corralled as securely as the old one in the lounge. No doubt, sitting here on the old sofa where the major decisions in their lives were discussed, decided and decisions taken, Margaret and Richard had decided that the tiny wireless which for some reason had been given this new name, radio, would be firmly relegated to the kitchen, perhaps so that the new could not challenge or compete with the old. Listening to a radio upstairs was unspeakable. It was enough in this room where they could hear or ignore the news of a progressively outlandish and dangerous world increasingly possessed of a vocabulary whose words they were sometimes organised enough to record on a piece of paper and ask Sal to translate: computer, digital, hypermarket, on-line banking, LibDem, pin number, laptop, video, on-line.

Sal's eyes slide back to the fireplace, the real centre, the real focus of the room. The sofa and the two easy chairs are angled towards it and, flanked either side like chief attendants, the printed world one side and the electronic world the other. Although it's high summer, coal lies in the scuttle ready for use. Who lights fires these days? Sal wonders. Her parents had been persuaded to have central heating put in, what, thirty years ago? But not oil. Even so, she could hear her mother saying, *'It's more cheerful to have a glowing fire in the winter, dear, and in the summer of a chilly evening.'*

Anyone entering the room, Sal sees, will be instantly drawn towards the mantelpiece with its photos left and right of the old clock: pictures of the central events in the life of the family. These proclaim themselves; these have pride of place; these define Margaret and Richard: in black and white and subtle tones of grey for their wedding. Then progressing, of course, left to right, to their first and only-born child in her christening robes. But it is at this point that her parents, Richard and Margaret, withdraw, are no longer featured in the triumphal parade of life because their final appearance is followed immediately by Sal as a toddler in an almost convincing colour touched-up photo before Sal is awkward in her first school uniform, but at last in Technicolor. As if over in a flash, fast forward *What's that, dear?* to Sal in full black gown and mortar board, clutching her scrolled degree against a dreamy blue background of the world thus opened up for her. It's as if her parents cannot compete with all this success, have withdrawn gracefully and gratefully from the race. *Over to you, dear*.

Sal wonders if they could have later on made a comeback with a point-and-press modern camera; but no, the arrival of Rachel, Penny and Oliver would have utterly obliterated any notion of their re-appearance on the mantle piece's stage, because the grandchildren utterly dominate the last one third of the display: newly born, then saggy-nappied, first school uniform, through to awkward teens when they didn't want to be photographed.

Looking back to the left, to the wedding photo in its silver frame with the chunky squared off corners, nodding at Art Deco, she sees for the first time how her parents married, delivered her to the world and then stepped back so that the next generation and the one after that could occupy not only full centre stage but most of the mantelpiece. Sally tries to see the mother she knew until a few weeks ago in the smiling girl just married to the tall thin young man whose almost bashful smile endured in a diluted, faded manner to the last. But it's her mother she's really looking at: there's just no connection, she thinks, between the young and the old. It's as if she's always seen her mother as she was right up to the moment of her death: small, slight, wizened, bent and apologetic.

A sudden impulsive thought re-intrudes - I've no one to share this with, I'm alone, it's as if I was the result of her one and only supreme effort, that after me there could never be anyone else because she had used up all her parturative strength, and from that moment became the post-menopausal woman I have always known. She knows this is ridiculous; but she also knows she's stuck with this notion. It'll have to fade in its own time like others, but until then will be another regret to drag down empty streets of the mind.

Breathing deeply, Sal feels the need to complete this rapid summary of the last sixty years. Because a little more than half way along towards the right hand side of the mantelpiece is the triumph of another wedding: Sal and Phil's: she as a gypsy nymph, he long haired in a white suit with flared trousers, a psychedelic tie unmistakably proclaiming the glorious 60s which hung on so tenaciously into the 70s.

Sal tries to smile, but it's a grimace. She wants to say, *Sorry Mum and Dad, we could have toned it down a bit, we could have played the wedding game.* She's near tears again and hasn't yet quite reached the very last photo on the right. Well, not a photo but a collage of pictures she made and arranged in a wooden frame, the snaps cropped and overlapping so that squares and rectangles cut into each other, creating other squares and rectangles, as allowed by Mondrian whose paintings Sal's father once confessed to liking. This shows the grandchildren from birth presented and celebrated in shawls knitted by their grandmother, then following the same sequence as their mother as toddlers, school uniformed, or in best clothes for some forgotten party, and finally graduation.

These visual biographies finish there, discreetly omitting the partners they're currently living with, the partners lived with and abandoned, the conspicuous lack of further weddings, the absence of the nappied bundles of a fourth generation despite the ticking of the biological clock.

Still acutely aware of the silence of the mantelpiece clock whose spring of life has spent itself, Sal's looking down at the sofa.

You two sit here, dear, on the settee.

Phil awkward, Philip for at least a year, hiding behind his shock of liberated hair, not knowing how to take anything, how to respond, where to put his hands, how to sit on a sofa next to her. Something he had to learn over the next months and years, which included keeping his hands to himself when in the presence of his future in-laws.

If Margaret was busy with the tea, signalled by muted clicks and chinks the other side of the closed living room door, Richard was probably down the garden gleaning the last of the radishes and lettuce. 'Let them be, dear,' she'd heard her mother whisper, then and only then could Phil put his hands where he liked. As long as they both remained upright for the call to tea, all was well. When Phil got too worked up, as she thought of it, she'd whisper about being back at college, about the bed waiting for them in the bed-sit and he'd try to grin, try to shrug it aside as a daring pretence of a violation in this her parents' domain.

Sometimes she'd stand and mince across the room. 'I'll see if I can help', she'd say. Sal squirms over the memory, feels her cheeks redden, feels surges of unidentifiable emotion rise in her body. But there's another reason she's avoiding this last involvement with the sofa.

Because that day, the Saturday, she'd come over as she had all that week to be with her mother, finding the week-long missing presence of her father almost more palpable than his quiet living self had been. If she kept expecting to see him in every room she entered; what, she wondered, was it like for her mother?

The Undertaker, Mr Whitaker, was a huge man whose puffy cheeks and wheezing throat seemed to suggest that he might at any time become one of his own clients. He came to the house in a funereal black suit and grey striped waistcoat with half its buttons popped open to accommodate his obesity. He sat on the sofa opposite Sal and Margaret, accessorised in black from his briefcase at his feet to his homburg hat for god's sake, who wears them now? His gloves and at ease on the sofa beside him, his silk scarf and stick balanced beside him on the arm rest. Sal shivers with recalled distaste remembering the presence of this man of death who seemed on the verge of participating personally in his own trade. There's a first for everything, she remembers thinking, the difference is you never get good at it, there's usually no repetition, just the one of, or two and that's it. Death forgotten, kept at bay. She thinks of the past when you were lucky enough to keep half of the children you produced over a what, twenty-year period? Spouses, siblings, uncle and aunts all tumbled into early graves - parents, well they'd already gone. Ninety- and ninety-two-year olds must have been rare, almost unknown.

Despite attempting to soften it, Mr Whitaker's voice growled and grated about telling them that you are doing the right thing by your dear husband and father. The cheapest coffin was thus not ordered, the name plate and coffin accoutrements were to be of the best brass rather than some baser metal, the coffin lining would have graced a bishop instead of the linen of a pauper. A few minutes into the meeting Mr Whitaker whispered abrasively, 'I hope you don't mind, my dear,' but lit up before either woman could object. Sal fetched the only ash tray she remembered seeing in the cupboard under the sink where it lived with bottles and plastic containers of the less mentioned kind: Harpic, Domestos, Mr Muscle, Toilet Duck, Loo Bloo, and an ancient cardboard drum of Vim.

'I'm so sorry that the funeral cannot take place sooner,' Mr Whitaker murmured through his lazy cigarette smoke as he collected himself and his papers together, 'but we've had more than the usual number of funerals to organize these last few weeks.'

To Sal's surprise, Margaret, though confused, in a day or two seemed to be gathering to her the threatened strands of living: these being a willingness and an ability to wash oneself as well as organise sheets and clothes. With this went a resumption of cleaning the house, washing kitchen utensils, crockery and plates, and the beginnings of a grasp of the monetary function of a single household.

Sal thought her mother, at ninety, was doing really well. The next step, therefore, was a gentle, low key expedition to the shops to prod her mother into a consideration of her future needs: the bread and butter of the following week, the money wherewith to buy it all. She was pleased that Margaret was not only up, but wearing a summer dress: a fresh, but muted, garden of light red, miniature roses. With her white hair gathered into its customary bun, her face a better colour, Sal had to congratulate herself for the time and effort her mother had put in to, as she saw it, achieving this picture book elderly lady effect. She'd be processing slowly down the High Street with her mother looking like everyone's picture of a benign, old-fashioned ideal, boiled egg and flowers granny.

And it worked. Sal was aware of the glances, not at her, but at her mother. The smiles, and a few waves from other elderly people Sal didn't know. But because the face of death was leering over the shoulders of mother and daughter, no one stopped to pass the time of day. with them. Margaret didn't seem to notice this. Her mother's bearing was as confident as she, Sal, had remembered from a long time ago, and her steps scarcely faltered. There was a moment when Sal wondered if she'd made a mistake in bringing her mother into the high street Tesco. But she reasoned that this first, this introductory widow's shopping spree should be as simple as possible - one place where everything could be found. Indeed, it could, and she prompted her mother to work out how big a packet of say, flour, sugar, butter or margarine she'd need.

There was a glitch over the bacon when she forgot and picked up a packet of streaky bacon, *I don't have it myself, dear, but it's your Dad's favourite*, only to replace it quickly as if hiding the mistake, as if hoping that Sal hadn't noticed. But she had noticed and had to turn and search among a whole shelf section of marmalade until her tears could be controlled.

While Margaret stood nearby, absorbed with the herb section with its serried little hourglass bottles, camomile, fennel, rosemary, turmeric, sage, nutmeg, Sal couldn't remember her mother ever using them. But this only reinforced her sense of loss - that she took her mother, her parents so utterly for granted that she hardly bothered to taste the food they offered her. It was a dash to get there, a dash to check up on them and pile through a meal and then a dash home to deal with a hundred-and-one-things a working wife has to cope with. Waiting parents forgotten until the next bout of guilt kicked in.

They walk slowly home, Sal lugging the bulging plastic bags. At home, she says, breezily, 'Cuppa?'

Margaret doesn't reply to the offer of tea. Instead she says, 'I'll just sit down for a moment, dear.'

Sal can see her mother heading for the sofa, so she takes the bags into the kitchen and heaves them onto the kitchen table. Should she put the packets, tins, veg, and fruit away, or should this be in the nature of a small organisational exercise for her mother? She could have asked, 'Shall I start sorting, or shall we do it together after the cuppa?'

But it seems to her afterwards as if she abandons all this because something impels her to lurch, almost fall into the living room, almost doesn't see that her mother won't be able to hear her, because she's sitting stiffly upright and her eyes are gazing into a distance that is through and past Sal who's standing there waiting for her mind to grasp the full implications of what she can plainly see has happened.

It is now, in the empty house, that real tears grab Sal, and she howls there and then in the centre of the living room staring at the dead clock and the procession of lives spread along the mantelpiece, deep inside the centre of the lives of her parents. Exhaustion suddenly washes through her body as if to cleanse her, wash away the last couple of weeks where she lost both parents, where she had to rearrange the funeral with that awful man, Mr Whitaker, so that it could be a joint funeral, so that she'd bury both her parents together. How people would later say how the Wards, Margaret and Richard, were always together and how appropriate this was. Then she'd had to see the keen, new young vicar who wanted to bring in his guitar-wielding music group to all and every service and ceremony, and how she'd had to repeat, No, just the organ - and repeat, Please could the words of the funeral service be from the old prayer book: the thee's and thou's my parents took such comfort in hearing. These two old people, these two old-fashioned people, these two old people so dear to her. And she'd want a proper burial so that she can visit them, and lay flowers on something as substantial as a large slab of stone where she will know,   and   find some kind of comfort in the fact that these her parents lie together. Above all, she feels as if she's backed into a corner: that there is all this to do to manage one death, let alone two. She knows how important it is to do the right thing or things, and that the eyes of all those around her will be watching and judging. It is as if the world, her world, is closing in around her and will not let go until this is all done: the house cleared and sold, the gravestone finally installed, and all the financial dust settled or blown away.

This weight of things to be organised and then done has Sal hold her face in her hands in this room where during her fifty-nine years she's been with, sat with her parents, where so much of life: birthdays, school, university, work, marriage, pregnancy, child rearing, resuming a career, was discussed, argued about, decided. With her hands unwilling to do anything else but encompass her face, she feels forces in her body trying to make her double up, fold her into a simpler, older shape as if that will contain her grief. She finds that she's full of an urge to do this on the sofa, but is then equally assailed by a revulsion to do so because in her mind her mother is still sitting there as if nothing has happened, as if completely accepting of this apparent change, this final act in her long life.

William English remembers the excitement of being a boy during World War Two, blissfully unaware of the stresses and tensions of the adult generation. Bombed out sites were playgrounds, there was shrapnel to collect, and children had considerable freedom to come and go, as long as they turned up for meals and bed time. As a young man in post-War Britain, William was more aware of the difficulties still being faced by a population which had lost so many men, and which was still suffering the aftermath of the conflict.

He is also the author of 'Peg's Pieces', a collection of short stories set in East Anglia.

Printed in Great Britain
by Amazon